Your Forever Love
(The Bennett Family, Book 3)

LAYLA HAGEN

Dear Reader,

If you want to receive news about my upcoming books and sales, you can sign up for my newsletter HERE: http://laylahagen.com/mailing-list-sign-up/

Chapter One

Eric

"Dad, can I meet Pippa *now*?"

Watching as my daughter runs her little fingers through her wavy blonde hair, I smile at her squirming in her seat. When I told Julie we would attend Sebastian Bennett's wedding, she announced she wants her hair styled in waves, not a braid, because the latter is for *little* girls, and she just turned twelve. She's growing up too fast.

"Not yet. She's busy right now." I suspect Pippa will be busy for the rest of the party since it's her brother's wedding.

Julie hero-worships Pippa Bennett—or more accurately, her designs. My daughter loves to draw, and lately, she's taken to drawing jewelry, which isn't such a surprise since I sell jewelry for a living. Callahan's Finest, of which I am the CEO, is the largest chain of high-end jewelry shops on the East Coast and has been for three generations. We work closely with Bennett Enterprises, and I admire the Bennett family. They started from nothing. Sebastian created Bennett Enterprises less than fifteen years ago, and it grew to be one of the most prestigious producers in the jewelry market. It takes a lot of determination and hard work to make that happen in such a short time.

Julie fell in love with their designs a while ago and insists on meeting the designer in person. If I am honest, I'm looking forward to meeting Pippa Bennett as well.

"This is a beautiful wedding," Julie comments, her eyes scanning the ballroom, and resting on the bride and groom's table. "Was your wedding to Mom this beautiful?"

Wham. Her words stab me, causing old wounds to resurface.

"Yeah, it was."

My life changed at twenty-one when Sarah told me she was pregnant. At that age, a kid was the last thing on my mind, but I wasn't about to leave the woman I loved to deal with the responsibility alone. Sarah and I got married. Julie stole my heart from the moment she was born. I held her in my arms, and I knew my life would change.

My life changed again five years ago when an accident killed Sarah and left Julie with a limp and a dependence on an inhaler.

"Hey!" I elbow Julie playfully, deciding it's time to cheer her up. "Do you want to do a movie marathon tomorrow?"

"Yeah. But you *can't* fall asleep again, Dad."

"I can't make you any promises."

Julie loves movie marathons. She also likes

watching the same movies over and over again, hence why I sometimes fall asleep.

"I will draw you a mustache with a permanent marker if you fall asleep," she threatens, barely withholding a grin. "Then you'll have to go to your office like that."

That's a thought. That would severely undermine my reputation as a business shark.

"I'd like to see you try."

Julie lets out a giggle, which turns into laughter. Her laugh is always contagious, so before long, I can't keep a straight face either. I love this little girl to pieces, and I would do anything to make her happy.

"Ooooh, look." Julie claps her hands excitedly. "The first dance."

I smile at my daughter, ruffling her hair, which garners me a frown from her.

"Let's watch it," I say. "Then we can go find Pippa Bennett."

***

Pippa

I love weddings. I love everything about them, from the vows to the dancing to the cake. *Oh, the cake.* I have a slight cake addiction, and I'm not doing a great job battling it. I really should, though. One of the downsides of being over thirty is that my metabolism no longer keeps up with my appetite.

My oldest brother and his bride are on the dance floor, and their happiness is contagious. My other seven siblings and my parents are scattered throughout the room, entertaining the guests. The ballroom is glamorous with a high ceiling spanning above us, and crystal chandeliers hanging from it. The place is vast, enough to house four hundred guests. The chairs are covered with elegant satin, and tiny twinkle lights adorn some of the tables. It looks like a fairy tale.

"Congratulating yourself on your matchmaking skills, Pippa?" my brother Max asks, appearing by my side.

"You have to admit, I'm great at it, little brother," I reply. I can't take full credit for my eldest brother being married, but I did give him a *nudge* in the right direction. "Why, are you looking to employ my matchmaking services? I'm warning you, I'm expensive. My payment is a lot of brotherly love and attention."

Max has been working out of our London office over the past few years, and I've missed him terribly. But now he's back, and I intend to take advantage of that.

"I can get my own date, no need for help."

"Yeah, that's what Sebastian and Logan said too." I wink at him, but Max merely shakes his head. Behind him, I spot Christopher. They are identical twins, and today they are particularly hard to tell apart because even their tuxedos and bow ties are identical. Luckily, Max has slightly longer hair that falls into his eyes. Still, I'm tempted to glue tiny, colorful dots on their clothes, as I did when we were kids because it was easier to tell them apart.

"You should get yourself a date," Max suggests.

I sigh. "Tried it once after the divorce. Didn't end well. I'm much better at finding dates for other people."

I believe in love. I truly do. But maybe I'm not destined to find my happily ever after. Maybe I already blew my chance. I was the first in my family to marry, almost five years ago, and that proved to be a mistake. Now I'm divorced.

The thought of being alone for the rest of my days leaves a dull ache in my chest. Watching Ava and Sebastian on the dance floor only intensifies that ache. I want someone to look at me as if I'm his whole world. Is that too much to ask?

Max pulls me into a hug, whispering, "You'll find someone, but you need to get back in the dating game. If you do it more often, you'll get better at it."

Drawing in a deep breath, I bite the inside of my cheek. The truth is I don't want to 'get back in the dating game.' For one, I'm not ready to open myself up again. More importantly, I clearly can't trust my own judgment when it comes to men.

"By the way, I want to introduce you to someone," Max says.

I chuckle. "Really? You want to become my matchmaking assistant?"

"I meant a business partner, Eric Callahan."

"The CEO of Callahan's Finest?" I ask in surprise.

"Yeah."

Callahan's Finest are among our biggest

distribution partners on the East Coast. Max has known Eric Callahan since college. Sebastian and Logan met him over the years, but I never got the chance.

"Isn't Callahan based in Boston? What is he doing here?"

"Callahan is looking to expand their chain of shops on the West Coast, so Eric will be here for about three months, overseeing the expansion."

"Got it."

"Anyway, he's here with his daughter, who is a great fan of yours. She can't wait to meet you. She's an aspiring designer."

"Let's go to their table."

"No need. They're on their way here." Max points to the other side of the room.

The girl catches my eye first. She has light blonde hair that falls in beautiful waves and walks with a pronounced limp. She wears a delicate pink chiffon dress, which bounces with every step she takes. What surprises me most about her, though, is that she appears to be eleven or twelve.

"I imagined his daughter to be younger," I murmur.

"He had her when he was twenty or something. His wife died a few years ago," Max explains.

"That's sad."

As they come closer, I hear the girl whisper, "Is that her, Dad?"

That's when I focus on the person next to her. I nearly do a double take when I take a closer look at her *dad*. Holy smokes and fires. This man is… *perfection*. He has deep brown hair and striking blue eyes. He's also muscular and tall—I'm talking at least six feet. His arms are strong enough that I imagine he could carry anything in them without effort… including me. *Where did that thought come from?* I haven't even met the man. Everything about him screams sexy, even the way he walks, as if he owns the place. He carries himself with a self-confidence that oozes raw power and masculinity.

"Eric," Max says. "This is my sister, Pippa." Someone calls Max's name, and my brother adopts an apologetic expression. "Have to go."

After Max leaves, the girl steps closer to her dad, as if wishing to hide behind him. Her father caresses her cheek, as though she's a delicate flower and the slightest wind could sweep her away. They are adorable.

Deciding to put her at ease, I hold out my hand to her. "What's your name? My brother told me you're an aspiring designer."

"Julie."

"Hi, Julie." I shake her little hand, feeling calluses on her fingers. Turning her hand palm up, I inspect the hardened skin—unmistakable signs of having held a pencil for hours at a time. "You have designer's hands. I have calluses too."

Julie's eyes widen as if she can't quite believe it. "But don't you have computer programs for designing?" she asks.

"Yeah, but I like sketching by hand better."

"Love your designs," Julie whispers to me, as if it's a great secret. "I am going to take a design course while Dad and I are here."

"Summer school?" I whip my head in Eric's direction, and he nods. His blue eyes rest on my face for a beat too long, and my skin heats from the intensity. *Holy hell.*

"I start in two weeks. It's a great program—specifically for jewelry design." Julie smooths her hands down her dress, adding in a small voice, "I hope I'll be good enough."

My heart stings as I watch Julie fret over this.

"Are you practicing every day?" I ask her.

"Yes, I have some assignments I have to complete before starting summer school. I hope I'll do them right."

"I have an idea. Why don't you come to my office every day before summer school kicks off, and I can teach you some techniques? That way, you'll be in top shape when you start the course."

"That's not—" Eric begins.

At the same time, Julie exclaims, "I'd love that."

She claps her hands, grinning from ear to ear, looking up at her father. "Dad, can I go?"

I suspect Eric wants to say no, but I can practically see his determination melt the longer he looks at Julie. If I'm honest, I'm melting too. I'm certain Eric is the kind of man who gets others to do exactly what he wants. Seeing him unable to resist his daughter's charm is adorable.

"I'll consider it."

"You are the best dad in the world. Thank you."

"Why don't you go back to our table, and I'll sort out the details with Pippa?" Eric tells his daughter.

Julie nods, politely shaking my hand again before leaving. Eric follows Julie with his gaze until she's seated at the table, then turns his attention to me.

"Thank you for offering to help her…."

"I sense a but coming." I smile, folding my arms over my chest.

Eric returns the smile and shrugs. "No offense, but I don't allow my daughter to spend time with people I don't know."

"Of course you don't, but you've met my brothers. You know me by extension. As to me, what you see is what you get."

"Who knows what you might be hiding under that pretty smile and elegant dress."

His gaze travels down my body with amusement, as if looking for any secrets. Yet somewhere along the way, the amusement turns to heat. He zeroes in on my hips, and I swear his nostrils flare. When he looks back up, surprise flickers in his eyes as if he's taken aback by his own reaction to me.

"It'll boost her confidence if I show her a few tricks," I say.

"Are you sure it's okay if Julie comes to your office?" he asks.

Is it my imagination, or is his voice a notch huskier? Imagination or not, it sends tendrils of warmth down my spine.

"It'll be my pleasure. I love children. I can't wait

for Sebastian and Ava to give me some nieces and nephews. I will spoil them rotten."

He laughs softly at my words. The sound fills me with joy. "You are the first person to find it perfectly acceptable to spoil kids. Everyone else is up my ass for doing so with Julie." He accompanies the last word with a wink. "I can't help spoiling her."

"As you should. You'll bring her to my office, then. It's settled. She said she has two weeks until summer school starts. I can teach her a lot in that time."

"You're stubborn," he remarks. There is a spark of a challenge in his tone, which riles me up.

"You have no idea." God, his eyes are too blue, and his lips too full. The combo should be illegal. Eric Callahan is six feet of sexiness.

"All right. Enjoy your brother's wedding now. I'll call you tomorrow, and we can talk about the details."

"You don't have my number."

"I'm a resourceful man." He gives me a crooked smile before taking off.

***

The wedding goes on without a hitch. The dance floor is full all the time, and the whole room buzzes with life thanks to the permanent chatter and laughter of the guests. I leave the dance floor when I can't feel my feet anymore, slumping in my seat and kicking off my shoes under the table. My sister Alice drops in the seat next to me a couple of minutes later, panting.

"The band is incredible," she says, fanning her heated cheeks. A waiter asks if there is anything he can do for us, and we both order a cocktail. After he leaves, Alice chuckles while glancing at my bare feet, then follows my lead and kicks off her shoes. Thank God we're alone at our table.

The waiter returns with the cocktails, and Alice smiles smugly as we clink our glasses. *Uh-oh.* That smile means trouble.

"Spill the beans," she says.

I sip from my glass, taking my time before answering. "What are you talking about?"

"What's up with you and Mr. Tall, Dark, and Handsome?" Alice presses.

"His daughter is an aspiring designer. I talked to him about meeting with her to teach her some stuff. Nothing else." I try to downplay the meeting even though my skin still simmers from the way he looked at me.

She leans in to me, dropping her voice to a conspiratorial whisper. "So, why did he give you a *hot* look?"

"Alice! I'm not sure it was a hot look."

"It was. I was across the dance floor, and even I could feel the heat."

Sighing, I lean forward, pulling the platter of sweets from the center of the table toward us. This conversation requires sugar.

"I asked Max about him. Did you know they call him 'the shark' in business circles?" Alice says, flashing her teeth.

"Yeah."

"He's the perfect candidate to help you with the cobweb situation down there." Alice announces this with such conviction you'd think she has research-backed data to support this statement.

"Stop using the word 'cobweb,'" I hiss.

"You used it first."

"I won't make that mistake again." Many moons ago, over too many cocktails, I admitted to Alice that I hadn't gotten laid in a while, and if that didn't change soon, I would have to start checking for cobwebs.

"He's perfect for the job. You're not ready for a relationship, and he's only here for a few months. You can just enjoy each other. He's single and hot."

Suspicion gnaws at me. I recognize this type of meddling; I did exactly this to Sebastian and Logan, my second eldest brother, back when they were still single. But Alice always kept away from my matchmaking activities. Is she now taking a page from my own playbook?

I had great plans for Alice tonight. Recently, I discovered she has had a crush on one of Sebastian's childhood friends for years, and he was going to attend the wedding, so I had the perfect opportunity to give them a *nudge*. Alas, he regretfully informed us that he couldn't participate two days ago. He received a job offer outside the country right before the wedding and had to start immediately. He'll be gone for months, maybe even a year.

"Sorry to break up your party, ladies, but I have a phone number to ask for," a male voice says from behind us. Alice and I turn in our seats at the same time. My breath stops as my gaze meet Eric's. He's standing not one foot in front of us, a mischievous glint playing in his blue eyes. I shift uncomfortably in my seat.

"I'll leave you two," Alice says, putting her shoes back on and then graciously disappearing.

"I'm surprised you're straight-up asking for my number. You said you're a resourceful man."

"I am, and this is the best use of my resources right now."

Eric hands me his phone, and I try—and fail—to ignore the flip in my stomach as his fingers touch mine.

I type my number. Without looking up, I ask, "Did you hear any part of our conversation?"

"A little. Something about tall, dark, and handsome. And about cobwebs."

"So, you basically eavesdropped on our entire conversation." My throat becomes dry.

"I did. Can I have my phone back now?"

"Sure." Snapping my gaze up to him, I return the phone. "This is my most embarrassing moment, and I have quite a few of those under my belt. I'll start digging a hole in the ground now. I should disappear off the face of the earth by the time the wedding's over."

"Pippa—"

"Sorry. My sister can be a bit meddling sometimes. I think she learned it from me. And I'm rambling. I do that when I'm nervous."

"I make you nervous?" He smiles.

"Obviously."

He eyes me in silence for an entire minute, which does nothing to soothe my nerves. "You are adorable." Tilting his head forward, he puts his lips to my ear and whispers, "Just to silence any doubts, it *was* a hot look."

My breath catches. "I... Well... I'm not sure if that's any less embarrassing."

Pulling back, he asks, "Why don't we talk that over during a dance?"

"What about Julie?"

"She's in good company." He points to the table, where Julie is engrossed in a conversation with Nadine, Logan's fiancée, and Alice. On a sigh, I realize I was right. My sister *is* playing matchmaker, and Nadine is playing along with her. They're beating me at my own game.

"Okay, let's dance, Mr. Tall, Dark, and Handsome."

Without further ado, he offers me his arm. I quickly put on my shoes, and then he guides us to the dance floor. The band has switched to an animated song, and this man *can* dance. My heart beats at a frantic pace from the quick rhythm of our moves. Being so close to him, I can take in his scent— sandalwood and mint—and it's addictive.

"You're a great dancer," I murmur as the song ends. The band switches to a slower song, and Eric immediately takes one of my hands in his, curling his other arm around my waist. I'd hoped my heart rate would slow down, but being in his arms has the opposite effect.

"Forgive me if I come across as curious, but you seem to know more about me than I do about you."

I laugh nervously. "What do you want to know?"

"Why is your sister trying to set you up? A beautiful woman like you shouldn't have any problems finding a date on her own."

Ah, going straight for the punch. "I'm divorced and haven't done well in the dating department lately. Alice is trying to be helpful."

We move to the music for a few seconds before he speaks. "About what she said about me… She made me sound like a catch."

"And you want to tell me you're not?"

"Well, I *am* tall, dark, and handsome, obviously." He winks at me.

I laugh. God, I love a man who can make me laugh. "Obviously."

The smile on his face morphs into a serious expression. "But I'm damaged goods, not a catch. Not at all. And I don't know you, but I think you deserve someone who is. Whether to take you out on dates, or help you out with that *cobweb* situation."

I burst out laughing, hoping it hides my embarrassment. I make a mental note never to use that expression again.

"So the hot look—" I begin, but he interrupts me with a headshake.

"Was a moment of weakness on my part. I am only a man, after all, and you are beautiful."

My cheeks heat up. "You are awfully articulate about your thoughts and feelings."

"I've always worn my heart on my sleeve. Not always the best thing, but I can't be any other way. And after my wife passed away, I saw a therapist for a few years. He helped me articulate—as you call it—my thoughts. Learning to do that was especially important for Julie."

"I'm sorry about your wife."

"It happened a long time ago." He gazes into the distance, emotions warring on his handsome face—pain, resignation, maybe hope. A deep frown stretches on his forehead, and I decide on the spot this won't do. I make it my mission to bring back that gorgeous smile of his.

I needn't have worried because the band switches to a fifties tune, and Eric wiggles his eyebrows.

"Another dance?" he asks.

"Rock-n-roll? Seriously?"

"I have moves," he assures me in a voice full of delicious promise. "I'm not a catch, but that doesn't mean I can't throw and catch you."

"Whatever you're planning to do, keep in mind I'm wearing a dress. I don't want to flash my thong for everyone to see, even if it is a gorgeous red from La Perla—"

"Stop talking about your underwear. I'm already

picturing it, and that's a slippery road." Without further ado, he lifts me in his arms and proceeds to steal the breath from my lungs. He half lowers, half throws me to his right and then to his left. I keep my knees firmly together until my feet are back on the floor. By the end of the dance, my head is spinning.

"Oh, my God," I say. "This was… I can't believe you pulled that off."

"Your lack of faith in me is insulting," he says as we step away from the dance floor. "I should get back to my daughter."

"You do that, and I'll see both of you on Monday. She'll love my office. I have samples all around."

"Why are you being so nice to us?"

"I'm nice to everyone," I reply a little too quickly. "But I like Julie. She and I will get along well."

"So it has nothing to do with the fact that I'm Mr. Tall, Dark, and Handsome?" His smile is priceless.

"You're never going to let me forget that, are you?"

"I haven't even started on the cobwebs. See you on Monday." He gives me a quick nod before returning to his daughter, leaving me breathless and smiling. Going back to my seat, I help myself to a cookie, stealing glances at Eric. That man is eye candy. I can't seem to look away from him, just as I can't seem to stop myself from putting yet another cookie on my plate.

At least eye candy has zero calories.

Chapter Two

Eric

"Dad," Julie says on Monday, as we eat our breakfast. "I want to wear lipstick."

I choke on my toast, looking at her across the table. "Wh—at?"

"I want a lipstick."

"You're too young."

She folds her arms over her chest, already taking her fighting stance. My daughter is lovely, but when she puts her mind to something she's more stubborn than I am. Folding her arms is the first step, frowning the second. By that time, I usually cower to her demands, but I will stand firm on this.

"Dad, I'm twelve."

"I allow you to wear lip gloss occasionally, but you're still too young to wear lipstick." Yeah, I know the difference between the two. Comes with the territory of being a single father.

"Says who?"

"I do."

"Well, you're not a girl. You don't understand." She sighs dramatically. "I want red lipstick."

"Finish your sandwich, Julie."

She verbalized one of my biggest fears: that she needs a feminine presence. I've always known this, but that doesn't make hearing her say it out loud any easier.

It took me a long time to piece myself together after Sarah died. After the worst was over, and at the encouragement of friends and family, I started dating. It turned out to be a bad move. Women feigned to be interested in Julie in order to get a second date, so I stopped. Until my daughter turns eighteen, she will be my priority. It's just the two of us, and that's okay most of the time. Until she starts asking me about wearing lipstick. At twelve years old. Dealing with boyfriends will be a bloodbath.

"I'm done," Julie announces when her plate is empty. "We can go."

"Are you sure you want to come to the office with me? I can ask Ms. Blackwell to spend the day with you."

Julie has two permanent nannies back in Boston, Ms. Smith and Ms. Blackwell, the latter who agreed to come with us from Boston to San Francisco over the summer. Julie isn't thrilled about having round-the-clock nannies, but she understands it's necessary.

"No, I want to see your office. It's funny to watch you scare people."

"I want them to do their job. I don't scare them intentionally."

"That's the funniest part."

"Okay, let's go. Did you put your inhaler in your

backpack?"

Julie nods, slinging the straps of her backpack over her shoulder. My daughter is a fighter. After the accident, I brought in the best doctors to treat her. Even so, they couldn't perform miracles. She had sustained heavy injuries to her left leg and hip, as well as the left lung. Despite their best efforts, my baby will always walk with a limp and have to carry her inhaler with her. She rarely has respiratory attacks—mostly when she's doing physical exertion—but she must carry it with her as a precaution.

The limp and the inhaler were a magnet for bullies, which is why she's changed four schools up until now, and she finally seems to be making friends there.

"I like this house, Dad," Julie comments as we walk out the front door.

"Glad you do."

It's a one-story with a garden and a pool in the heart of San Francisco. The house is simple, yet elegant. The exterior walls are painted in a light green, and white shutters are on the windows.

I could have rented a more luxurious house; I can certainly afford it. However, I grew up with others who came from old money, and I've seen that financial security offers opportunities but also destroys lives. A number of my childhood friends got involved in gambling, drugs, or simply wasted their lives away because they never had to work. I plan to teach my daughter what the right way is. I owe that to Sarah.

As I drive us to the office, I wonder if bringing Julie to San Francisco was a good idea after all. She says she's excited to travel with me, but she knows no one here. Let's hope that will change once summer school starts. I can't help feeling that bringing her to San Francisco was a selfish decision. I need to spend a few months here to oversee the expansion, and I scheduled this trip to coincide with her summer holiday because I couldn't stand the thought of being apart from her for three entire months.

"This is a *huge* building," Julie announces once we get out of the car. A skyscraper stands in front of us in the buzzing business district. We arrived in San Francisco on Friday morning, and I came into the office shortly thereafter to meet the team, but it's the first time here for Julie.

"Only four floors belong to us."

"Why? Your office is an entire building in Boston. Though the building's smaller."

"The team here is much smaller. We're just starting out on the West Coast."

My great-grandfather started Callahan's Finest as a one-man shop selling jewelry. Since then, the company grew to a multi-million-dollar juggernaut. We own hundreds of shops on the East Coast and even in Europe, but none on the West Coast. Recently, one of our competitors went bankrupt, and we bought their assets on this coast—and their team.

Julie and I take the elevator and ride up to the fifth floor. When we step out of it, I switch to full-on business mode. This is a new team, and seeing me arrive with my daughter might give them the impression I'm a softie. I'm not—when it comes to business. They don't call me 'the shark' for nothing.

"Veronica," I tell my secretary. "Please tell the team we can start the meeting in five minutes."

"The meeting room is prepared. Will your daughter go in with you?"

"No. She'll remain in my office."

I lead Julie to my office—a corner room with floor-to-ceiling windows on two adjacent walls.

"I'll be gone for an hour," I tell her. "You can stay here and draw. If you need anything, Veronica will be outside. After lunch, I'll take you to Pippa."

As I make my way to the meeting room, I try—as I tried all weekend—not to think about Pippa Bennett. That woman is something else. Everything about her tempts me, from her kindness to Julie to her addictive laughter. Her rambling tendency is adorable—except when she casually speaks about her underwear. Then it's dangerous.

Damn it, Callahan. Pull yourself together. I'm here for three months, so dating Pippa is out of the question. Still, I smile at the memory of dancing with her. In those moments, I wasn't the concerned father or the stern businessman. I was just myself, and it was refreshing.

Stepping into the meeting room, I scan the party before announcing my presence. The atmosphere in the room is relaxed, the two dozen employees around the oval table sharing jokes and chattering. Well, that's about to change. Since I bought the company in a hostile takeover, I don't imagine they look forward to working with me.

"Good morning," I say loudly, and the chatter dissolves to whispers. "Let's start this meeting. We have three months to make Callahan's Finest run like a well-oiled machine on the West Coast. The clock starts ticking as of this moment."

The whispers instantly die. I glance around the room at everyone's stricken expression. Perfect. Mom made a bet with me that the team will call me 'the shark' by the end of my stay here. I bet against her—I plan to earn that moniker by the end of the week.

***

Julie and I walk into Bennett Enterprises five hours later. The doorman informs me that the Creative department is on the first floor.

Two things shock me when Julie and I enter the Creative department. One: the mayhem. Two: Pippa Bennett—specifically the way she runs this mayhem, with severity. I wasn't expecting this from the sweet woman who trusted me to dance wildly with her at the wedding.

There are ten desks in this open-space area, and each of them is cluttered with poster-sized papers with designs and unfinished pieces of jewelry.

Pippa is right in the center of the room, wearing a snug blue dress that highlights her delicious curves.

She's talking to a twenty-something guy who's a head shorter than she is. He's biting his nails, glancing at Pippa while she comments on the paper he's holding in front of her.

"Luke, I love you, but if you ever hand me something this half-assed again, we will have a serious conversation." Even though her voice is stern, I detect a hint of warmth in it. Interestingly, the poor schmuck she berated doesn't look terrified, just ashamed. The people I berate usually look like they're about to pee their pants after I'm done with them. Of course, I don't soften my criticism with *I love you*, either.

"I'll have a new design on your desk in thirty minutes. Sorry." He mumbles something more before scurrying to one of the desks. Pippa turns to a redhead sitting behind a computer, typing furiously.

"Kathy, how are we doing on the prototypes?"

"I'm on it," the redhead answers. "Riley's trying to buy time, but I'm on it."

"Ride his ass if you have to," Pippa says briskly. "I need that done today."

That's when Pippa sees us. We're still standing by the door, and it's a miracle Julie kept quiet this long. One look at her and I solve the mystery—she's mesmerized by the jewels all around the room.

"I didn't see you there," Pippa exclaims. She walks toward us, a large smile on her face. Her long, blonde hair falls in waves over her shoulders, covering her breasts. As she pushes her hair back, I have a moment of weakness, studying the delicate curve of her neck as discreetly as I can. Another moment of weakness follows as I drink in the perfect way her hips sway.

Pippa stops in front of us, directing all her attention to Julie.

"Like them?" Pippa asks her. My daughter's eyes are glued to the nearest stand of jewels.

"Are these diamonds?" Julie asks. She's been in a few of our shops, but we don't have precious stones lying around like this.

"Yes, they are," Pippa answers. "I also have rubies and sapphires on my desk."

"Wow," Julie exclaims.

"Say good-bye to your dad, and we'll get started. I've prepared everything. That's my desk." Pippa points with her thumb behind her to the largest desk at the far end of the room. "I brought in a second chair for you."

Julie gives me a quick good-bye kiss before running off to the desk. Pippa follows her with her gaze, then turns to me, keeping her focus firmly on a point on my shirt. Is she avoiding my eyes?

Not one to beat around the bush, I ask, "Pippa, are you avoiding looking at me?"

"Yes," she whispers, snapping her gaze up.

"Why?"

"You did it again," she replies, this time in a stronger voice.

"What?"

"The hot look," she clarifies. "Earlier."

"Right." I run a hand through my hair, mentally

cursing. Guess my moments of weakness weren't as discreet as I thought. Pippa pushes a strand of her golden blonde hair behind her ears, and that's when I see the tip of her ear is red. Can this woman be any cuter? She's a goofball, sexy goddess, laughing partner, and stern businesswoman all rolled into one.

"I'll try my best not to do it again. Can't make any promises, though. You're too damn beautiful."

Pippa licks her lips, looking away. It's time for me to give her some space.

"Are you sure it's all right if I leave Julie here the entire afternoon?" I press.

"Yes," she answers. "And before you ask, it's also okay if she comes every day for the next two weeks until her classes start. I promised her."

"If it gets too much, tell me. I'll make something up to get you off the hook."

Pippa crosses her arms over her chest. "I don't make promises I don't intend to keep. I won't disappoint her. She has plenty of time to be disappointed when she's older."

A shadow crosses her eyes, and my protective instincts kick in. She doesn't deserve to be disappointed or hurt. I barely know her, but someone who shows so much kindness to strangers deserves the best.

"At what time do you finish work?"

"I'll be here at six."

Pippa lifts one corner of her mouth in a smile. "I thought you'd work longer hours since they call you 'the shark' and all."

"I try not to," I admit. "If I don't give myself a strict deadline, I'd end up staying way too long, and I'd barely see Julie. I usually stay up late and work after Julie goes to bed. It works in Boston most of the time. Not sure how it'll be here since the workload is much higher."

She nods, and that's when I remember she was wearing red lipstick at the wedding. I admit my business instinct doesn't help jack shit when it comes to my daughter, but I can put two and two together. Julie wants lipstick—a red one, at that—because that's what Pippa was wearing at the wedding.

"Can I ask your advice on something?" I inquire.

"Sure."

"Julie told me today she wants to wear lipstick."

Pippa throws her head back, chuckling. "What did you tell her?"

"That she's not old enough."

"I'm guessing it didn't go to well?"

"Which is why I'm asking for your help. She wanted a red one, like the one you wore at the wedding."

Pippa nods in understanding. "Leave it to me. See you at six."

I'm usually picky with the people I allow my daughter to spend time with, but I'm glad I followed my instinct when I allowed her to come here. Pippa swirls on her heels, striding to her desk with confidence and whispering something in Julie's ear. My daughter bursts out laughing. I smile and wish I could stay longer. I have a hunch I could watch this woman smile all day, which is dangerous.

***

Pippa

Julie is lovely. She listens to my instructions and does her best to follow them. The girl is talented, and with the right training, she'll do great.

"I'm not as talented as you are." She props her head in her hands, sighing.

I'd love nothing better than to hug her. I'm a hugger. When I have kids of my own, I'm going to be that parent who embarrasses them by hugging them in public long after they're old enough to drive.

"When I first started drawing, I wasn't good. But I persisted, worked hard, and honed my skills."

"Did anyone tell you that you weren't good enough?" she asks in a small voice, lowering her eyes to her hands. My heart aches for her—obviously someone told her that. But she's a kid, for God's sake. She has plenty of time to practice.

"As a matter of fact, yes. I had a teacher at school who told me I should concentrate on math or another subject because while my art was decent, it was nothing to brag about."

"What did you do?"

I pause for a few seconds, remembering that day. "I cried a lot and was unmotivated for weeks. Then I made a pact with myself. I'd work hard and give it my best shot, and if nothing came of it, at least I'd tried. Also, it was about that time I heard the phrase, 'Opinions are like assholes. Everyone has one.' I became very fond of it."

Julie claps her hand over her mouth, giggling. "You're not supposed to use the a-word around me."

Oh, crap. Right, I'm not up to date with Parenting 101.

"Sorry. Will you rat me out to your dad?"

"No, it can be our little secret." She lightens up, and she's evidently thrilled at the idea of keeping a secret. Ah, a girl after my own heart.

"Anyway, back to our conversation. If you're determined enough and work hard, you'll get where you want to."

"You really think that?" she asks hopefully.

"Yes."

Luke takes Julie to his desk next, and I send an e-mail to my brother Logan. He is the CFO of the company and Sebastian is the CEO. Logan has taken over some of Sebastian's responsibilities until the latter returns from his honeymoon.

Six o'clock comes all too soon, and the ping of the elevator announces Eric's return. He strides into the office with his chin held high, as if he owns the room. The man is pure masculinity and confidence, and I start hyperventilating just by *looking* at him.

He's more than eye candy because candy can be resisted. Eric Callahan is eye-cupcake. Delicious and utterly irresistible. What a lethal combo.

As he finds Julie—who's currently at Luke's desk—his expression lights up. The more I study his face, the more similarities I find between him and Julie. She is so taken with what Luke's showing her on his computer she doesn't even realize her dad is in the room.

"How was she?" Eric asks me, stopping in front of my desk.

"Great. She's a well-behaved kid."

His shoulders are hunched with tension, and I don't like it. I'd rather see him the way he was at the wedding: carefree and happy. "How was your day?"

"Working with a new team is always tough." Winking, he adds, "Have to do justice to my nickname."

"Why *do* they call you 'the shark,' anyway?"

Flashing his teeth in a wide smile, he says, "I bite. Often."

I have no idea why these three words cause me to bite my lip, but I only realize I'm doing it when Eric's eyes zero in on my mouth. *Jesus.* I haven't reacted to a man this way in a long time. Is there anything he can say or do that won't set my nerves on edge? I doubt it.

"Dad," Julie exclaims, noticing her father's presence. "Can we stay a little longer? Luke's showing me an *awesome* computer program for designing."

"Sure." Eric observes his daughter before turning his attention to me.

"You'd say yes to anything she asks, wouldn't you?" I inquire.

He doesn't hesitate. "Yes. If it makes her happy.

The things I've endured to see my daughter smile…." He shakes his head. "Let's say that standing here talking to a beautiful woman is a pleasant way to spend the time while indulging Julie."

His gaze lingers on me for long seconds, and I can feel the tips of my ears heat up. *Damn my ears.*

Ignoring the 'beautiful' remark, I ask, "What did you endure? Humor me."

"Let's see. Once, she asked me if I'd dress up as a character from *Beauty and the Beast*. Turns out I had to play Belle. I rocked that costume like you wouldn't believe it."

It's a good thing I'm sitting because his words liquefy my muscles. This man is eye-cupcake with a side of chocolate sauce, and if he talks about playing Belle for his daughter for one more second, my ovaries might jump him.

I try to keep from laughing, but a giggle finds its way past my lips anyway. "It's blowing my mind that you even know who Belle is, and I can totally see you rocking a dress. Your secret is safe with me," I assure him. "It must be hard, being a single parent."

He clenches his jaw. "We manage. I don't do everything on my own. My mother helps, and Julie has nannies. Still, she misses her mother daily."

There's a finality in his tone that clues me in not to question him further. The silence stretches for a few seconds, and then he points at the designs in front of me, asking, "Are those yours?"

"Yes."

Rounding the corner of my desk, he stands next to

me, looking at my sketches.

"I drew them this afternoon between giving Julie instructions," I explain. "We won't be using them for the current collection because they don't match the direction, but I like to play around, and I can always keep them and see if they'll fit in future collections."

"They're very...." He pauses as if searching for the right word. "Happy, optimistic."

I nod. "My drawings and my mood go hand in hand."

"This means you were happy today." He rests a hand on my shoulder, and the touch warms me. In fact, it more than warms me. It sends tendrils of heat along my nerve endings.

"Yes. I had a lot of fun with Julie. I'm happy you allowed her to come here."

Since my divorce, I've been careful around men—deeming any man who doesn't share my last name as distrustful even before he opens his mouth. But something about Eric completely disarms me. I feel at ease around him, and that scares the living shit out of me. Probably because I have a hard time believing that a man who has no qualms putting his ego aside for his daughter, dressing up as Belle, deserves to be mistrusted. Or maybe the reason is simpler—I haven't learned my lesson yet.

"Dad, we're done," Julie announces.

"All right, let's go."

The pad of his thumb connects with my shoulder and the touch feels loaded with tension, almost intimate. When he retracts his hand, cold grips me. I walk them both to the elevator, and as the doors open, Eric says, "See you tomorrow."

The fact that I'll see him every day for the next two weeks sinks in. Something in his gaze tells me he's thinking the exact same thing. The air between us is instantly charged, and I avert my gaze as Julie bids me good-bye, and they disappear in the elevator.

What have I gotten myself into?

Chapter Three

Pippa

"Hey, sis," Alice says into the phone as I enter my apartment later.

"Hey. Do you want to drop by?"

"Are you out of food again?" Alice asks, her voice both stern and amused.

"No. Do I need a reason to invite my sister over?"

The last couple of times I asked Alice to come over, I *was* out of food and asked her to bring something from the restaurant she owns. I love cooking. As a kid, I helped my mother in the kitchen. Cooking daily for eleven people was a true team effort, but a lot of fun. Cooking for myself is no fun, hence why I've rarely done it over the past months. It makes my loneliness almost palpable.

"I guess not. So, how was the meeting with Mr. Sexy Pants today?"

"Stop calling him that," I answer. Kicking off my heels, I open my fridge and discover I have some leftover pizza from yesterday. It'll have to do.

"Why? You have a better name?"

"Mr. Sexy Ass, Sexy Lips?" I suggest.

"I see you've given this some thought."

"Yeah, but I'm still not ready for a relationship, and neither is he." I press the phone to my ear with one shoulder as I walk to my living room, a plate with pizza in one hand, a glass of soda in the other.

I moved into this one-bedroom apartment after my divorce. The spacious living room is decorated in warm shades of brown and cream. The L-shaped couch and the library dominate the space, and the two things are probably a reflection of me. I love few things more than curling up on the couch with a glass of wine and a steamy romance novel.

On the wall opposite the couch hangs a painting by Summer, the younger of my two sisters. The vibrant turquoise on the canvas contrasts beautifully with the rest of the room.

I love the place, but I wasn't cut out to live by myself. I can't get used to the quiet after growing up with eight siblings. However, moving in with one of my sisters at my age would be ridiculous.

"Who said anything about a relationship?" Alice asks. "Wham-bam, thank you, ma'am."

"Alice!" I admonish, slumping on my couch. "I don't do one-night stands, and you know that. You don't do them either. Where is this coming from?"

"You need some fun, and you could do multiple one-night stands. At any rate, he'll only be here for a couple of months. You have the perfect excuse. Then he'll be out of your life, and you'll solve the cobweb situation."

I freeze in the act of taking a bite of my pizza.

"Okay, stop using cobweb. My skin is starting to crawl."

"He seems like a good guy, and they are a disappearing species."

"Yeah, they are," I agree with a sigh, remembering my ex. His betrayal left me with deep scars. As a lump settles in my throat and my eyes sting with unshed tears, I admit something to myself—I'm afraid I won't find love again. Hell, I'm afraid I don't *deserve* to be loved. Taking a deep breath, I close my eyes, refusing to cry.

"So, what are you gonna do?" Alice asks.

"Nothing. I'll teach Julie the ins and outs of designing, and that's all."

"Damn, you're stubborn."

"I've gotta go," I say. "I have some pizza leftovers to concentrate on, and you're killing my buzz."

"Fine. Just tell me you won't be daydreaming about the *ins and outs* of his probably fantastic lovemaking skills."

"I won't," I reply before clicking off.

Liar, liar, pants on fire.

***

As I drive to work the next morning, I decide the best course of action is to minimize the number of interactions between Eric and me. Over the next two days, whenever he drops off or picks up Julie, I pretend to be busy, barely sharing words with him.

The intense exchange of hot looks makes up for the lack of conversation, though. The man is impossible to ignore whenever he's in the room. His presence is like a magnet, oozing testosterone and masculinity, drawing me to him against my better judgment.

"You've been avoiding me," he states on Thursday morning. I'm sitting behind my desk and Eric stands on the other side, propping himself with his fists on the wooden surface, leaning slightly forward, a naughty smile playing on his lips.

I like to read people, so I tend to overanalyze body language. His appearance now is domineering, which messes with my hormones. The curiosity in his eyes messes with my mind. I have to give it to him; he doesn't tiptoe around. He goes straight for the target.

"Guilty as charged." Dropping my voice to a whisper, I add, "Why have you been flirting with me?"

Eric rounds the corner of my desk until he's next to me, invading my personal space. Then he casually leans with his ass against my desk, crossing his arms over his chest, pinning me with his gaze. "We've barely talked over the last few days."

"Eye-flirting is still flirting," I inform him, stubbornly holding his gaze. "I've been out of the dating scene for a while, but I can still read the signals. So, what gives? You said you were off the market at the wedding."

Eric doesn't hesitate. "I can't seem to help myself around you."

Well, what can I say to that?

"Your honesty is disarming."

"Maybe it's my weapon." The words roll off his tongue so sexily it nearly takes my breath away.

"Why would you need one?" I mumble.

"To make you blush and squirm." Leaning forward, he says, "You look delicious when you do that."

I'm unable to hold his gaze anymore. Jesus. His words affect me too much.

"You can't talk to me like that," I whisper.

"Why?"

"We're at the office." My desk is far enough from everyone else that they can't hear our conversation, but that doesn't mean I can't use them as an excuse.

"Not a good reason," Eric answers.

"Because I don't know how to handle it." I swallow, my skin humming at his proximity. To my astonishment, he doesn't utter a witty comeback, just nods.

"Fair enough. I'm leaving now and will be back at six. Will you be avoiding me when I pick up Julie?"

I chuckle. "Probably. It's safest. I might do something silly otherwise."

Not taking his eyes off me, Eric lowers his voice. "We wouldn't want that, would we?"

***

Eric

"Let's take a break," Max says, punching the pause

button on his treadmill. We're at a gym downtown, letting off steam. Working out is my number one choice for putting a stressful day behind me. I keep running for fifteen more seconds before pressing pause.

"You're not as fit as you used to be Bennett," I tell him after I step off the treadmill. "You kicked my ass every time when we were doing laps in college."

"I was on the polo team back then. It's hard to keep that level of fitness."

I met Max when I was doing my MBA. He was a junior in college, while I was a married man with a kid. Our friendship started with me giving him shit over his weird beard phase, and him calling me old man, despite the fact that I'm only a few years older.

"Let's hit the bench press. I don't have much time."

"Why are you in such a hurry?" He drinks with large gulps from his water bottle as we walk to the nearest free machines.

"I'm picking up Julie in half an hour."

"She's with Pippa, right?"

"Yeah. Your sister's been great, helping Julie."

"Cut the crap. I saw the two of you at the wedding. She's been through enough, so don't mess with her."

"I'm not planning to."

We don't say anything more as we start with the bench press, but his warning pisses me off. The last thing I want is to mess with Pippa. I only met this woman a week ago, yet her well-being is surprisingly important for me. Maybe it's because she's shown so much kindness to my daughter, but she's gotten under my skin, and I like how it feels. Against my better judgment, I find myself looking for a reason to keep seeing her after Julie's time with her is over.

Once we're done with the bench press, we proceed to do sit-ups. I want to close off the training session with another round on the treadmill.

"I'm gonna run another fifteen, and then I'm leaving," I tell Max.

He shakes his head. "No more running for me today."

"Who's the old man now?" I toss at him.

"The birth certificate would indicate it's still you. Afraid you can't change that. Don't forget what I said about my sister."

"I would've expected this from your brothers, not you." I break into a light jog on the treadmill, increasing the speed with the buttons. "You're my friend."

"Pippa's my sister. Family trumps friends, sorry." Max is grinning now. I give him a thumbs-up, concentrating on my sprint. Yeah, I know about the Bennetts' unspoken rule. *Family comes first.*

It sums up my view about life, which is probably why Max and I became friends in the first place.

I leave the gym shortly after, heading straight to Bennett Enterprises. With Max's warning in mind, and Pippa's earlier hesitation, I walk inside her office determined to simply pick up my daughter and head back out. Then I see Pippa and Julie *dancing* in the center of the room, and my determination flies out the window. Julie loves dancing, but because of her leg problem, she's shy when other people are present, and the office is full.

"What's going on?" I ask when I reach them.

"We're celebrating," Pippa answers, not stopping the dance moves to whatever imaginary music she's dancing to.

"Ms. Watson wrote that she saw a great improvement in my design." My daughter's grin is contagious. Ms. Watson is the program director of the design course she'll be attending starting next week, and Julie has to send in designs periodically. "I'm going to get my things now so we can leave."

Pippa stops swinging her hips after Julie turns her attention to packing.

"This is a miracle," I whisper to her. "My daughter never dances in front of strangers."

"Have you ever danced *with* her?"

"No," I admit.

"See, that's the secret. If you make a fool of yourself, she won't feel like the spotlight's on her."

I have to admit it makes sense.

"How come none of your employees seemed surprised by the dance?" I inquire.

Pippa blushes, and then it hits me why.

"You dance in the office on a regular basis?"

"No, only when there's something to celebrate." She shrugs. "They got used to it."

"You have the most unusual leadership style I've ever seen."

Pippa cocks an eyebrow, folding her arms over her chest. "And I suppose you're the ogre type who doesn't feel in charge unless everyone's afraid of you?"

"Hey." I hold up my palms in mock defense. "We can't all dance our way to the top."

Her expression is full of playfulness and warmth, and I find this refreshing, even though I'm not going to dance in front of my team anytime soon. Or ever.

"You should try being nice to your team. You'd be surprised how far that can get you," she says.

I should step back and leave with my daughter, but instead, I lean forward and tell Pippa in a low voice, "You look sexy dancing."

I watch with satisfaction as she inhales sharply, and her eyes darken. She turns around, walking to her desk with purposeful strides, giving me a perfect view of her round, perky ass. Damn her pencil skirt for showing off her curves. It weakens my determination to keep my distance.

I'll try again tomorrow.

***

Pippa

Eric and I make it through Friday without spending time with each other, and as the second week starts, I'm optimistic it'll go by the same way.

Then, of course, my family decides to intervene. At noon on Wednesday, the entire creative team heads out for the weekly lunch we have at the nearby

French restaurant. I don't join them because I promised Julie we'd stay in and get a head start on the drawings for the day. She's not here yet, but Eric usually drops her off during the lunch break. I'm debating if I should order Chinese or tacos for Julie and me when Alice steps in my empty office, holding two bags of food. At first, I think she decided to have an impromptu lunch with me, but something about her smile tells me she's plotting against me.

"What are you doing here?" I ask her.

"Why, hello to you too. I've brought lunch for you and Eric," she announces, as if it's the most natural thing in the world.

"You—"

I swallow my words as the elevator opens again and Eric and Julie walk in, chatting animatedly about some movie they went to yesterday.

"Hi, Alice." Eric doesn't appear surprised in the slightest about her presence.

"I brought roast duck, as promised," she tells him. Turning to Julie, Alice asks, "Are you ready to go?"

Julie nods.

"What is going on?" I ask, bewildered.

"Julie and I are meeting Nadine at the aquarium, the one that opened five blocks away. They have a special program today, and I figured Julie would love to see it."

"You don't mind, Pippa, do you?" Julie asks. "We'll be back in an hour."

"I don't mind," I reply.

One glance at Eric tells me he knows about all of

this. My mind is racing. *What is going on?* I recognize this for the setup it is. I've staged 'accidental lunches' before, but being on the receiving end is different. Evidently, in the face of my stubbornness, Alice and Nadine have decided to take matters into their own hands. I should have known karma would do a number on me eventually. What goes around comes around. And looking at Eric, I have to admit, karma could do a lot worse.

As my sister and Julie leave, Eric heads toward me, carefully placing the food Alice brought on my desk.

As if anticipating my question, he says in an amused voice, "Your sister called me last night, asking if she could take Julie to the aquarium today. It was such an obvious attempt to get the two of us alone that I barely made it through the conversation without bursting into laughter."

"So, why did you agree?" I'm genuinely intrigued.

"She bribed me with roast duck. I couldn't say no," he says with humor.

"Perfectly legitimate reason. That duck is to die for."

"And Julie was listening to our conversation. She started jumping up and down when Alice mentioned the aquarium. I was going to say no, mostly because I've only met your sister and Nadine once before, but I lost the battle."

I help him unpack the food and gesture for him to sit in the chair on the opposite side of my desk.

As we both sit, he says, "You look gorgeous

today, Pippa. You'll forgive me if I slide one or two inappropriate looks your way during lunch. *Completely unintentional*, of course." He says this with a straight face, and my cheeks and ears heat up. He's in the mood for flirting openly today, and for some reason, I'm looking forward to whatever lunch might bring. This will be fun.

"You're welcome to try," I say. "But I warn you, the result might be more than you can handle."

God, he's beautiful. I allow my gaze to roam freely over his luscious lips and broad shoulders. My senses go into overdrive as I imagine the well-built muscles underneath his shirt, every ridge and every line. That's when I realize he's watching me while I'm watching him. He raises a brow, letting out a whistle.

"You're undressing me with your eyes, and we're not even halfway through lunch." His voice reverberates in a lower octave than before. It sounds unbelievably sexy.

"It's the testosterone you're oozing. It clouds my mind, does unspeakable things to my senses." The second the words are out of my mouth, I nearly choke on them. *Did I really say that out loud?* I'm on a slippery slope. I can feel it in my bones… and other places.

His hand freezes in the motion of cutting a slice of the duck.

A girl must always land on her feet. If I pass this as a voluntary comment, it'll be less embarrassing.

"You're not the only one who can use honesty as a weapon," I inform him.

"Clearly."

"Why did you say you're damaged goods at the wedding?"

"Losing someone you love leaves a mark." Judging by his clipped tone, he doesn't want me to insist on this topic. I *will* drop it, but I want to make a point before.

"That doesn't make you damaged goods. I wouldn't call you that."

"What would you call me?"

"Alice nailed it," I answer, deciding to lighten the mood. "I can't think of a better description than tall, dark, and handsome."

"I see. Are you flirting? 'Cause last week, you admonished me for giving you hot looks."

"I think I am, although I haven't flirted in a long time, so I can't be sure. Can I test this out some more on you? Maybe I can get my game back."

"You want to exercise your flirting muscles on me and plan to actually flirt with another man?" Eric sets his jaw, his gaze igniting me. "'Cause then we're having a problem."

"Did you just go alpha on me?" I ask, fascinated.

"Do you like it?"

"Yeah." I giggle, completely embarrassed. We focus on our food for the next few minutes, wolfing it down in no time, which leaves us with another forty minutes to kill until Julie and Alice return. My dirty mind supplies me with a wealth of options that would keep us busy. Kissing, ripping clothes off... *Goddammit. What has gotten into me?* I've never had such sexual thoughts about a man I wasn't dating. It's Eric's fault entirely. Why does he have to be so tall, dark, and handsome?

I rack my brain for a safe topic.

"I've bought something for Julie," I say, rummaging in my bag. "Before you start protesting, I bought it from the kids' section at the store. It's a tinted cranberry lip balm, packaged to look like a lipstick."

"She was very specific about wanting a lipstick," Eric says skeptically. He eyes the object in my hand with utmost distrust. I recognize that expression; I've seen it in Julie before.

"It's all about how you sell it to her," I explain.

"What do you mean?"

"You can tell her that it was in the section for adult women, and that even her favorite actress wears it."

He frowns as if weighing the merits of my suggestion. "Why don't you give it to her?"

"Trying to buy your way out?" I tease.

"No, but she'd believe you more, since she looks up to you. Also, she threw in my face that I don't understand her because I'm not a woman."

"Ah, I see. How about her nanny?"

"Julie doesn't go to her for advice. Apparently, she's too old. The woman is forty-five!"

"Yeah, but to a twelve-year-old, forty-five is ancient. When I was her age, I considered everyone above twenty to be from the age of the dinosaurs."

"You're amazing. How come you speak teenager

language?"

"I saw some of my siblings grow up, and my inner twelve-year-old is still a big part of me. I take it Julie isn't that close to your mother either?"

Eric runs a hand through his hair, leaning back in his chair. "Mom adores Julie, but her idea of spending time with her granddaughter is teaching her manners, or drinking afternoon tea together. Not exactly a hit with a twelve-year-old."

"Okay, I'll talk to her," I assure him. A shadow crosses his face, and I don't like it one bit. "What are you worried about?"

"I keep wondering if bringing her here was a good idea. She has no friends her age in San Francisco."

"Yes, but she'll meet some next week when her course starts."

He nods, but it's obvious he's still not convinced.

"Why didn't you leave her in Boston?"

"She would've had to stay with Mom, and she didn't want that. I have to be honest. I couldn't bear the thought of being away from Julie for almost three months. I'm an egoist when it comes to my daughter. I planned the trip here so it would coincide with her school vacation."

"Your idea of egoism sounds like love to me." I like this man more with every word he utters, and this is dangerous for too many reasons. Eric's eyes light up, and he looks young and almost carefree, like he did when we danced at the wedding.

"She stole my heart from the moment she was born. I was twenty-one, so I had other things on my mind, but I did a 180-degree change the moment I held her in my arms. Every time I have to make a decision in my personal life—and even in my professional life—I first think about how it will affect her."

It is precisely at this moment that I realize it's not only Eric's good looks that cause me to think about him so often. His ability to be completely selfless as well as downright adorable with his daughter beckons to me.

"That's very commendable of you." My heart sighs, a multitude of emotions overwhelming me.

"Which brings me to my self-imposed ban on not giving hot looks, which doesn't work when I'm around you."

"How shameful of me to tempt you like this," I reply playfully. "So, you're basically a monk?"

He smirks. "My plan is for Julie to believe that until she's eighteen."

It doesn't escape my attention that he hasn't given me a straight answer, which can only mean one thing. He's *not* a monk.

"Good luck with that," I murmur.

"I don't want her to ever think she's not the most important person to me."

"Eric, you don't owe me any explanations. For what it's worth, though, it's a great explanation."

He studies me for a beat but doesn't say anything else. The air between us grows thick with tension again. I hold his gaze until it becomes too much, and then I break the eye contact. Luckily, Julie, Alice, and

Nadine arrive.

"Dad, Alice and Nadine had an awesome idea. I told them I love the *Harry Potter* series, and that we're rewatching it on Saturday, and guess what?"

"What?" Eric asks. My stomach clenches. I have the nagging suspicion I know where this is going.

"They told me Pippa loves it too. We should invite her to watch it with us."

Eric and I turn to my sister and Nadine in unison.

"Please, Daddy," Julie insists.

Uh-oh. She's making those puppy eyes Eric can't resist. He'll agree to it before he utters one word.

"Pippa, if you don't have any plans this weekend, would you like to join us on Saturday afternoon?" Eric asks.

"Sure," I reply out loud, my heart stuttering in my chest. *Bad, bad idea.* I can barely resist Eric in an open space like my office or a party with hundreds of people. Being in his home feels too intimate, especially for two people who can't keep their eyes off each other. What will happen with the lights out? The mere thought makes me shiver.

As Julie and Eric negotiate whether to do a marathon of all the movies or select a few, I push Alice and Nadine to the side.

"Girls, I know what you're doing," I murmur. "Stop."

"Yeah, we thought you'd say that," Alice replies.

"I'm not just saying it. I mean it." I use my *bigger sister* tone, but unfortunately, it stopped being effective a million years ago.

As calmly as possible, I say, "Neither of us is—"

"You two need a push," Nadine interrupts. "How was lunch?" She smiles suggestively. *Ah, damn.* Nadine and my brother Logan were the ones I staged the accidental lunch for about six months ago.

"Full disclosure," Alice says, "I didn't insinuate to Julie to invite you just to set you and Eric up. You need a distraction this weekend. You already turned down our offer for a girls' night out."

All my annoyance with my sister dissipates. Always looking out for me, even though the last thing I want in the world is to worry her.

"I'm fine," I say a little too cheerfully. This Friday would have marked my fifth wedding anniversary. "I'll be fine."

"If you say so. Anyway, if you two don't want anything to do with each other, how hard will watching a few movies be?"

Almost involuntarily, I glance over my shoulder and find Eric sizing me up. As his eyes find mine, I have my answer.

Very, very hard.

Chapter Four

Pippa

"These are wonderful," I say, admiring the shoes I'm trying on. I'm in my favorite shoe shop in downtown San Francisco. The red pumps look ridiculously good on me.

"I set them aside especially for you," the clerk says, winking at me.

"Oh, you're a bad influence," I tell her. I walk around in the store, admiring the shoes in the mirror. I don't know why I love shoes as much as I do, but I'm sure it can be classified as an addiction.

"I can bring you more to try on," she offers.

"No, no, or I'll end up buying all of them."

"So, you're taking these?"

"You need to ask?" Toeing them off, I bend to take the shoes, then hand them to her. "Pack them up. On second thought, don't. Pack my old ones. I'll walk away in these."

"Got it. Nothing like a new pair of shoes to brighten the day, right?"

"Amen to that."

When I walk out of the store, I'm smiling ear to

ear, which is what I needed today. I have fielded invitations from my family for the past two days. They all tried to convince me to join them for dinner on Friday evening, but I declined every time, assuring them I'll be *fine* on my own. But today is Friday, and I'm not so sure I'm fine.

I remain in my office long after Julie and the team leave, drawing like a madwoman. It's dark outside when I finally lift my head from my sketch. I put down my pencil, flexing my wrist. A glance at the clock tells me it's ten. Sighing, I lean back in my chair, staring at the ceiling. I'm not ready to go home, not yet. Today of all days, I don't want to be alone in my apartment. Maybe I should have taken my parents up on their offer to sleep at their house tonight, but they'd worry about me again.

Rubbing my temples, I flex my stiff neck to the right and the left. Thank God, this isn't my fifth wedding anniversary.

On our first anniversary, Terence forgot to show up at the restaurant we had reservations at and bought me flowers the next day to apologize. On our second anniversary, he forgot about the reservation and didn't even apologize for it. On our third one, I didn't make any plans, and he didn't bother to pretend he cared about the damn anniversary anyway. On our fourth one, we were in the process of getting divorced.

Today, on what would have been our fifth anniversary, I received a call from my lawyer. He informed me that Terence got himself a new lawyer and wants to appeal the court decision, which was in favor of not giving Terence a single penny, as was stated in the prenup. But apparently, this new lawyer found a loophole in the prenup, and Terence wants to fight again. Well, good. Let him fight. I will do the same. That bastard won't get one cent.

Sighing, I pick up my pencil again, wanting to lose myself in my drawings again. The ding of the elevator doors startles me.

"Who's—" I begin, but stop when I see the intruder. Eric.

"Pippa, what are you doing here?" he asks.

"I work here," I reply, rising to my feet. "Why did you come? Did something happen to Julie?"

"No. She forgot some of her sketches here, and she wanted to work on them during the weekend."

I inspect my desk, and sure enough, I find her sketches buried under my own.

"Here they are," I announce. "Why didn't you tell me? I would have brought them tomorrow."

"I didn't think you were still here. Thanks." His fingers touch mine as I hand him the sketches. I've been antsy for the past few hours, and the contact both calms and electrifies me at the same time. "Why are you here so late?"

"I stay up late sometimes. I have a lot of work, and I didn't want to go home." Pointing to the cupcakes near my keyboard, I infuse my voice with extra cheer as I add, "I have plenty of cupcakes to keep me company."

Eric's gaze holds mine for a few seconds, but it's

not a hot look; it's a concerned one. He breaks eye contact, staring at my designs instead.

"You're upset," he says finally.

"How can you tell?"

"You said your designs vary according to your mood. These are dark. Scary."

"These are scary? Not much of a horror movie man, I take it?"

"Nope," he admits. "They scare the crap out of me. Always have. Want to tell me what's wrong?" His voice is low and smooth, almost like a caress. It beckons me to open up to him. I debate brushing him off, but there is no reason to lie to him. Yes, he knows my brothers, but it's unlikely he'll tell them anything.

"Five years ago on this date, I married my ex. To fill you in, the reason behind our divorce was that I discovered he'd married me for my money."

Eric raises his eyebrows, his expression unreadable. Then, to my utter astonishment, he gives me a thumbs-up.

"In that case, I'm surprised you're taking out your feelings on your designs and not a voodoo doll or throwing darts at his picture."

I chuckle, grateful for his reaction. No additional questions, no brooding. Just laughing. *God, I can use some more of that right now.*

"I should have taken my sister up on the offer of going on a girls' night out instead of staying here by myself," I admit. "But I didn't want to worry anyone."

Eric taps his fingers on my desk as if considering something. "Let's you and I go out."

"What?"

"You need a distraction. I'd like to provide that. Besides, I'd like to see a more adult version of San Francisco. Until now, I've only seen the twelve-year-old version."

"How about Julie?"

"She's asleep, and Ms. Blackwell is at the house with her."

"Are you sure?"

"Yeah. Don't overthink this, Pippa," he says in a calm voice.

Oh, why the hell not? This man can make me laugh, and that's exactly what I need. "Okay. Give me Julie's sketches. I'll carry them in my bag."

"What do you want to do?" he asks.

"I want to dance," I tell him. "But no weird fifties music." I hold up my forefinger, accentuating every word with a swing. Eric looks on the verge of bursting out laughing.

"Why, you're wearing inappropriate underwear again?"

"Maybe I'm not wearing any at all," I tease. Big mistake. His eyes darken, his lips parting with a heavy exhale. In a fraction of a second, the air between us charges, a blanket of tension settling over us.

"You're not?" His voice is low and husky, and I shudder listening to it.

"I was kidding, Eric. Let's go."

"Before we go," he says, "let's set some ground

rules."

"I'm all ears."

"No hot looks, and no flirting."

I tilt my head to one side, barely holding back my laughter. "Why do I get the impression you're talking to yourself, not to me?"

"Because I am, but it's on you to keep me accountable."

"That sounded businesslike. Are you going to shark out on me if I don't hold you accountable?" I inquire.

"You bet I will." His tone is cheeky, almost challenging.

"You can count on me. It'll be easy-peasy."

As I grab my purse, slinging it over my shoulder, I steal glances at him and have to swallow hard as I take in his equally imposing and consuming presence. Okay, so maybe it won't be *that* easy. Eric's hand drops to the small of my back, guiding me as we head outside the building. I lean in to his touch, amazed by the warmth coursing through me.

A stubborn wind rustles the leaves and I turn my eyes skyward, searching for any signs of an upcoming storm. The sky is remarkably clear, though, with stars shimmering here and there. I inhale the smell of nearby roses and smile. It's a beautiful and peaceful evening, almost magical.

"Do you have any place in mind?" he asks me while signaling a passing cab to stop.

"I know a place that opened last month. They have three dance floors and a rooftop bar."

"Sounds great," he says after we climb in the car. I tell the cabbie the address, and afterward, we're on our way. We're halfway there when my phone rings.

"It's Alice," I tell Eric before pressing the phone to my ear and muttering, "Hi!"

"Where are you?" she asks. "You said you'd be working, and your office is empty."

"I—You're at the office? Why?"

"I wanted to check on you."

I love my sister to pieces. "I'm great, Alice. Don't worry." In the background, I hear Nadine's voice and Summer's unmistakable laughter. "Alice, why are the girls with you?"

"No one's with me," Alice replies a little too quickly.

"I can hear them."

She sighs. "We all came to check on you."

"You organized a girls' night out, didn't you?" Guilt gnaws at me as I eye Eric.

"Sort of. Depends. What are you doing right now?"

"Eric and I are going to get some drinks."

"You're on a date?" She practically screams the last words, so of course Eric overhears her. I sneak a glance at him, and sure enough, he smiles.

"No. It's not a date. It's as nondate as it can be."

"Right. Then I was absolutely not planning a girls' night out. Go back to your nondate. Bye." The line goes static. One glance at Eric and I confirm he's about to burst out laughing.

"That was my sister," I tell him.

"Do you want to go out with her?"

"No," I answer. "I love girls' nights out, but I want something different this time."

Winking, he says, "Let's enjoy the hell out of this *nondate*."

The venue is packed when we arrive, which is not surprising, given it's Friday night. Eric and I enter through the VIP area. A friend of mine owns the club, and every time we speak, she reminds me that I'm permanently on the VIP guest list. I've never taken her up on her offer before. There are three floors, and the first two are too packed to breathe. The third one is for VIP guests only, and even so, it's crowded.

"What do you want to drink?" Eric asks me.

"Red wine."

He nods and heads to the bar, leaving me on my own. Several men ogle me with what are clearly unorthodox thoughts, and after a few minutes, one of them walks up to me. He's wearing a black shirt with a white pattern that resembles an uninspired combination of a zebra and a Dalmatian.

I immediately put my fight face on.

"Can I buy you a drink?" he asks.

"Thank you, but no." I cross my arms over my chest and look away from him, hoping he'll get the appropriate *unavailable* vibe from me. He doesn't.

"I bet you're a vodka type," he continues.

I groan. "Please don't insist. I'm not interested in anything."

The guy doesn't budge. Unbelievable. I do the

only sensitive thing and walk away, but the idiot follows me. Right. I knew I should have gone to Judo classes with Alice when she asked me to.

"You can't—" he begins, but a deep voice interrupts him from behind me.

"Are you deaf?" Eric bellows. "She said no. Fuck off."

"And you are?"

I have to give it to the guy; he's got balls. Despite Eric looking every inch an alpha—and a pissed one at that—the guy doesn't back off.

"Her fiancé. Leave, unless you want to have a black eye to match your shirt."

At the word 'fiancé,' the muscles in my entire body clench. The guy blinks, panicked, and scurries away.

Eric hands me a glass, his gaze following the schmuck through the crowd.

"I was handling him. I can deal with things like this." I take a sip of my wine, and it tastes delicious.

"I don't doubt that," he answers, finally snapping his gaze to me. "But just because you can doesn't mean you have to."

"Why not?"

"You have enough on your mind tonight without having to fend off idiots." He raises his glass at me. "I'll do that for you. The expression on his face when I said 'fiancé' was priceless."

I tense again at the word, and this time, Eric takes notice.

"I crossed a line saying that?"

I shrug. "No, I'm—I don't…." I don't finish the sentence because I honestly don't know why hearing that word makes me anxious. Probably because it brings back ugly memories. "Anyway, his face *was* priceless."

"I'm surprised he bought it," Eric says.

"You looked scary," I assure him.

"Yeah, but I'm not acting like a fiancé should."

This piques my interest. "And how's that?"

Eric drums his fingers on his glass and the back of my neck prickles, as if he was doing that exact motion on my skin. I let out a heavy sigh as a cold shudder runs down my spine.

Eric steps closer. "If you were my fiancée, everyone here would know it, trust me."

"How so?"

"I wouldn't take my hands off you. I'd touch you every chance I got."

My breath catches, yet somehow I manage to whisper, "That would be very indecent."

"Oh, I'd be indecent all the way." Leaning in, he brings his lips to my ear. "And you'd love it."

I push him away. "You are full of yourself, fake fiancé, given that this is a nondate."

"I know my strengths," he retaliates with nonchalance. "I've got game."

"Prove it," I say.

This catches him off guard. "Come again?"

The two words have an atomic effect on me. A wave of heat washes over me, starting in my center and spreading all through my fingertips. He didn't even mean it in a sexual way, but my mind is in the gutter. So is Eric's, judging by the dangerous glint in his eyes.

"Dance with me," I say. "Dancing is part of having *game*."

Eric nods. "Your wish is my command," he says. "Fiancée."

We put our glasses on a nearby table and he takes my hand, intertwining his fingers with mine, leading me to the center of the dance floor. He looks delicious in his suit. We're surrounded by men and women in business attire. Consultants, bankers, and whatnot have come to let loose and relax after a week of hard work.

The music has an addictive rhythm, and as I start moving my hips to it, I realize dancing was a bad idea. Eric's eyes rake over my body, setting me on fire. Then he turns me around, so my back faces him. Maybe it's the inviting music or the dim lights, but my thoughts drift away, leaving room only for sensation. He pushes my hair to the side, baring a part of my neck to him. His hot breath lands on my skin as we sway our hips in tandem. Mimicking the couples surrounding us, his hands reach for my hips, gripping me strongly. Pulling me to him, he flattens my back against his chest. An electric current zips through us, setting my nerve endings on edge.

"Whoa," I say, taking a step forward, at the same time Eric exclaims, "Damn."

"Okay, so touching is out of the question."

He nods in agreement. "Yeah, let's make that

dancing is out of the question. I won't be able to keep my fingers away from you here with the dark lights."

"I really wanted to dance, though." I pout a little, shrugging.

"Stop pouting or I'll damn everything and kiss that beautiful mouth of yours."

His honesty is so disarming. I'm not even sure how to answer. I expect every man to have a secret agenda, to have trouble keeping his lies from surfacing. Eric's different in the best possible way.

"You always say what's on your mind, don't you?" I ask him.

"Yep. Big fault of mine. Lost a few business deals because of it."

"Let's go on the rooftop, have drinks, and talk. Talking is safe, right?"

"I hope so."

The rooftop is lined with cozy outdoor couches and dove-shaped lamps, and it's remarkably uncrowded. It becomes clear why within seconds; the wind is stronger than it was down on the street, and it's almost chilly. I rub my arms vigorously, and without a word, Eric shrugs out of his suit jacket, draping it around my shoulders.

"Thank you," I murmur. We find a corner that is shielded from the wind and take refuge there. "We didn't bring our glasses."

"I'll buy us new ones. Wine again?"

I nod. As Eric walks to the rooftop bar, I pull his jacket tighter around me. It smells amazing and fills me with a strange sense of safety. He returns with two glasses a few minutes later, handing me one and sitting next to me. I approximate there are eight inches of distance between us—not nearly enough to be considered safe. I can practically sense the testosterone oozing off him.

"What do you want to talk about?" I ask him, trying hard to keep my mind out of the gutter.

"Anything," he replies. "Tell me about you, but please, make an effort to find something vile and repugnant. So far, I've learned that you get along with my daughter, are funny as hell, and have a body made for sin. Bad combo for my determination to remain a monk."

I laugh out loud, as he continues, "There's something I meant to ask you after your phone call. Why are you keeping your family at arm's length?"

Coming from anyone else, this question would set me on edge, but instead, I sink in my seat. My muscles loosen up one by one. I love that I don't feel the need to pretend around him, or keep up the bravado.

I take a sip of wine, wondering how to best formulate my answer.

"I'm not used to having my siblings fret over me. I mean, sure, Sebastian and Logan have made it their mission to hover over us, but I'm the family's official worrier." I take another sip then play with the glass in my hands, focusing on the way the liquid swirls inside. "When we were little, I worried there wasn't enough of anything for everyone. When money ceased to be a problem, I worried if I was setting a good enough example for them." I chuckle, remembering one particular incident. "On my twenty-eighth birthday, Summer told me that whenever she's in a dilemma, she asks herself, 'What would Pippa do?'"

"You're a remarkable woman," Eric says in a soft voice.

"How can you tell? We met two weeks ago."

"I've seen you with Julie. That's all I need to know. You should cut yourself some slack." He hesitates for a few seconds, before adding, "I have a hunch you keep punishing yourself for something."

I raise my glass to him. "Nice to meet a fellow people reader."

"So, what are you punishing yourself for?" he insists.

"Being stupid," I admit. Eric raises his hand, obvious from his expression that he wants to contradict me, but I stop him with a headshake. "I sensed in my gut that something was wrong with Terence, and still I went through with the wedding. All the signs were there, but I wanted to be blind. I wanted a family like the one I came from so badly, with lots of kids running around and many happy moments, that I ignored the signs."

"You weren't stupid, but you wear your heart on your sleeve, and you can't fathom that anyone else can have hidden agendas. You will eventually have everything you wish, Pippa."

I shrug. "It's okay. I'm happy with the family I

already have. They've been my rock through all of this. I relied on them and on plenty of sweets, good books, and occasional trips to a therapist, which didn't do much for me, if I'm honest."

"Ah, yes, therapists. It's hard to find the good ones." Eric's voice is so conversational, as if we're exchanging impressions about the weather. "Even the great ones can only help so much. You have to find things that ground you. For me, it was Julie. No matter how hard it was I had to pull myself together for her."

"You are a great father," I assure him. We're kindred spirits, he and I, and my heart clenches for him.

"I try. Do you want another glass?" He points to my empty one.

"No, I'm good. We should go. Long day ahead tomorrow."

"How so? You're only joining us after lunch."

"Sebastian and Ava are back from their honeymoon, so we'll have a family brunch at Alice's restaurant tomorrow morning."

We leave our corner and I shudder in the wind, despite the jacket. As we step out onto the street, he says, "Come on, I'll take you home."

"Nope. This is a nondate. I will take myself home."

"But—"

"We're not negotiating," I interrupt. "I'll grab a cab. There are plenty in this area. Oh, I almost forgot. What's your address? I need it for tomorrow."

I frown as he tells me the name of the street. I know it. It's a residential, no-fuss area. My surprise must show on my face because he asks, "Why do you seem so taken aback?"

"I was expecting you to live in one of the most expensive areas." Eying him with appreciation, I add, "But you're okay."

"I'm *okay*," he says stunned. "This is the most insulting non-insult I have ever received."

I snicker. "You understand what I mean."

He shakes his head. "I'm trying to set an example for Julie."

"Very commendable of you."

He steps forward, signaling to a cab approaching our spot to stop. The car pulls a few feet in front of us. Eric walks me to it, opening the back door for me.

I lean closer to him, dropping my voice. "This is by far the best anniversary I had."

As I slide in the backseat, he says, "Glad I could be of service. See you tomorrow. Looking forward to *talking* more with you."

He shuts the door and as the car lurches forward, it dawns on me that talking isn't safe. Not at all. Talking, hearing him pour his heart out is more dangerous than dancing or touching. Tomorrow will be interesting, to say the least.

Chapter Five

Pippa

I wake up with a jolt the next morning, hugging my pillow, enjoying the lazy morning. But my happiness slowly morphs into uneasiness. I can feel it even in my state of semi-sleepiness. Something's nagging at me—

"Shit."

Sitting upright in my bed, I grab my phone from the nightstand and stare at the display. It's ten past eleven. I was supposed to be at Alice's restaurant for the family brunch ten minutes ago.

That was my conscience nagging at me. I send a quick message to Alice.

Pippa: I'll be fifteen minutes late. Sorry.

Alice: Liar. You'll need at least half an hour.

Being on time for family gatherings is on my bucket list. I manage fine in my professional life, but utterly fail when it comes to punctuality in my personal life. I shower quickly but spend an inordinate amount of time deciding what to wear. I'll be going directly to Eric's after this and choosing the right dress is crucial. I need something that can spell out the message *No flirting* better than I can. In the end, I go for the most unflattering dress I own. A grayish mumbo jumbo that's large enough to be a tent. I have no idea how it ended up in my closet, but it'll save the day. Summer and Alice will make fun of me for weeks to come for wearing this.

The entire clan will be there, and I can't wait to see them, especially Christopher. He lives in Hong Kong, overseeing our operations in Asia, and is only here for a short time. I dearly hope he'll follow Max's lead and return home soon. Max was in London for a few years, but returned to San Francisco before the wedding, resuming his old position of International Operations Manager.

My sister's restaurant is high up one of San Francisco's hills, and the view is to die for. When I arrive, I linger outside for a few minutes, my eyes sweeping over the hills in front of me. The sun shines brightly, turning the foliage covering the hills a vivid green. Up here, San Francisco seems to be a different city than downtown. Nearby, birds sing happily, and I'd like to think they agree with me; it's a perfect early July day.

Walking inside, I expect everyone to already be stuffing their faces. Instead, my siblings are sitting at a long table with Sebastian heading it. Logan, Alice, Summer, and Daniel are on one side, with Blake, Max, and Christopher on the other. I hug Sebastian tightly before taking my seat between Max and Blake.

"Is this an unofficial board meeting?" I ask, ogling the stack of papers in front of Sebastian and ignoring

Alice and Summer's incredulous stares at my hideous dress.

"Yes," Sebastian answers.

"Well, let's start. Everyone's here, even both of the nice brothers," Blake says.

Max chuckles.

The friendly rivalry between the two sets of twins is always fun to watch. Christopher and Max are the older set. They ended up with the nickname 'the serious brothers' while Blake and Daniel are 'the party brothers.' While the moniker completely fits Blake and Daniel, Christopher and Max aren't *serious*. They're the biggest pranksters in the family. But they work hard with us at Bennett Enterprises, while Blake and Daniel don't have steady jobs. They do projects of their own from time to time, living off the dividends they receive from the company.

I straighten up in my seat and rest my elbows on the wooden surface. From across the table, Alice and Summer flash a smile, shaking their heads at the twins. I sneak a glance at Christopher and Max. For the millionth time, their resemblance strikes me. If they didn't have slightly different haircuts, I couldn't tell them apart. Maybe this makes me a bad sister, but it's always been like this. Now I finally accept it. When they were about ten, they started hating their likeness, so they made a point to always dress differently and get wildly different haircuts. Later they turned into teenagers and realized they could use being identical twins to their advantage. The year they turned fifteen will forever be known in our family as 'the year of the pranks.' They kept this up until they went to college, and even then, they liked to do a number on us from time to time. A dull ache settles in my chest at the thought that Christopher will leave again soon. I *really* want him back here. I need more brothers to hover over or simply to annoy.

"I want to run something by you," Sebastian says. "Ava's birthday is coming up, and I want to gift her shares in Bennett Enterprises. I will give them away from my own part, so your shares won't be diluted at all, and neither will your decision power."

There is a beat of silence, after which Logan says, "Great," which sums up how I feel in the best way possible.

"Brother," Blake tells Sebastian, "I don't give a fuck about dilution, but that's the most unromantic present ever. And that's coming from the least romantic brother in the family."

Blake winces at the word 'romantic.' Ah, one of these days I will plot his downfall as well. That will be an interesting challenge.

"Yes, but it's the perfect present for Ava," I say. The shares are distributed exclusively among our siblings and parents, and extending that courtesy to Ava... Well, I know how much family means to her. I look at Sebastian with renewed admiration. He certainly knows how to make gifts. Almost two years ago, he surprised my parents by buying them the ranch where we grew up. My dad had built it with his own hands, and my parents sold the ranch when

Sebastian needed capital for Bennett Enterprises. The new owners didn't put it up for sale until two years ago, and my brother immediately snatched it.

"Pippa's right," Alice agrees.

"She'll be thrilled," Summer adds.

"And she deserves it," Christopher says. "From what I've seen, she works as hard as we do."

"Plus, she is family," I finish.

Sebastian nods, his shoulders slumping slightly, tension ebbing away from his posture. I wonder why he thought we'd object to this. I've heard of families who fight over shares and money like sharks, but that has never been an issue in our family.

"So, everyone is all right with this? Mom and Dad already agreed," Sebastian says.

"Yeah, like anyone's going to tell you no," Blake remarks, echoing my thoughts. "We don't have schmucks in the family." He looks around the table once half-threateningly, as if daring anyone to contradict him. No one does, of course. "Anyway, I still think it's not the best present for a lady."

"I never said it'll be the only present. The shares will be accompanied by some jewelry."

I perk up at this. "I'll get on it right away." I've created unique engagement rings for Ava and Nadine, and their wedding rings also. I can't wait to do something like that again. "Do you have any specific requirements?"

"No. I trust you completely," Sebastian says.

"It'll be perfect," I assure him.

"Didn't Ava brush you off a long time ago when

you tried to give her jewelry?" Logan asks casually.

"Yeah, but that was before we got married. That gives me the license to buy her expensive gifts."

Both Blake and Daniel burst out laughing. Logan merely shakes his head.

"Bennett logic," Max remarks.

"It's completely foolproof," Christopher adds.

Sebastian passes the documents around the table, telling us where we have to sign.

"Now, there's something else I wanted to share with you," Sebastian begins after we're done. "Blake gave me some good news, which I already shared with Logan. He wants to involve himself more with Bennett Enterprises."

"Wow," I exclaim, turning to Blake. My word echoes throughout the room.

"I wish people would stop reacting like this," Blake says in a low voice.

"Can you blame us?" Logan asks.

I chuckle, imagining how Logan must have reacted when Sebastian first told him. He is the eternal pessimist, thinking Blake and Daniel will waste their lives away with parties.

"Sorry," I say. "This is a great thing."

"I'd like to talk out some details about Blake's entry before we eat," Sebastian continues. "Logan, Pippa, Blake, and I can do it. The rest of you can start the brunch."

"Isn't Ava joining us for this?" I ask.

"She said she'll be late, and that we can start without her."

The room empties quickly afterward. Daniel pats Blake's shoulder before he leaves. Sebastian and I exchange furtive looks and share a smile, but we both remain silent. In contrast to Logan, the two of us never doubted that the twins would come around eventually. Sebastian insisted they are Mom and Dad's sons after all. They know the value of hard work and taking nothing for granted, even though they've had a much easier childhood than we had. My personal philosophy was that everyone grows up eventually. If I'm honest, the twins never were that wild. Sure, they've lived off the dividends and partied wildly, but neither ever dabbled with drugs, nor have they flaunted their wealth. Neither are assholes, and family is important for them. That's enough for me. Blake's come around, and I'm sure Daniel will too eventually.

"What's the plan?" I ask.

"Blake will spend two months in each department before deciding where he wants to stay," Sebastian replies.

"Sounds great to me," Blake answers immediately.

"You'll have to work, Blake," Logan says in a stern voice. "There will be no favors."

Blake rubs his jaw. "Relax, I got it. I'd love to start in whichever department has the most beautiful women."

Sebastian, Logan, and I all stare at him.

Blake merely shakes his head. "Man, things here need some shaking up. You're lucky I'm joining you. No one can even joke with you."

"You'll start in my department," Logan tells him. "Finance."

To his credit, Blake appears to be looking forward to it. "Excellent."

"Welcome to Bennett Enterprises, brother," I tell Blake. He breaks into a grin, and of course, I hug him. A long time ago, Logan and Sebastian sat with me at a small round table, welcoming me to the company. We were in a different location, on the outskirts of San Francisco, in a one-story building with small windows. The team consisted of ten people, and my brothers asked me to be the eleventh. The company was doing well enough to support the family, but Sebastian and Logan had dreams of international fame, which meant that costs had to be kept as low as possible, so the profits could be used for expansion. They told me that each member of the family has shares in the company, regardless of the choice of work they'd do. The goal was simple: make sure our family never suffers from financial hardships again. There's no better motivator in the world. The three of us worked like there was no tomorrow to turn the company into a success.

As the years went by, Max and Christopher joined us. Alice and Summer opted to do something else, which only left the other set of twins. I know that Logan and Sebastian are as proud as I am that Blake will be joining us at the company.

The sound of the door opening snaps me out of my melancholy. Ava and Nadine slip inside the room, big smiles on their faces.

"Well, hello, handsome Bennetts," Nadine says.

Logan's face lightens up instantly, as does Sebastian's. He takes his wife's hand, bringing it to his lips and kissing it gently.

"We already talked about Blake's first placement," Sebastian tells Ava.

"Aaaand that's my cue to leave before I become a sixth wheel," Blake says, before slipping out.

I'm about to follow, having no wish to become the fifth wheel, when Nadine suddenly asks, "How was lunch at the office the other day?"

I chew the inside of my cheek, wondering for a brief moment why she's bringing this up in front of my brothers. Surely they're going to throw a fit and flex their protective muscles. But they both look at me curiously. That's when it hits me.

"Wait a minute. You're all in on this, aren't you? Trying to bring me and Eric together?"

"Well," Logan says patiently, "I wouldn't say Sebastian and I are *in* on this, but the girls are scheming, and we didn't… disapprove."

I snort despite myself. "As if they need your approval. They're both badasses."

"Why, thank you," Nadine says.

The sound of the door opening startles the four of us, and Alice peeks inside. "Nadine, Ava, I need both of you out here."

The girls hesitate but join my sister outside, leaving me in the room with only Sebastian and Logan.

"Pippa," Sebastian says in his most gentle tone, "if

you're uncomfortable about this, we can ask the girls to back off."

"Rest assured, we can convince them," Logan adds.

"I'm not…." I take a deep breath. "I like Eric. We hit it off at the wedding, and every time I'm with him, I'm happy."

"That's good," Sebastian says gently. "You haven't been happy in a long time, and you deserve to be."

"I'm afraid," I answer. "And he's only here until Julie's school starts again in the fall."

"You don't have to go into every relationship thinking it must lead to marriage," Sebastian continues.

"You have to give yourself a chance, get back in the game," Logan adds. I can't help but smile at this. About six months ago, I made an attempt to date someone. Midway through the date, I panicked and asked Logan to come pick me up. I usually like to lick my wounds on my own, but I felt like such a failure for not being able to make it through a date that I couldn't stand being alone.

"All we're saying," Sebastian concludes, "is that you shouldn't close yourself off to anything."

"Wow," I exclaim. "I never thought I'd talk to you about this without you threatening to harass whoever I plan to date."

Sebastian shrugs. "Things change. Maybe we did too."

"And he seems like a decent guy," Logan adds. "We checked him out."

I giggle. "Of course you did."

"We're doing business with him, so he probably checked us too," Logan says.

For the hundredth time, the door bursts open, and Christopher sticks his head in. "Okay, freaky family council over. We need all of you out here to start this party properly."

Recognizing defeat, the three of us leave the room. Max waits beside Christopher. Taking advantage of the opportunity, I wiggle myself between the twins and take each one by the arm.

"What are your plans for the next few weeks?" I ask them.

"We have quite a bit of work, but we're planning to spend some time with Mom and Dad at the ranch," Christopher answers. My parents decided to turn the ranch Sebastian gifted them into a B&B and are now busy overseeing renovations there. The ranch is about an hour away from where they currently live, so they commute every day.

"Make sure Dad isn't overworking himself, thinking he's still in his twenties," Max adds.

"That's a great idea," I say.

Dad is micromanaging everything, but that's because he built that ranch with his own hands. "So, Christopher, when can I expect you to follow in Max's footsteps and return to San Francisco?"

"No idea," he says.

"We have to talk Christopher into changing his mind," I tell Max, then drop my voice to a conspiratorial whisper, acting as if Christopher isn't with us. "What do you think? Simple persuasion techniques or blackmailing?"

"Sentimental or actual blackmail?" Max asks. "I have some dirt on him."

We launch into a debate on the merits of each tactic until Christopher gets fed up with us and says, "Hey, I'm right here."

I love my family.

Chapter Six

Eric

Julie woke me up at seven o'clock today, dragging me to the zoo and a shopping mall. We arrive back home shortly after one o'clock. I carry Julie's shopping bags in her room, which looks as if a hurricane swept through it. Clothes lie everywhere, along with sketches and shoes. It looked like that this morning too, but I hadn't had enough coffee in my system to admonish her for it.

Before I even open my mouth, Julie dutifully starts picking up her clothes, folding them neatly like I've shown her a hundred times.

"What are you doing?" I ask her. Usually, I have to negotiate with her for at least ten minutes to convince her to clean up.

"I want my room to be clean when Pippa sees it. If she likes it, maybe she'll come again."

Something catches in my throat. "You want her to come again?"

"Yeah. She's cool. I can talk to her about stuff like girls do with their moms."

Her words stab me. "Sweetheart, you can talk to

me about anything."

Julie sighs, peering at me. "Not *everything*. It doesn't work like that." The pseudo lipstick Pippa bought her lies on her desk. My daughter didn't even contest Pippa's explanation.

"Okay. Need help?"

She shakes her head. "Go make the rest of the house pretty for Pippa."

"Okay. I'll order pizza. Do you know if she likes it?"

"Everyone likes pizza."

"Right." Trying not to be too obvious, I fish for more information. "Any dessert?"

"I want cheesecake. Oh, and Pippa loves tiramisu. She ordered it a couple times."

"I'm on it."

Bingo. The least I can do for Pippa is make sure I order her favorite dessert. The urge to find out everything there is to know about her hits me hard. I thought the outing yesterday would be enough to satisfy my curiosity, but far from it. The more she spoke, the more I wanted to know. Most of all, I wanted to erase that sadness in her eyes when she spoke of her ex. It's incomprehensible to me how that moron could spend years with her and not love her. I'd worship her. Hell, I'm worshiping her already, and she isn't even mine. This is the first time in years that I don't feel the need to keep a woman at arms' length. On the contrary, I can't seem to get enough of her. I'm walking a dangerous line—we both are. We also can't seem to help ourselves.

Julie crawls under the bed, emerging with a neon pink sock after a few seconds. She pushes her hair out of her face, frowning. Then she dives under the bed again. Leaning against the doorframe, I ask, "Honey, why's all your stuff under the bed?"

No answer.

"What are you looking for?"

"Nail polish," her muffled voice comes out. "I promised Pippa...." The rest of the sentence fades, and I leave her to finish her search.

***

At three o'clock, the doorbell rings. Opening the front door, my jaw nearly drops. What in God's name is the woman wearing? That thing looks large enough for five Pippas. She barely steps in when Julie storms down the hallway, holding a small bottle of nail polish in front of her like it's a diamond.

"I found it," Julie announces.

"Awesome." Pippa gives her a genuine smile. "I'll do your nails if you do mine."

"Deal."

Opening her purse, Pippa takes out a foil with what appear to be tiny stickers on it, and my daughter sighs. "Oooh, they are nice."

"Promised you I'd find half-moon nail stickers, didn't I?"

They talk about the stickers for a few minutes, completely ignoring me. I simply watch them, amazed by the intense excitement on my daughter's face. I instantly tune out whenever Julie starts talking about this stuff. Pippa listens and shares her opinion. Hell, she even seems to enjoy the conversation.

Finally, Julie heads into the living room, and Pippa turns to me, offering me a shy, "Hello, Eric."

"Welcome."

"Where is Ms. Blackwell?"

"She has the day off."

Even though her dress doesn't show anything, I know exactly where the curve of her waist meets her breasts, and my eyes linger there. I've been paying attention to her more than I like to admit. When I look up again, she draws in a sharp breath.

Then Julie calls her, and they spend the next fifteen minutes doing each other's nails. Afterward, we settle onto the couch, enjoying the movie and eating pizza. Julie sits between Pippa and me, looking happier than I've ever seen her. I watch the two of them more than the movie. At some point, Pippa stretches her arm on the backrest of the couch. I mirror her stance and our hands meet in the middle. I stroke the back of her hand with my thumb, and intertwine our fingers. Pippa stares at the TV, but I can see her chest rising up and down with labored breaths. We stay like this for the rest of the movie. I'm not sure where I'm going with this, but it feels right. I like having her here, watching her have fun with Julie, as much as I liked spending time with her yesterday. I think I could watch Pippa do nothing at all and still find it fascinating.

After the first movie finishes, Julie leaps off the

couch, announcing it's time for dessert.

"What's for dessert?" Pippa asks.

"Cheesecake for Dad and me, and tiramisu for you," Julie answers. "We ordered it especially for you."

"Thank you."

"We can bring the dessert," Julie says, taking Pippa's hand and directing her to the kitchen.

"All right. I'll prepare the second movie."

Low chatter comes from the kitchen as I pull up the second movie, and then I hear a scream. Instantly, I jump to my feet and stride their way. Julie emerges from the kitchen, looking pale.

"Blood," she mutters.

"Are you okay?"

She nods. "Pippa cut herself." With that, Julie rushes past me into the living room. She hates the sight of blood. As I step into the kitchen, I discover she's not the only one. Pippa holds her finger over the sink, looking away from it. There is only one small cut on that finger. I grab the first aid kit from one of the cabinets and take out a Band-Aid. Standing in front of her, I carefully wrap the adhesive bandage around her finger, fighting not to laugh.

"Stop it," she says.

"What?"

"You know what. You're laughing at me." She's still looking away from the finger and away from me.

"I'm sorry. I thought people get over the fear of blood after a certain age."

"Weirdly enough, I don't have a problem with

other people's blood, only my own." She breathes slowly as if trying to calm herself.

"There, done," I say. Slowly, Pippa turns her head, glancing briefly at her finger. This close, her feminine scent catches me off guard. It's sweet and spicy.

I caress her jaw, tipping her head up a notch. "I like your perfume."

"Thanks." She shifts slightly, and her full breasts press against my chest. My reaction is instantaneous. A groan I mask poorly reverberates in my throat. Pippa licks her lower lip, averting her gaze, but she doesn't pull away. Her sweet, warm body is nestled against mine as if we belong together. I'm fighting against my every instinct.

"Fuck." My voice trembles. "I want to kiss you so badly."

Pippa shakes her head, almost imperceptibly. "Bad idea."

"Yeah, very bad," I agree. "Because I couldn't stop at one kiss. I'd want to taste every inch of your skin, find out what you like and take you over the edge."

"Eric," she whispers, fisting my shirt. My name in her mouth stirs a movement in my boxers. She is so close to me that I feel her pressing her thighs together. I nearly lose my control.

That's when I realize she's trembling lightly in my arms. She's fighting this as much as I am. I kiss her forehead, my mouth lingering on her skin for a few beats until we both calm down.

"Is the blood gone?" My daughter's voice

resounds from the living room.

"Yes," I reply. "We'll come with the desserts in a second."

Except we don't. We need longer to pull ourselves together, and when we finally return to the living room, Julie says, "Dad, I miss your grill." Turning to Pippa, she continues, "He makes delicious chicken wings with honey and ketchup sauce."

"Sounds delicious," Pippa says. She senses no danger, but I already know where Julie's going with this.

"Why don't you cook some tomorrow? I'm sure Pippa will love them."

Yep, exactly as I suspected.

"I have plans tomorrow," Pippa says quickly, throwing me a pleading look. "Alice and I are doing something together."

"Next weekend?" Julie pushes. I almost laugh as realization dawns on Pippa. I briefly wonder if Alice and Nadine corrupted my daughter when they went to the aquarium with her.

"I suppose I could stop by next Saturday," Pippa mutters.

"Excellent," Julie exclaims.

Pippa and I exchange a glance, and one thing becomes clear. Next time I am alone with this woman, I won't be able to hold back.

Chapter Seven

Pippa

"What do you mean you're not coming to the gym?" I ask Alice, clutching my phone tightly. I'm standing in the foyer of the gym, my usual meeting point with Alice. The place is surprisingly empty for a Tuesday afternoon.

"I have a meeting, sorry," she replies.

"And you didn't tell me because…?" I tap my foot with impatience, eying the exit.

"You would've skipped the gym. Admit it."

I sigh into the phone. "Fine, I admit it."

"But now you're already there, so be a good girl and work out."

"Your motivational speech isn't working unless you're here with me," I volley back. I hate exercising with a passion, but I love my sweets. I spent my early twenties avoiding any kind of exercising, relying on a young metabolism to get by. I was twenty-six the first time my sister dragged me inside a gym. I'd like to say I never looked back, but I have. I look back every time, hoping I can talk Alice out of it. Now that I'm alone… Well, I was a very good girl before

Sebastian's wedding, working out three times a week, keeping my eyes on the prize: rocking my dress. I've been floundering ever since the great event.

"I want a picture as proof that you worked out today," Alice says.

Damn, my sister knows me well.

"No need to be so controlling." I let out a dramatic sigh.

"Suck it up, sis. Think about the Jell-O."

"Eww. Fine, I'll work out."

"Have to go," Alice says. "My appointment is here. You might run into Max and Logan. They said they'd hit the gym in the afternoon." That wouldn't surprise me. All my brothers are sporty, and the gym is two blocks away from Bennett Enterprises.

I shut off my phone, securing my equipment bag over the shoulder, and walk to the changing rooms' area. *You can do this, Pippa. Think about the Jell-O.* After coercing me into my first ever gym visit, Alice and I went out for drinks. I was complaining about my sore muscles when my sister pointed to a Jell-O the woman at a nearby table had ordered.

"That's how your ass will end up looking if you don't exercise," she said. To this day, that remains a strong motivator. I like my sweets, but I like having a firm booty too.

I change into my sports bra and Lycra pants, putting my hair up in a ponytail. Then I brace myself for an hour of hell.

I start with the treadmill, putting on earbuds, turning up the volume, and listen to my favorite songs. I'm halfway through my set time (fifteen minutes) when I peek up from the timer and glance at the entrance. Max and Logan hover at the reception. Eric is with them. I haven't seen him since last Saturday because Julie has started summer school, so she won't come to my office anymore.

I stop the treadmill, happy for a reason to interrupt my running, and head to the reception.

"Well, hello, fellow Bennetts," I tell my brothers. "Alice told me I might see you here."

They each kiss my cheek and then hop on the stairs leading to the upper floor, which is where they sometimes do their workouts. Eric stays put.

"I didn't know you work out here," I say.

Eric gives me a crooked grin, and I fidget in my spot. "I signed up a while ago. I work out four times a week. It's the best place to clear my mind, and it gives me energy."

Oh, so he's one of those weirdos who thinks the gym is therapy, coffee, and cake all rolled into one....

My skepticism must register on my face, because he asks, "You disagree?"

"I'm not a believer. I think the gym is a necessary evil."

"Working out is good for relieving stress," he continues.

"So is eating sweets. I prefer that. Exercising can be dangerous."

"How so?"

"Look around. Every machine here is a potential death trap."

"So, what are you doing here?"

"I've been tricked by my sister. But I'll take your advice and try to relieve stress. This week will be rough."

"How so?"

"I'm trying to finalize some new designs that have been giving me headaches," I explain.

"Good luck."

"See you around," I tell him, and continue with my routine. Over the next half hour, I discover one of the few advantages of the gym—spying on Eric.

He's alone because my brothers do their entire workout on the floor above us. The man is a work of art, and he dedicatedly works out every muscle group. Seeing his skin damp with sweat while he occasionally grunts out with efforts is torture. I'm almost salivating as I watch him. Once in a while, he looks at me as if he can feel my stare, and a white-hot current runs through me every time.

After I finish my routine, I stop by the health bar behind the reception and drink a fresh orange juice. This is my favorite place in the entire gym, mainly because I'm allowed to sit and do nothing, but also because it's empty most of the time.

Since I'm the only one here right now, I kick off my sneakers and prop my feet on the armchair in front of me. My heart slams against my ribcage with nauseating speed, and not because of my run on the treadmill. Knowing Eric is here does *things* to me. It makes me nervous, and at the same time, it gives me an odd reassurance. I love being around him, and I haven't even remotely *liked* being around a man in a long time. In fact, ever since I filed for divorce, whenever a man not related to me entered a room I made a point to avoid any interactions beyond the necessary ones. My *danger* radar was up at all times, and all men failed it. But when Eric enters the room, I instantly look forward to *any* interaction with him. It might be because until now, everything he's said prompted one of three reactions in me: laugh, swoon, or melt. Sometimes all three.

"You're cheating," Eric says, startling me. He stands before me, holding a glass of orange juice himself. I rise to my feet, almost flattening myself against the wall behind me in an effort to put some distance between us. All I manage is to trap myself between the hard wall and Eric. His shirt sticks to him, and it's a damn fine sight.

"What do you mean?" I ask, trying hard not to look below his jawline.

"You're breaking the rules," he replies. "We said no hot looks. You gave me plenty."

"We broke some other rules too on Friday and Saturday. It's your fault anyway. You're wearing clothes that show off your best parts, and you were making manly sounds."

He laughs, placing his glass of orange juice on a nearby table. "What's that supposed to mean?"

I lower my voice. "You know… grunting and stuff." Without thinking, I add, "It sounds sexy." How do I always talk myself into a hole when I'm around this man? Not only is my danger radar not working, but my hormones are wreaking havoc on my thoughts.

"You have a dirty mind, Pippa Bennett."

"Only when I'm around you," I add. "I promise not to do it again."

"Don't." He latches his eyes on mine, and the intensity is so powerful it weakens my knees.

"What?"

"Don't promise. You won't be able to keep that promise, just like I'm not." His fingers find their way under my chin, and he tilts my head up.

Without breaking eye contact, his thumb inches up my skin, reaching my lower lip. My chest heaves up and down. He drags his finger from one corner of my mouth to the other with exquisite slowness, setting my lower body on fire.

"I'm a man, Pippa Bennett. I thought I could resist you, but I was wrong. I want to taste you. I want to kiss you until you tremble beneath me."

I'm shaking already. "Bad idea," I mouth, as I did on Saturday, but it has no effect on him this time. What makes it especially bad is that I want this so much it hurts.

"I know. Very bad." His voice is a whisper. "Just one kiss."

Dropping his hand to my waist, he tilts his head forward until I can feel his hot breath on me, and it undoes me. Our mouths meet in a clash, his lips covering mine with desperation. His tongue searches, probes, tastes, turning me into a bundle of need. Eric is fierce, and I love it. His kiss spurs something deep inside me—a desire for more. Every inch of my body screams for him. I become acutely aware of his hard chest pressed against mine, his fingers digging into my waist.

When we pull apart, gasping for air, his eyes hold the same kind of heat his kiss did. He rests his forehead against mine, cupping my cheek with one hand. I want to memorize everything about this moment, the warmth of his body, the tenderness of his touch.

"Say something," he whispers.

"I don't know what to say, except that I want more."

He pulls back a notch.

"I'm going to kiss you again," he announces. "Since we're on that slippery slope anyway. You need to be thoroughly kissed, and I'm up for the task. All good things come in twos. One kiss wasn't nearly enough."

This time, when his mouth claims mine, his hands don't rest on my waist anymore. One reaches for my thigh, the other for my neck. My fingers find their way up his chest, feeling him up shamelessly until they reach his neck and then his thick, soft hair. I tug at it, pushing him closer to me. God, this isn't enough. Two kisses will never be enough. The longer I feel his mouth on mine and his hands on my body, the more I want. A loud bang in the background startles us, and we pull apart, both breathing heavily.

The girl in charge of the bar looks at us apologetically. "I dropped my tray. Sorry." Then she scurries away. Eric and I are standing a few feet away from each other. I don't dare to walk closer to him. Seeing his messed-up hair and luscious mouth while his taste is still so fresh on my lips might push me to do something reckless... like kissing him again.

His next words confirm that I'm not the only one entertaining such thoughts. "I will not come near you again now, or I'll kiss you senseless."

"Yeah. It's best if we stop at two kisses." I beam, finally looking at him. Eric smiles back.

"See you at my house on Saturday."

Oh, crap. I'd forgotten about that.

"See you," I whisper as he leaves.

How on earth will I go through with it?

Chapter Eight

Pippa

"Morning, everyone," I say as I step into my department on Thursday.

Blake and Logan are sitting in front of my desk, and they're both wearing suits. Logan always wears a suit, but seeing Blake in one comes off as a shock. He only wears them at special events, such as weddings. My little brother means serious business.

"What are you two doing here?" I ask as I round the table.

"Why, I thought she'd be happier to see us here," Blake tells Logan.

I notice an orange pouch on my desk. It contains cookies from my favorite store. There is a card next to it.

A little bird told me these are your favorite cookies. Hope they make your day better. Don't stress too much.

Eric

I read the text over and over again, the corners of my mouth lifting in a smile. I inspect the pouch again, then raise my eyebrows at my brothers.

"So, which one of you stole three of my cookies?"

"You know how many there are inside?" Blake asks, flabbergasted.

"Told you she'd notice," Logan tells him under his breath.

I jut my chin forward. "Yeah. I know the package sizes. Small white organza pouch—five, red organza—seven, orange organza—nine. Brother, I love you, but if you have any preservation skills, you won't come between me and my sweets again."

"Duly noted," Blake says.

"So, both of my brothers are visiting. To what do I owe the pleasure?"

"I'm not staying," Logan says. "Blake will finalize analyzing the budget for the new generation of mock-ups with you."

My jaw nearly drops. "Impressive. Blake's been here for a few days, and you already send him to do your dirty work." Moving my glance to Blake, I add, "Spoiler alert. I hate talking about numbers."

"No problem," Blake says. "I love numbers."

Freaky thing is he does. He majored in finance and partying in college. Graduated with honors in both.

"Right on track to become Logan's henchman," I tease.

"Henchman?" Blake says, his face stricken. "I'm better than that. If there's a Batman-Robin situation here, I want to be Batman."

"You're drifting off the point, Blake," Logan remarks.

"Why are you so pissed off?" I ask Logan.

"Because this asshat was hitting on my secretary," he informs me, pointing with his thumb at Blake and darting him a menacing glare. "You will not sleep with anyone on my floor."

"Can you repeat that, please? I haven't heard it the first twenty times you said it." Blake looks bored. "I wasn't hitting on her. I was being polite. You're tenser than usual, brother. If I hadn't had firsthand evidence of Nadine's sexual appetite, I'd say she's keeping you on the dry."

I stare at them. "What is going on?"

"I caught Nadine preparing herself to give him a striptease in his office months ago," Blake says, clearly proud of himself. Logan sets his jaw. *Oh, man.* It's only their first week of working together.

"How often will you repeat that story?" Logan asks him.

"Ideally, I'd tell every family member individually, in your presence, just to see your expression."

"Time-out," I say, looking from one to the other. "Logan, you can leave me with Blake now. We'll have everything finished in about an hour."

After Logan leaves, Blake points to my cookies. "I couldn't help but notice that those are from a certain Boston import."

"So?" I challenge.

"I want to make sure I don't have to kick anyone's ass," Blake answers.

I let out a loud whistle. "This is usually Sebastian's role. Are you channeling him?"

"That's twice you offended me today, sister," Blake says with humor. "And I look much better in a suit than Sebastian does, anyway. My ass is much sexier." He leans forward over the desk. "Ask your girls here. They've been checking me out since I arrived."

Scanning the room, I realize he's right. At least three of the girls are looking at him with a dangerous longing, practically drooling.

"You are not sleeping with anyone in my department," I warn him, barely moving my lips.

Blake sighs. "I can't believe I'm saying this, but let's start with the budget. If I hear that warning one more time, I might lose my good humor and actually become Logan."

***

After finishing with Blake, I talk to my lawyer, Oliver, about Terence and his new lawsuit. Oliver informs me that my ex has hired one of the sharpest lawyers in San Francisco, but in his professional opinion, he has no case. Terence is simply hoping that I'll settle so I won't go through all the hassle of mediation meetings and court visits again. Well, the asshole is in for a surprise, because I'm not changing my stance. He won't get one cent. I don't care if I have to go through hell for this—and being in the same room with Terence is hell for me—but I won't let him touch what belongs to my family.

It's only when I see a hand shoving a sandwich

under my nose that I realize it's lunchtime.

"Turkey sandwich," Luke says.

"Thank you, thank you, thank you," I reply before I dig in. My stomach rumbles violently as I down the first bite.

"Can't let you starve, boss. You haven't even eaten the cookies on your desk."

Oh, wow. I completely forgot about them, which goes to show how much the Terence issue stresses me out.

I lean back in my chair as I continue to munch on my sandwich, eyeing the sweets. *I will not eat them until after my workday is done.* I repeat this mantra a few times, but the more I eye the cookies, the weaker I become.

I'll have one.

I fail, of course. Once I taste one, I can't stop. I need more. In my defense, though, these are really tiny mini-cookies. They are mini mini-cookies.

I'm on my second one when I decide to text Eric.

Pippa: I received your cookies. How did you know they're my favorites?

Since it's lunchtime, I'm keeping my fingers crossed that Eric's also taking a break and can text back. My wish comes true less than a minute later.

Eric: Alice. Are they helping with your stress?

Pippa: They are. But I remember you telling me that exercising is the best stress reliever.

Eric: After what happened yesterday, I agree with you. Exercising is dangerous.

I hover with my fingers over the letters, unsure

what to write to him. Then I see the little dots indicating he's typing, and I wait.

Eric: I don't regret it. Those were some fantastic kisses.

I hesitate, still unsure what to write back, so I concentrate on devouring another cookie. After a minute or so, my phone beeps again.

Eric: I was not expecting radio silence. If you don't think it was at least one of the best kisses in a while, by all means, lie to me. Honesty is not required this time.

I chuckle, shaking my head. *Okay, I can do this.* My flirting skills are rusty, but phone flirting seems less challenging than if we were face-to-face.

Pippa: Someone can't stand having his ego wounded. Sorry, I was too busy eating cookies. They're like your kisses. As soon as I have one, I need more.

Eric: This comparison is the best thing that could happen to my ego today. My team should be thankful to you.

Pippa: Ah, so you're on the friendly end of the shark-o-meter today.

Eric: I'm still debating that. Can't wait to see you on Saturday.

Oh, yeah… Saturday will be dangerous, because I have a suspicion that all bets are off.

Chapter Nine

Pippa

When I step out of the cab in front of Eric's house on Saturday, my heart is beating fast. I jam my hands in my pockets, surveying the one-story home. I feel like an impostor as I walk to the front door because I'm here supposedly for Julie. But the memory of Eric's kisses still lingers in my mind. I can still sense the rough touch of his lips on mine, as well as his taste.

I shouldn't want a repeat of the gym incident. I should be more cautious. I'm not ready to trust a man again, and Eric has his own issues, which I respect. The biggest issue? He's going to leave when Julie's holiday ends. No matter what, I'll end up heartbroken, and I couldn't piece myself together a second time. But all the arguments in the world can't subdue the way my nerve endings are buzzing at the mere prospect of being in Eric's proximity. Drawing in a deep breath, I knock at the door. I hear footsteps from the other side and Julie's excited voice. "She's here. She's here." Seconds later, the door swings open.

"Hi, Pippa," Eric greets me. "What did you bring?"

"Dessert, of course. Ice cream."

Eric steps back as I enter the house, and our fingers brush by accident. The slight touch sends tendrils of heat through me, singeing me. I catch my breath as Eric pulls his hand behind him. Damn it. If this is what a simple brush of his fingers does to me, how will I survive the evening? The answer comes in the form of a bubbling twelve-year-old who wraps her arms around me. I will focus on Julie.

"Come on, Pippa," she says without further ado. "The wings are almost ready."

She takes my hand, leading me to the backyard. Eric tags behind us, and I can feel his eyes on me. I'm wearing a simple blue dress. The fabric is light, perfect for this weather, but it shows no cleavage, though it highlights my curves. I was out of tent-sized dresses, and it didn't seem to do much good last time anyway.

"Won't Ms. Blackwell eat with us?" I ask.

"No, she has the evening off," Eric answers. "She'll be back in a few hours."

We eat in the backyard, next to the swimming pool. As we eat, Julie begins to talk about her week in the design class.

"And there is this girl, Sophie Ann, who keeps saying anyone who doesn't wear a headband like she does isn't cool, and I don't know what to say back. I hate headbands."

"Well," Eric says, "you should tell her exactly that.

No reason to pretend."

"Yeah, I guess. What do you think, Pippa?"

From the moment I met her, Julie struck me as a sheltered girl, even acting a little young for her age. Eric is very overprotective, which I assume is because of the accident. But she's growing up, and he's going to have his hands full once she's a teenager.

"Your dad is right," I tell her.

Julie gives a quick nod and remains silent throughout dinner. After dessert, she disappears inside briefly, returning with a kite.

"I want to fly this kite," she announces, holding up the bag.

"You can do that tomorrow, pumpkin," Eric tells her. "It's almost dark. You won't even see it."

"No, it has to be now," she insists. "It glows in the dark."

Eric and I exchange looks, and I know we're thinking the same thing. Julie could hurt herself if she runs around in the dark, because of her leg.

"What if your dad and I raise it?" I offer. "You can sit at the table, eat a second portion of ice cream, and watch the kite."

Julie considers this for a moment. "Okay."

Eric and I inspect the kite and read the instructions for the next few minutes.

"Have you ever done this?" he mouths to me.

"No," I admit. "How hard can it be?"

As it turns out, it's very hard. Getting the thing into the air truly requires a team effort. Eric holds the rope, running from one end of the yard to the other to gain traction while I give him directions, so the kite doesn't collide with any tree.

"If I wanted to work out, I would've gone to the gym," he complains after yet another lap around the yard.

"We've almost got it," I encourage. I walk backward, keeping my eyes on Eric, and gesturing him to keep his current direction.

"It's beautiful," Julie calls to us, and Eric smiles, advancing with renewed energy.

"It's nearly up," I announce. "You have to—"

Splash. Splash.

***

Eric

We fell into the goddamn pool.

When I surface from the water, my daughter's shrieking with laughter.

"You were supposed to give me directions," I tell Pippa, who's standing a few feet away from me in the water and laughing even harder than Julie.

"I was," she explains between chuckles. "And I somehow directed both of us into the pool. I'm sorry. I was too busy making sure the kite didn't end up in a tree to pay attention to our feet."

I break into laughter too, and man, it feels good. Julie looks between Pippa and me as if we're two big idiots—which, of course, we are. Two grown adults up to their navels in the swimming pool because they didn't watch their step. Damn kite. Which reminds me....

"Anyone see the kite?" I ask.

Julie points to a spot beyond the pool. "There. It's high up in the tree, though."

"I'll get it down tomorrow," I assure her.

"I don't know about you," Pippa says, "but I'm cold." She swims to the steps. I suck in a breath as she climbs out. Sweet Jesus. Pippa in a wet dress is irresistible. It sticks to her body, showing off every delicious curve: her round, perky ass, her waist, and beautiful breasts. My imagination supplies images of all the other delicious parts of her that are not on display. Images so vivid that I have a full-on boner. *Damn it.*

"Aren't you coming out?" Pippa says, swirling around to me.

Her blonde hair clings to her translucent skin, and bless her, she's so unaware of what she's doing to me that she's not even bothering to hide her body. My daughter joins Pippa at the edge of the pool, a curious expression on her face.

"Why aren't you coming out, Dad?"

"I'll be out in a minute," I inform them, looking away from Pippa to try to calm the situation in my boxers. Numbers. Yeah. If I think about the sales reports I was reading before I left my office today that should work. Except it doesn't. My dick twitches with awareness just knowing Pippa is a few feet away. *Okay, think, Eric. Think.* I need Pippa to know what's going on, so she can leave my sight. That's the only way I'll calm down. But I can't exactly spell out the reason with my daughter here.

"Bones," I blurt out. "Some of my bones hurt. The water helps."

Julie raises her eyebrows. "You're not making sense, Dad." Of course not. I'm trying to bullshit my way out of this. I'm the worst father in the world.

Pippa looks crestfallen. *Come on, Pippa. Adult code. Replace the* s *with an* r. She continues to stare at me questioningly, so clearly she's not getting it.

"There's some wood here in the water. I'll pick it up." *Wood. Come on, Pippa.* Finally, her eyes widen in understanding, as Julie says, "I think Dad hit his head when he fell in the pool."

Pippa giggles, then tells Julie, "Let's you and I go inside. I'm cold and I need a towel."

"Okay."

Pippa throws me a furtive glance over her shoulders, winking at me as the two of them head back in the house.

***

It takes me about ten minutes to calm myself. Afterward, I leave the pool and hop in the shower inside the bathroom adjacent to my room. I use the time to cool down. After I put on dry clothes, I head to the living room. The snippet of conversation I overhear stops me in my tracks shortly before entering the room.

"Do you ever feel lonely, Pippa?" Julie asks.

"Sometimes." Pippa's voice is calm and smooth. "Do you feel lonely? It's okay if you do. Everyone does once in a while."

"I'm okay, but I think Dad feels lonely lots of times."

I flatten myself against the wall, barely believing what I'm hearing.

"What makes you think that?" Pippa asks calmly.

"He spends a lot of time with me. In Boston, I have friends at school who only have one parent. And their parent goes out on dates."

Wham. I feel as if someone punched me.

"Would you like for your dad to date?"

"I don't want him to be lonely. I want him to be happy, and if he meets someone nice, both of us will be happy. You're nice. Do you like Dad?"

"I, well… Um," Pippa stutters. "Everyone likes him."

"Why don't you ask him on a date?" Julie continues. I smile, imagining how red Pippa's ear tips must be.

"I—Wait, what?"

Julie continues in a serious tone. "The high school students at my school had a spring dance where the girls asked the boys out. You should ask Dad. He doesn't know how."

"Why do you say that?"

"If he knew, he wouldn't be so lonely."

My daughter is the best kid in the world. I listen intently for Pippa's reply.

"We should hurry up with the nail polish," she says. "Let's try the red one."

They delve into a discussion about colors next, and I stay hidden for a few moments longer, digesting this new piece of information. I drag my hands across my face in disbelief. All these years, I thought my self-imposed ban on dating was for my daughter's own good. Apparently not. Remembering Pippa's non-answer when Julie asked her if she likes me, I chuckle. I can't believe even my daughter is trying to set us up.

I have a rule in business: When too many people tell me the same thing, I get my head out of my ass and listen to them. Maybe it's time I applied it in real life as well.

I step into the living room to find Pippa and Julie sitting on the floor with their fingers sprawled on their legs.

It strikes me as odd until Julie looks up and says, "We're waiting for our nail polish to dry."

I nod, but Pippa captures my attention. She's wearing one of my shirts and sweatpants, her hair up in a ponytail. She looks homey. More than that, she looks like she belongs here, with Julie and me.

"Sorry for hijacking your shirt and pants," she says with a shy smile, pointing to a small transparent bag on the couch, which contains her wet dress. "Julie's clothes don't fit me, and Ms. Blackwell isn't here, so I couldn't ask her for clothes. Julie brought me these."

"Don't worry. They look good on you."

"Our polish dried, honey," she tells Julie. "Seems

like the label wasn't lying. It does dry fast."

"Can we watch a movie?" Julie asks, making full use of the doe-eyed expression she knows I can't fight.

Pippa replies before I even open my mouth. "If we start now, it's going to get too late. Isn't it bedtime for you?"

I watch Pippa with renewed admiration. She's better at resisting Julie's charms than I am.

My daughter wrinkles her nose. "I suppose it is."

"Ms. Blackwell should be here any minute now. She'll—"

As if on cue, the front door opens and Ms. Blackwell steps inside the house.

"Time for bed, Julie," she says in her usual no-nonsense voice. She greets Pippa, frowning slightly as she takes in her clothes, but doesn't comment on it.

Julie sighs, then goes to her room.

"I have to call a cab," Pippa says. "I didn't come here with my car."

"I'll give you a ride home," I tell her, employing a tone that breaches no argument. *Usually*.

She dismisses my words with a wave. "Nonsense. I'll be fine with a cab."

"Yeah, but I'll need those clothes back." I actually don't need them, but it's as good an excuse as any. I want to spend more time with her.

"Ms. Blackwell is here. Maybe I can borrow some clothes from her?"

"I'd need to bring those back to her too," I say.

"You're right." She takes a deep breath, rolling her

shoulders. "Okay, let's go."

Spending time *with* her turns into spending time *next* to her. Pippa falls asleep in the car within five minutes of typing her address into the navigator. As I drive, a faint wheezing sound fills the car. It takes me about two seconds to realize the sound comes from Pippa. Tiny snores. I chuckle and, in a stroke of genius, whip out my phone and record the silly sound. Ah, this will be excellent blackmail material. I'm not sure when I'll need it, but it's good to have it.

She wakes up before we arrive, yawning. Then she sees me, and she startles in her seat.

"I'm sorry I fell asleep," she said. She's very cute with her frazzled hair and I-just-woke-up eyes. And just like that, I wonder what it's like to wake up next to her in the morning. No idea where the desire comes from, but this seems to be a recurrent theme with Pippa. She creates in me the longing for things I haven't wanted—or searched for—in years. She makes me want to live again.

"Did I say something inappropriate while I was asleep?" she asks in a shy voice. Ah, so she's a sleep talker... and all I got were snores. No reason for her to know that, though.

Deciding to tease her, I say, "You might have professed your love for me."

She narrows her eyes in suspicion.

"There was definitely something about my muscles in your mumbling."

"You're so full of shit." She chuckles, but the tips of her ears are red. *Aha.* The cat's out of the bag now.

"Are you telling me that you dubbed me tall, dark, and handsome, and you haven't fantasized about me?"

"Alice dubbed you."

"You didn't contradict her." I park the car in front of her building, but we don't move from our seats.

Pippa sighs, shifting in her seat. "Why are you suddenly so flirty?"

I hesitate for a second, then decide to be straightforward. "I overheard your conversation with Julie."

"Wow, so eavesdropping *is* one of your superpowers," she says with a smile. "I can't believe Julie thinks you're incapable of asking someone on a date."

"Yeah. My plan for her to believe I'm a monk worked too well, apparently. Time to change that."

"Eric… I'm still…." Her words fade. After a few beats of silence, she continues in a small voice, "I mean, you know all my baggage."

I cup her cheek with my hand and look her directly in the eye. "We both have baggage. So what? We're strong enough to carry it. If not, we'll hire a bellhop or buy a forklift. I want to learn everything there is to know about you."

"That's a big goal," she whispers.

"We'll start small. I want to make you smile."

"It's been a long time since someone whose last name isn't Bennett had this goal," she says sadly.

"I can assure you that I'm up for the task."

She licks her lips, the corners of her lips lifting in a smile. "So, your daughter's blessing was all it took for you to change your mind?"

"Maybe." I drop my voice to a whisper to give it a more conspiratorial feel. "Or maybe you're irresistible."

She chuckles, pulling back. "In these clothes?"

"Especially in them. I mean it. Seeing you in my clothes does things to me."

"Let's go upstairs." Her voice is low and husky. "So I can change and give them back to you."

When we enter her building, the doorman greets us, jerking his head back as he sees Pippa.

In the elevator, Pippa mutters, "Great. Now the doorman thinks I'm doing the walk of shame."

"Well, you should be ashamed. You directed both of us into the pool."

She blushes violently, probably remembering my out-of-control rambling. Pippa lives on the eleventh floor in a spacious condo with a generous view of San Francisco.

"So, this is my lair," she says proudly. "Sorry about the mess. I wasn't expecting guests."

There are sketches *everywhere*.

"You've transformed it to a workshop?"

She shrugs. "I take my work home often."

Leaning against the living room doorframe, I observe her as she picks up sketches from the floor. "I have a proposition for you."

She straightens up, clutching the pile of sketches to herself. "Let's hear it."

"Obviously, neither of us is ready for a date yet. Julie's more ready for the two of us to date than we are." I laugh, remembering my daughter's words. "So let's go on another nondate."

"You're persistent." She winks at me. "I'm that irresistible, huh?"

I walk up to her until there are just inches between us. "Maybe neither of us is ready, but we can take a risk and see where that leads us."

Pippa's expression is unreadable for a few long moments, before she breaks into a beam. "Can we preemptively bring a bellboy to our nondate?"

"I'm not sure. He might witness some very inappropriate things. A forklift would be safer."

Pippa hugs her sketches tightly to her chest and swallows hard. The sound nearly undoes me. "What will we be doing on our nondate?"

"I can't tell for sure but expect kissing. A lot of kissing." I lean closer to her, caressing the side of her neck. "I'm not telling you where."

She swallows hard. "I'll go change."

"No need. Keep my clothes. It was a ruse. I wanted to spend more time with you."

"Are you sure?"

"Yeah."

"Okay."

"I'll leave you for tonight."

With that, I turn around and leave her apartment, wondering all the way to my car what the hell I'm getting into. My phone beeps with an incoming message the second I climb in the driver's seat.

Pippa: I'll sleep in your shirt tonight.
Eric: Is that all you'll be doing?

Knowing she's naked underneath my shirt makes it hard to concentrate on driving. I'm jealous of my own fucking shirt. Fantastic.

Pippa: There will be touching. A lot of touching. I'm not telling you where.

Chapter Ten

Pippa

I wake up with a big smile the next morning and remain under my covers for a few minutes. I slept in Eric's shirt. It's soft and light, the only downside being that it doesn't smell like him. Still, wearing it feels as if he slept next to me. There was a shift between us yesterday, and I can't define it or what to make of it. All I know is that while part of me is still afraid of moving forward, another part wants to dream and hope again.

I hug my pillow and decide to text the man responsible for my renewed hopefulness. To my astonishment, I find he texted me already.

Eric: I've found the perfect place for our nondate.

Pippa: You're fast.

My phone buzzes with an incoming message within seconds.

Eric: I stayed up late last night researching.

Ah, I can gauge a lot of teasing potential from this sentence alone.

Pippa: Had trouble falling asleep?

Eric: Nah. Just had to wait for my balls to go back to normal. They were blue after I read a certain message last night.

Giggling, I type as fast as I can.

Pippa: You asked for it. So, where are we going?

Eric: I'm not telling you. It'll be a surprise. You'll love it.

Pippa: That's a cocky statement.

Eric: Please. My romance skills might be rusty, but I've still got game. Still deciding what size the forklift should be, though. Between the two of us, we can probably do with a large one.

I fiddle with my phone in my hands, debating what I should write back. I love talking to him. Maybe it's because he's so open with me, but I don't feel the need to keep up the bravado when I'm with him. Eric puts me at ease with nothing more than a smile and a few words, but I don't want gloom to hang over our date.

Pippa: No forklift needed. I want us to have fun.

Eric: You sure? I can bring a tiny one.

Pippa: No need. Besides, tiny never does the job. Haven't you heard? Size does matter.

I get no answer for one whole minute—I count the seconds—and I'm wondering if there's anything inappropriate happening on his side of the line.

Eric: STOP the dirty talk right now, or I'll start with the blue you-know-what again.

Ah, definitely inappropriate. I bite my lip, wishing

more than ever that he could be here with me right now.

Pippa: You're going all bossy on me. It's sexy.

Eric: You haven't seen anything yet. Wait until our nondate. Any chance I'll see you at the gym before then? I'll stop by later today. There'll be plenty of opportunities for you to stare at me.

Pippa: Are you selling your body? You're cheap, Callahan.

Eric: Merely interested in your general health and well-being.

For a fraction of a second, I debate going to the gym just to ogle him again, but not even the perfection that is his ass is worth all the sweat and muscle cramps.

Pippa: Doubt it. I have a full day with Alice today and a lot of work next week. Not sure if I'll make it to the gym at all.

Eric: That's a long-winded way of saying you're too lazy to work out.

He nailed it, of course. What a waste of letters. There's no way I'll admit it, though.

Pippa: Get over yourself, Callahan. Got to go.

I put the phone back on the nightstand and grudgingly get out of bed to start my day. I'm grinning like an idiot the entire time I get ready to meet Alice. There's something to be said about flirting upon waking up. It fills me with an infectious energy, and I love it.

Alice and I have our hands full at the charity

center, but of course, my sister manages to question me about Eric. I have bestowed my butting-in ability on both of my sisters. Summer usually joins us, but she couldn't make it today.

"What do you mean, a nondate?" Alice inquires while we're on a break and sitting on a bench outside "You've said that before, and I still don't get it. What is that?"

"The term used by two people who aren't emotionally prepared for a date," I explain, soaking in the sun.

"By the looks of your grin, you're hormonally prepared for one. I bet he is too. So, where is he taking you?" Alice asks.

I shrug. "He wouldn't say."

"Oh, you've got to love a man who knows how to keep you on your toes."

"You have no idea," I murmur.

***

When I get back home, the doorman tells me there was a delivery for me, which awaits me in the foyer. To my astonishment, I find a large bouquet of roses there. Beaming like an idiot, I take the flowers and step into the elevator. I text Eric as soon as I step inside my apartment.

Pippa: From cookies to flowers? That's an interesting change of tactics.

My phone rings right away.

"I thought about sending cookies along with

them, but I have a hunch you would've ignored the flowers," Eric says without further ado.

I'm grinning so much I'm genuinely afraid I might pull a muscle in my face.

"You're a smart man," I answer. "Sweets versus flowers? The flowers never stand a chance."

"Looking forward to Saturday?" Eric asks.

Sitting on my couch, I press the phone to my ear. "Why don't you tell me where we're going?"

"That's the purpose of a surprise," he says in an amused tone.

"But I'm not good with surprises. I mean, I'm excellent at organizing them for everyone else, but—"

"It's time someone planned one for you. Relax. Let me woo you, Pippa. Stop fighting it so much."

His amused tone sends my heart into overdrive, and my stomach flips in excitement. It's been a long time since I felt as giddy as a schoolgirl for an upcoming date.

"That's a lot of effort for a nondate," I remark.

"You deserve it."

"Can I get some clues at least?"

"Don't be impatient."

"Can I have a tiny one now? I'll even take clues in Eric code-language like the one you used in the pool."

A groan resounds from the other end of the line. "I'm never going to live that down, will I?"

"Not if I have a say in it." And behold, I'm grinning like an idiot again.

"I've got to go, but I can't wait to see you on Saturday," he whispers.

"Me too."

***

Saturday morning, my alarm clock rings at eight o'clock sharp. Amazingly, the usual sleepiness that plagues me in the mornings is not present. Instead, I feel as full of energy as if I'd drunk three coffees already. Who knew? The antidote to morning grogginess is a nondate with Eric.

I have four hours until he picks me up, which gives me plenty of time to go through several of my trusted beauty routines. My stomach rumbles the entire time I prepare, and sweat breaks out on my palms in regular intervals. I can't believe I'm having first-date jitters.

I remember Alice's words. *You're hormonally prepared for a date.* Truer words were never spoken. Every nerve in my body is alive with need and anticipation. At twelve o'clock, my doorbell rings. Taking a deep breath, I open the door. I'm rocking this outfit—a light pink sundress—so there's no reason to be nervous. He said I should go for casual, which I did. If casual also includes high heels.

When I see him, my face instantaneously cracks into a grin.

"Someone's happy to see me," Eric remarks. He wears a white polo shirt and black jeans, looking *yummy*.

I hold my thumb and forefinger very close together. "A little bit."

He chuckles when he sees my shoes.

"Do not mock my shoes," I say in a warning tone. I place my hand on my hips, emphasizing my words with a glare.

"I wouldn't dream of it. Let's go."

He takes my hand, leading me to the elevator without any further words. I'm giddy with happiness all the way to the car.

Eric opens the door for me, but I don't climb in my seat right away.

I place a kiss on the corner of his mouth, whispering, "We're going to have a lot of fun today."

"We are. Per your instructions, I didn't bring a forklift."

"Great. Forget the forklift and concentrate on the cobweb remover." I look suggestively under his belt, and when I snap my gaze back up, his eyes are dark and hooded.

"I'd never thought I'd use the words 'cobweb remover' and 'forklift' on a nondate. You're an interesting woman. Now, get in the car, or I'll take you upstairs and we won't come out for a few days."

I exhale sharply, the sensuality of his words nearly undoing me. Swallowing hard, I obey, climbing in the car.

Eric joins me and I pout as soon as he guns the engine. "Please give me a hint where we're going at least."

He's sneaking glances at me, so I bat my eyelashes

in an attempt to soften him up.

"Nope."

"Is there any way I can convince you to tell me where we're going?"

He shakes his head, smiling. "I might be bribed into it."

"By?"

"A peek at the lovely skin under that dress."

My mouth forms an O. "Eric Callahan! Are you asking me to strip in your car?"

"Absolutely. A peek at one thigh, and I'll give you a clue. If I get to see both of them, I'll tell you the location right away."

"You're asking me to strip and negotiating? You've got balls."

He lets out a small groan at the back of his throat. "Right, I changed my mind. No more balls or striptease talk, or we won't make it to the date at all."

"Should I take it as a challenge?" I ask, feeling naughty.

"Please don't. I'm trying to be a man of honor here."

We talk about Julie and my family for the better part of the drive, and after about an hour, he pulls off the highway. Ten minutes later, he pulls into the parking lot of a small harbor.

"Ah," I exclaim, as understanding dawns on me. "Are we going out on a boat?"

Eric turns to me. "Come on. Let's get down to business."

I lick my lips, his words igniting a spark deep

inside me. "You have a dirty mind."

"You turn my words into innuendos, and I'm the one with the dirty mind?"

"This coming from the man who wanted to bribe me with clues to strip in his car?"

"I've got my weak moments," he says with a shrug. "Come on. Let's go. Our nondate officially begins."

"You look so smug. I don't know if I want to smack that smile off you or kiss you."

We leave the car, and Eric leads me down a narrow stone path past the cabin that presumably houses the reception desk. Suddenly, unease slithers down my spine, and I dig my nails in my palms. To calm my nerves, I take in my surroundings, inspecting the magenta flower buds lining the narrow alley leading down to the harbor. As we approach the water, the smell of salt and sea is thick in the air. Eric extends his hand out to me, his eyes warm. I can almost read the promise in them: *I will take care of you.* I can do this. I can enjoy this beautiful day with this beautiful man. Smiling, I take his hand.

There are rows of luxurious yachts and boats, and we come to a halt in front of a six-person speedboat. Eric helps me inside, and that's when I see the small picnic basket tucked behind the driver's seat.

I sense that he's expecting me to say something, but I remain silent for some time. The fact that he put so much effort into this reaches somewhere deep inside me.

"I had someone arrange this for us," he says,

pointing at the basket. "I debated renting one of the bigger yachts, but this is cozier."

When I still don't say anything, Eric gently squeezes my hand, and I squeeze it back.

Finally, I murmur, "You've still got game, Eric Callahan. You can be sure of that."

Leaning in to me, he whispers, "I know." Then he pulls back, tilting his head to the right as if debating something. "Though for a while there, I feared you were silently preparing your exit strategy and were brainstorming for an excuse."

I laugh, elbowing him. "I wouldn't do that with you. If I'd wanted to leave, I would be honest."

"I appreciate that. I'm an upfront guy, and there aren't many people who respond with the same kind of honesty."

Within minutes, we're speeding out into the open sea. The water is remarkably still, reflecting the sunlight almost as perfectly as a mirror would. I admire the water for a while and then resume my favorite activity, ogling Eric. I'll never tire of doing this. He has a determined expression on his face, and it looks delicious on him.

It seems forever before the boat slows down, and I notice that we're not that far out into the sea. In fact, we're remarkably close to a deserted section of the coast.

As soon as Eric stops the boat, I rise from my seat, stretching. He produces an umbrella from under the bench at the back of the boat and opens it. Fantastic idea, because the sun is scorching hot.

"Let's see what goodies you brought." I point to the basket, rubbing my stomach.

Five minutes later, we're sitting on the rear bench under the umbrella, the basket at our feet. I broke first date and nondate protocol when I started stuffing my face with a delicious donut, but in my defense, it's filled with apricot jam.

"I love apricot jam," I remark.

"Yeah, I know. I asked Alice."

I sigh, my heart squeezing. "Stop being so nice to me." I realize too late that I said this out loud.

Eric puts his thumb under my jaw, lifting up my chin.

"You deserve nothing less." Shifting closer to me, he swallows, and I watch the dip of his Adam's apple. "I don't know where this will lead, but I can tell you I plan to treat you right every moment of it."

"You're a classy charmer, Mr. Callahan," I reply with a smile.

"Not sure about that. If you keep licking your lip, I might lose the class."

"That's a sweet challenge." I close my eyes, leaning my head back as I enjoy the jam's texture in my mouth, along with the rich flavor. I only open them again after I finish this little piece of heaven, and discover why Eric's been silent all this time. The bastard's been too preoccupied staring at my chest.

"So, checking out my boobs is your way of showing me your non-classy side?"

"I'm doing an in-depth study," he answers seriously. "Can you blame me? They're exquisite."

I scoff. "You haven't even seen them without clothes."

Finally looking up at me, he wiggles his eyebrows. "I plan to change that today."

Slowly but surely, my cheeks catch fire. "Okay."

"But later. No pressure." He says this with such nonchalance, as if he's talking about the weather, and I can't help but laugh again.

"I want to know a secret of yours," I inform him.

"Why?" He looks at me suspiciously.

"I'm the keeper of secrets in my family. I thrive on them."

Eric leans back, glancing at me. "I'll consider it. If you're done with eating for now, let's swim. I even brought goggles for snorkeling." He dips one hand deep inside the picnic basket, retrieving two pairs of glasses and placing them on the edge of the boat. "The water is clear here. You can see the fish, and even some corals."

"I didn't bring a swimsuit," I state, even though he knows this.

"Couldn't tell you or I would have spoiled the surprise. There's always skinny dipping."

I fold my arms over my chest, tapping my foot. "That's an indecent proposition for a nondate."

"I figured you might say that, so I bought a suit for you."

He jams his hand inside the basket again and retrieves a light yellow bathing suit.

"Impressive," I admit. "What else do you have stuffed in there? A white rabbit?" *Condoms*, my dirty mind supplies. By the loaded look Eric gives me, he knows exactly what I'm thinking. Blushing, I take the suit from him and inspect the label of the top, which is precisely my size. "Did Alice tell you my size?"

"You're offending me. I could tell your size by looking at you. Today wasn't the only day I studied you."

And behold the return of the blush. This time, the heat spreads to my neck as well. Eric takes in my reaction to him with satisfaction. I lick my lips, stubbornly holding his gaze, until it becomes too much.

"Right," I say. "Will you change too?"

"Sure. When you do." He points to some swimming shorts on the driver's seat.

"Turn around, so I can change. I'll do the same."

He does as I ask, and I change quickly, half-expecting him to turn around and kiss me senseless. Except he doesn't. I can't decide if he's being a tease or a gentleman.

"Done," I announce.

We both turn around at the same time. His gaze is so intense that my knees nearly buckle. His eyes travel up and down my body, leaving no room for interpretation. This man wants me, and the knowledge sets my nerve endings on fire.

"After you," he says in a low voice, pointing to the small metal ladder that leads into the water. I walk past him, intending to climb down, but I stumble over my own feet and grab both his arms for support. I clumsily pull myself straight and accidentally brush my breasts across his chest. A moan slips past my mouth, as Eric sucks in a sharp breath. We both lose control at the same time.

Cupping my cheek with one hand, Eric pulls me so close to his face we nearly touch. Then he covers my mouth in a raw kiss, his tongue exploring my mouth greedily while his hand slides into my hair. His other hand grips my waist, flattening me against him. I can feel his heartbeat, strong and furious. I can feel something else too, his hot and hard erection pressed against my belly. I become putty in his hands and, driven by blind need, I grind against him. Eric digs his nails in to my skin and cups my ass with both hands, pushing himself hard against me.

"I want you so much it hurts," he says as we pull apart to breathe before we lock lips again. Lost in his kiss, I barely notice that we're moving backward. When we reach the couch, we tumble over it, and a striking sound followed by a splash startles me. I pull back, looking around wildly.

"The snorkeling goggles fell in the water," I remark.

"I don't give a damn," Eric says. "I want you." He leans his forehead against mine, breathing hard against my lips. "You're all that matters." He claims my mouth again. First, he swipes his tongue over my lips, sending a jolt of heat right between my thighs. When he deepens the kiss with unrestrained passion, I become so aroused I barely know what to do with myself. "I'll never have enough of your lips. You taste so good."

Pushing my knees apart, he settles between them. I lean back, propping myself up on my elbows on the couch. Eric caresses one of my inner thighs with his fingers, turning my skin to goose bumps. He lowers one hand, stroking me with one finger over my bikini. I moan, shuddering at his touch.

"You're soaked," he whispers.

I drag my tongue across my lower lip, letting out a shaky breath. "I need you."

He strokes me again, and I wantonly curve against his fingers.

"Greedy girl."

"More, Eric. I need more. I need everything. Now."

He stops the caress and moves over me, watching me intensely. His chest is shaking lightly, as if he can barely restrain himself from taking me.

"I didn't bring any condoms," he says.

"What? Why?"

"It's a good way to curb the temptation. I don't want to rush things with you." Touching my cheek, he says, "I want you to be ready and trust me completely when we make love. You've been through a lot, and I want you to be absolutely sure."

Emotion clogs my throat, but I know he understands how much this means to me. All I can do to show my gratitude is nod and lean forward, searching for his lips. He kisses me again, tenderly at first, but it quickly spirals out of control.

"I have a problem," I whisper, smiling against his mouth. "My body won't listen to reason."

Eric chuckles. "I will give you what you need, and I will make it so good you'll ache for days." The promise in his voice prompts a new wave of heat that I feel in every inch of my body. Pushing himself back in a sitting position, he peels the top and bottoms of the bikini off me with exquisite slowness.

"You're shaved clean." His words come out more as a groan.

"All ready for you," I tease.

Eric turns his attention to my boobs, taking one puckered nipple in his mouth, running his tongue over it, driving me crazy. He moves on to the other breast, lavishing it with even more attention. He traces the skin on the underside of my breasts with his tongue, and I involuntarily arch my hips against him. I'm so turned on I can barely form a thought. When he finally seals his lips over my nipple, while flicking his fingers over my other hard, sensitive nub, I almost lose it. Can someone orgasm just from foreplay? Because I might. The sensations are so intense I will combust.

"I want to kiss you here, Pippa." He nudges my legs apart, cupping between them.

My body arches at his mere words. "Do it." I lick my lips as he lowers himself until he's inches away from my core. Feeling bold, I hitch one leg over his shoulder, giving him better access.

"Feisty," he murmurs. "I like it. Look at you, all dripping and ready."

"Too much talking," I tease, my breath wavering. "Prove it."

He rubs his fingers up and down my folds, deliberately avoiding my clit. I writhe and tremble, my toes curling in anticipation. I draw in my breath as he lowers his head, planting his lips straight on my slick spot.

"Eric." I grit out his name, fisting his hair with one hand. This man is a wizard with his tongue. I'm so aroused I might come in one minute flat. His tongue circles my clit again and again, driving me crazy. At the same time, he slips one finger inside me. I clench around him, panting. Tiny beads of sweat form on my temples as he slides in a second finger, stretching me. Every nerve inside me flexes in anticipation, need splintering me. He moves his fingers in and out of me, then curves them in a motion that drives me crazy. I am close… *so* close. Abruptly, he pulls his fingers out, leaving me empty and exposed.

"No," I protest. "What—oh!"

Eric blows a breath on my hot flesh. As the cold air reaches my drenched sex, I curl my hands into fists.

"I love seeing you like this," he murmurs. "All wild and hot."

Eric startles me by letting out a groan. That's when I notice that one of his hands is inside his boxers, moving up and down. *Oh, my.* Seeing him touch himself while his mouth is on me does unspeakable things to me.

He licks me once from my entrance up to my clit. Every swipe of his tongue brings me closer to my release. I ride the wave of pleasure until every inch of my skin is on fire. My climax sears me, and I moan and writhe, his name on my lips. Eric lies next to me on the couch, placing one palm on my chest, which is rising and falling with every heavy breath I take.

"You're so beautiful when you come," he whispers in my ear. I cuddle against him, needing the warmth of his body, and that's when I feel his erection against me.

"He's happy," I tease.

"Yes, he is."

"I want to make him even happier," I announce.

"Bad idea," Eric mouths. "I'll want you even more."

I pout, looking down at his boxers. "If you say so."

"Stop pouting, or I won't stop imagining those gorgeous lips of yours somewhere else."

"Your call," I say.

"Come here." He pulls me against him in a loving embrace.

"You prefer cuddling over an orgasm? You're a strange man."

"I want to feel you up." He cups one of my ass cheeks with his strong hand. "I'm an opportunist."

I pinch his shoulder. We can't keep our hands off each other, and I love it.

"I love your smile," Eric says. "You look happy."

"I am. I wish we could stay like this for the entire weekend." I rest my head on his chest, forming circles with my fingers around his navel.

"Pippa." His tone is so serious all of a sudden that my heart leaps in my chest.

"Yes?" I whisper.

"I like spending time with you, but I have to be honest. I don't know what I can give you."

"Why don't we find out together?"

He takes my hand in his, kissing my palm. "I don't know where this will go, and I'm well aware that in less than two months I'll be back in Boston, but while I'm here, I want us to explore this."

"Excellent." I ignore the way my heart clenches at the mention of his departure. I'm not afraid of giving him my body; I'm afraid of giving him my heart. Lifting my head, I glance at him, taking in his strikingly beautiful features. "I'll put on my explorer glasses and join you."

He hoists me up closer to him, planting a kiss on my neck. "You're so fun to be around. It's addictive."

"I'm banking on it."

I raise one arm above my head, stretching like a cat, and Eric runs his fingers over my underarm.

"Not there." My words come out on a screech.

He grins like the little devil he is. "So you tickle easily. This is very important information."

"Why?"

"I can use it as a persuasion technique."

I stand up, eyeing him suspiciously as he follows my lead. "Keep your hands where I can see them. I don't trust them."

He lifts his hands, chuckling. "You seemed to

trust them all right earlier."

"Different circumstances," I fire back. "Tickling me is out of the question. Now, an orgasm? You can give me one of those at any time."

"Noted."

"So, since we're here, why don't we get on with that snorkeling thing?" I suggest. "Unless, of course, you want to discuss the possibilities of more orgasms. No pressure or anything."

Stepping in front of me, he pushes a strand of hair behind my ear. "No can do. If I see you come one more time, I will lose it. There's only so much restraint I can have around you."

"Snorkeling it is, then." I look in the distance, at what appears to be a cave. "I think that's a cave there. Do you want to explore it?"

Eric frowns, touching his jaw. "No. Here's a secret. I don't like caves. They're dark, creepy, and scare the shit out of me."

"Wow... I wouldn't have thought anything could scare you. You're so tall and big."

"Many things scare me. Closed places, snakes, losing the people I love." His smile falters when he utters the last part. "I'm just a mere mortal."

"I've never met someone who wears his heart on his sleeve the way you do." Pointing to the water, I add, "No cave, then. Let's snorkel."

It's when we head to the ladder again that I remember we did away with the glasses during our passionate kiss.

"Oh, no," I groan, looking around the boat. Eric

seems to realize what I'm looking for, because he joins me in my search.

"The currents carried them away. I don't see them anywhere."

"Oh, plastic in the ocean. That was irresponsible of us," I say.

"Let's swim."

We spend a long time in the water, swimming, fooling around, and touching each other on every occasion. Before sunset, we climb in the boat again, dress, and drive back to the shore. We walk to the car holding hands, and as we let go of each other, I can't help the sinking sensation forming in my stomach. Come fall, I will have to let him go for good.

Chapter Eleven

Pippa

The next few days are like a dream. Eric and I don't see much of each other, but we text and speak whenever we get a chance. I'm counting down the days—and hours—until we'll be together again, which should be tomorrow night. Just thinking about it makes me feel giddy.

It's late in the evening, and I'm at home when my phone rings. *Max.*

"Hi, brother."

"Where are you?" he inquires. His tone instantly sets me on edge.

"At home. What's wrong?"

"Dad had an accident."

I gasp, a shiver running through me. "What happened? Is he all right?"

"He was with the renovating team at the farm, and he fell from the roof."

"Oh, my God." I try to calm myself and take deep breaths, but no air seems to reach my lungs.

"They brought him to San Francisco General Hospital. He broke several ribs, has a collapsed lung, and torn knee ligaments. They're getting him ready for surgery."

"But a collapsed lung can usually be fixed bedside with a chest tube, and torn ligaments aren't operated on an emergency basis."

"Yeah, but there's been some significant injury to the lung."

It takes me a few seconds to pull myself together before I can speak again. "I'll get there as fast as I can."

"I'll pick you up in ten minutes. Don't want you to be alone right now."

"Thank you."

I could have taken a cab, but I appreciate my brother's foresight. Heart thundering in my chest, I gather my things and head outside the building. My pulse races to the point I fear I might throw up. In the few minutes I spend waiting for Max, I manage to scare myself into imagining the worst scenarios. I try to reason with myself. The injuries Max listed, while bad, are fixable. *But my dad is not that young. A surgery at his age is no small thing.*

Max is pale when I climb into his car.

"Any news?" I ask as soon as the car lurches forward.

"No." He sighs, frowning.

"What is it?"

"I should've stayed at the ranch with him."

"What?"

"I went there last weekend to help out. He was overworking himself."

"You mean he was his usual self," I say as calmly as I can, trying to soothe him. "Don't blame yourself, okay? Dad's stubborn. Even if you stayed there, you couldn't keep him from doing whatever he wanted."

Max nods, but he doesn't look quite convinced. We remain silent for the rest of the drive. I try to convince myself not to give in to panic and am almost successful. But when I walk into the hospital a while later, an avalanche of feelings hits me. I sway on my feet, suddenly more nauseous than before.

Max eyes me with worry, and I somehow manage to give him an encouraging smile.

Tears spring at the corners of my eyes as we step into an elevator. I wipe my tears away, hoping Max hasn't seen anything. I can't let this happen. I'll cry later, when I'm alone. My family can't see me like this. I have to pull myself together. The elevator doors open all too soon, and I force myself to put one foot in front of the other, urging myself to go on. The corridor seems to grow narrower with every step, closing in on me. My brother is behind me. I force myself to take deep breaths, but the opposite happens. The waiting room is completely white. Even the air *smells* white. Austere and stinging, a mix of medicine and alcohol that raises the hair at the nape of my neck. Bile rises up my throat as I try to shut off the smell. I hate hospitals.

With each breath, less air reaches my lungs. I stop dead in my tracks when I see my family. The image before me is jarring. My mother sits on the first chair, her eyes vacant. Alice has an arm around her; the other one clutches the phone in her lap. Summer sits on the chair on Alice's other side, hugging her knees to her chest, her nose red. My baby sister has cried. Daniel and Blake occupy two chairs on the other side of the room, sitting next to each other in silence. Sebastian and Logan are both at the far end of the corridor. Sebastian leans against the wall, his arms crossed over his chest, and Logan paces back and forth.

Seeing them like this, all my fears come crashing down on me. Dad is in a surgery. *My daddy.*

I don't know where to start, whom to comfort first. Mom, who looks more lost than I've ever seen her, or Summer, whose fresh tears break my heart.

I decide to find out more details first. Pulling myself together, I stride down the corridor, right to Sebastian.

"How is Dad?"

"In surgery," he replies in a seemingly calm tone. To an outsider, this might be reassuring, but I know my brother. This is his alarm voice—trying to keep anyone else from panicking.

"How long will it take?" A knot settles in my throat.

"No idea," Logan replies in a whisper, joining us. "Apparently, they're not certain about the extent of the damage. Lung surgeries can take anywhere from one to six hours."

"There's nothing we can do but wait," Sebastian continues. I can tell by his voice that this frustrates him more than anything else. Sebastian isn't one to sit by and wait. Neither is Logan.

"Did anyone tell Christopher?" I ask.

"I talked to him," Max answers, appearing by my side. "He's on his way from Hong Kong."

"Okay," I say, pulling myself together. "I'll go buy supplies for everyone. Water, sandwiches—"

"Nadine and Ava are taking care of it," Sebastian interrupts.

"Oh, great. That's great. Then I'll…." My voice fades as I point at the rest of our family, but I don't need to spell out to my brothers what I want to do. Sebastian and I always could communicate with our eyes only, and Logan learned the language over the years. As the oldest trio, it's our duty always to be there for our younger siblings. This time for Mom too, it seems.

"Mom and Summer were at the ranch," Max tells me. "They rode with him in the ambulance."

Which explains why both of them are more affected than the rest of us.

Biting the inside of my cheek, I walk over to Summer and sit next to her. Without saying anything, my sister leans her head on my shoulder, still hugging her knees to her chest. A little sob escapes her mouth, and I hug her tightly with one arm like I did when she was a toddler and came seeking comfort. I often forget my sister is a grown woman, and this is one of those times. Now she's just my sister, the family baby, and I can't stand to hear her cry.

"Dad will be okay. We have the best doctors here." Even though I say this in a whisper, Alice,

Blake, and Daniel look up at me. They all want to believe this.

"Pippa," Alice whispers, pointing to Mom. "Can you talk to her a bit? She hasn't said one word since they've taken Da—" Her voice wavers. "Since the surgery started."

I nod, and Alice and I quickly trade places. Up close, my mom appears even more disheveled.

"Mom," I say softly, "do you want to take a walk with me outside?"

Mom doesn't reply, and Alice darts me a worried glance.

"Mom?" I press. Ever so gently, she turns to me.

"No. What if the doctor comes out and—"

"The surgery will go on for another few hours. Come on. Let's go out."

"Not outside," Mom whispers. "It's too far away."

"All right."

We go to the cafeteria on the sixth floor, and I leave her to sit at a table while I buy her a tea. In the short time it takes me to buy it, Mom's stare becomes vacant again. I shove the hot tea in her hands and search for the right words to soothe her.

"I'm afraid he will die," she says unexpectedly. Her words whip my breath away. "I don't know what I'll do if he—"

"Mom," I interrupt, because I cannot bear to hear the word again. "Please don't fall apart. You're the strongest person I know."

A sob is her only answer.

I hug her tightly. "Everything will be fine, Mom,"

I say lamely, but I'm not sure what else to say. I can comfort my siblings, but Mom has always been my rock. Seeing her come apart like this, my own tears threaten to spill.

I make her drink all the tea, and by the time her cup is empty, she looks more like herself. Looking up to me, she asks, "How are you, child?"

Scared is what I want to say, but I'm afraid Mom will fall apart again. So instead I go with, "Optimistic. Dad's a fighter. He'll get through this and tell us he wants to fix the house himself in one week."

"I bet he will. I'll give that stubborn old mule a piece of my mind when he comes out of the surgery."

I smile and Mom puts her hand over mine, squeezing it slightly.

***

When we return to the others, Ava and Nadine have joined my siblings. I take the sandwich Nadine hands me and then sit next to Blake. A heaviness forms in my chest, and I hug my knees, mirroring Summer, hoping to quench the uneasy feeling. The wait is killing me.

Thank God for Ava and Nadine. They run around, making sure everyone's all right. After a while, though, there's nothing more for them to do, so they wait too. Sebastian sits next to me with Ava on his other side, holding her hand.

My eyes travel from their hands to my brother's

face, and his expression startles me. Sebastian is the master of the poker face. He's so good at hiding his feelings that sometimes even I can't read him. But right now, he's let his guard down, and the emotion stretched on every line on his face is crystal clear— fear.

"Pippa, I forgot to tell you," Alice says about an hour later. "Your phone has been beeping while you were away with Mom." She hands me my bag. I fish my phone out of it and find quite a few texts from Eric.

Eric: Give me a call when you're out of the office.

Eric: You're still working? You're more of a workaholic than I am.

Eric: Now I'm worried. Is everything all right?

Eric: For Christ's sake, write something back, or I'll go to the police.

There are two more messages from him, but I don't read them, just type quickly. **We're all at the San Francisco General Hospital. Dad had an accident, and now he's in a surgery. I'll call you later.**

I put my phone back in my bag and resume holding my knees, rocking back and forth. A heavy silence falls over the group, interrupted only by Summer's sobs. My own sobs are locked in my throat, and I refuse to let them out.

If I can't find any words to comfort my family, the least I can do is not break down in front of them.

I don't know how much time passes before I hear

Alice saying, "Eric."

My head snaps up and I immediately rise from my chair, dashing to him.

"What are you doing here?" I whisper.

He takes my hands in his, pulling me a few feet away from the rest. "How's your dad?"

"We don't know anything. He's in surgery."

"How are you?" he asks.

"Fine." My voice breaks on the word, so I clamp my mouth shut. My hands start shaking in Eric's grip.

"I'm going to take Pippa downstairs. She needs some air," he calls to the group. "Anyone need anything?"

There's a collective *no*, and the next thing I know, Eric leads me to the elevator, holding my hand. I'm too tired to question anything, and maybe stepping outside is a good idea after all. The knot in my throat threatens to suffocate me. We ride the elevator in silence and Eric slides closer to me, curling an arm around my waist, keeping it there as he walks me outside.

The air is warm and heavy outside, but it soothes me. I take what feels like the first real breath in hours.

"Better?" Eric asks.

I nod.

"Will you tell me now how you really are?" His eyes bore into mine, and the worry in them is the straw that breaks the camel's back. I burst out crying. Ugly crying, with blubbering and everything.

"I'm so scared," I manage to say between sobs.

Eric hugs me tightly, and I weep uncontrollably into his neck. "I've never been more afraid. I don't want to be afraid." I lose myself in his arms, drawing strength from his hug.

"Shh, calm down, baby. It's okay to be afraid. It's okay to show it too. You don't have to bottle things up."

Pulling myself out of his hug, I press the back of my palms on my lids, hoping to calm the tears.

"Are my eyes red?" I ask Eric after I take my hands away.

"Very. Your nose too."

"Oh, no." I groan. "Everyone will see I cried."

"As they should." He cups my face. "You don't have to only show them your strong side, even though you're the oldest sister."

"Hey," I admonish. "I'm the people reader. Stop psychoanalyzing me."

"Why, because I'm right?" His mouth curves into my favorite grin. "From one people reader to another, let me tell you, reining everything in eventually wears you down. You have a big family. Let them comfort you too, Rudolph." He kisses me straight on the tip of my nose.

"You know the names of all the reindeer?" I tease.

"The hazards of helping my daughter prepare for Christmas recital auditions. You have no idea about all the things I know. Now, let's change the subject before my masculinity takes a hit."

I laugh, something I never imagined I'd be doing, given the circumstances.

"Thank you for making me laugh," I tell him. Now that I've put the ugly cry behind me, I can focus on Eric. He wears a dark blue suit with a white shirt underneath, oozing an amount of testosterone that should be illegal. But there are also signs of tiredness stretched all over his face, and yet, he still took the trouble to come here. "It means a lot to me that you stopped by."

"Stopping by? Oh, no, honey. I'm stayin' here."

"What?"

"You heard me."

"You don't have to stay," I say stubbornly.

"I want to. I'm here for you. Anything you need. You want to take care of everyone else, and I want to take care of you."

I shake my head, pulling myself straighter. "I don't need anyone. I can take care of myself."

"I'm not asking for your permission. I want to be here for you, and I will be. No matter what you say, I'm not leaving."

"What about Julie?"

"She's asleep, and Ms. Blackwell is at the house with her."

"Eric—"

"There's no point arguing. I'm not leaving."

"You're bossy."

"You have no idea."

He takes me in his arms again, and I allow his body heat and strength to soothe me. I revel in his tenderness and don't argue anymore, because deep down, I want him here. I want him to stay, and that scares me because soon enough I'll have to let him go.

When we return upstairs, Sebastian tells me that nothing's changed. But as Eric and I sit next to each other, holding hands for the next hours, I can't help feeling that something has.

The chief surgeon comes out at precisely one o'clock in the morning. He informs us that the surgery has gone well, and Dad will remain in ICU for tonight. They will move him to a regular room tomorrow. My dad is in stable condition, but they have to monitor him closely.

"We expect him to recover well," the doctor finishes in a tired voice. Almost in unison, the room breathes with relief.

"Thank you," Mom tells him while Alice and Summer hug her.

"There is no reason for anyone to stay here. You're not allowed to see him tonight anyway," the doctor adds before leaving.

Everyone, myself included, murmurs about how we aren't leaving until Mom exclaims, "Nonsense. I'm his wife. I'll stay here, in case there's any news. One of you can stay, but no more. We can take turns keeping watch."

Sebastian and Logan protest, but I smile, glad that Mom returned to her normal self. In the end, Alice and Mom remain at the hospital, and they all but kick the rest of us out.

"I'll take you home," Eric tells me.

I smile, almost amused. "I came here with Max,

but what if I had driven my own car?"

He shrugs. "I wouldn't let you drive."

"I change my stance. You're not bossy. You're a downright caveman, like my brothers."

"It wouldn't be safe for you to drive. You're too tired."

I don't move, taking in his commanding body language, which contrasts so starkly with the tenderness in his eyes. As if reading the question in my mind, he steps in front of me, cradling my head between his hands.

"I protect and take care of what is mine, and you're mine, Pippa. Mine. Let's go."

Chapter Twelve

Pippa

Eric pulls his car in front of my building a while later, and I sigh. As if sensing my unease, he puts his hand over mine.

"If you don't want to be alone, tell me. I'll come upstairs with you and sleep on your couch."

His eyes are hooded with desire, yet under it all is warmth and concern for me. "Why, you don't think you'll like my bed?" I tease.

"I was trying to be a gentleman."

"Let's go upstairs."

He nods, and the gesture unleashes a thick tension between us. Wordlessly, we exit the car and walk inside. Once we step into the elevator, the tension grows, intensifying with every breath, every stolen glance. As I unlock my door and push it open, the tension climbs to an unbearable high.

Once inside, Eric places his hand on my shoulder. "Are you sure you want this?"

"Where is he?" I pretend to search his pockets, first dipping my hands in the pockets of his pants, then those of his suit jacket.

"Who?" he asks in bewilderment.

"The caveman. Right now, I prefer him to the gentle guy."

"He's right here, ready to strike. He's always here."

The twinkle of mischief in his eyes is delicious. Eric is sweet and caring, but underneath that is a passionate and fierce man. I want all sides of him for as long as I can have him in my life.

"But I warn you," he continues, "your neighbors will know my name after tonight."

I shudder at the promise in his voice and tease, "Your first or last name?"

"Both. And you, Pippa Bennett… You will forget your own name."

"Good." I fist his shirt, drawing him closer to me. "That's what I want. To forget everything." Realizing how this might sound, I add, "I mean, I'm not planning to use you…."

He caresses my hair. "You can use me all you want, darlin'. However and in whatever position you want."

"Don't go all yoga on me." I slap his shoulder playfully. "I want sex, not acrobatics."

"That was a straightforward command."

Taking his hand, I lead us to my bedroom and turn on the lamp on my nightstand. The smell of jasmine and honey fills the space from the incense I often use in this room. All my senses are on hyper alert.

***

Eric

The fly of my pants is nearly bursting. I need her, right now. Cupping her cheeks, I capture her mouth hungrily. With every inch of her lips I claim, she places more of her trust in me. Gripping her waist, I guide us both backward until we reach the bed. Pippa lowers herself on it, peering up at me.

I put one knee on the bed, then lower myself until my face is level with hers. "You're the best thing that has happened to me in a long time, Pippa," I say, and she simply nods, smiling. "I want you naked."

"Back at you," she whispers.

I yank away her dress and underwear within seconds, congratulating myself for not ripping apart either. Pippa's fingers work furiously on the buttons of my shirt. When she's done undoing them, she pushes it down my arms and away. I kick off my pants and boxers myself, then push Pippa on her back, climbing in bed next to her. Fisting her hair, I tilt her head so I can kiss her jaw, descending to her neck and further down, lingering on her breasts. I knead them with my palm, then swipe my tongue on the underside. I move further south, kissing around her navel. Laughter bubbles out of her. God, I love this sound. I'd do anything to keep this woman happy and make sure no one hurts her again.

Flicking my tongue over one of her delicious nipples, I part her knees with my hands. She lets them fall to the side without inhibition, opening for me. Surrendering to me. *Fuck, that's a turn-on.* I drop my hand between her thighs, running my fingers up and down her ripe flesh as Pippa wraps her palm around my erection, moving her hand up, running her thumb over the tip.

I groan loudly, and she bites my shoulder. "You are so beautiful. I want to worship every inch of you."

But I'm about to lose control. My voice is hoarse as I peer at her. I give her a quick chaste kiss before lowering myself to her thighs, peppering her legs with kisses until I reach her ankles. I observe with satisfaction her toes curling. Pushing myself up on my knees, I take a second to admire her. She's on her back, spread open, the glistening heat between her thighs signaling she's ready for me. I grab the pants I discarded next to the bed, looking for my wallet, and take out a condom.

"I had bought some too."

While I roll the condom on, Pippa pushes her hips forward.

"Not so fast." I grab her hips with my hands, pinning her to the bed. "I'm not done teasing you, love."

"Not fair," she whispers.

"I like seeing you like this. On edge."

With the last vestiges of self-control, I place the tip of my erection on her clit, circling it while she writhes and moans.

"Eric." She arches up, closing her eyes. When I

slap my tip across her pink flesh, she gasps, and her thighs wobble slightly. Her folds are clenching, and she cradles me between her thighs, unleashing my primal instincts. Unable to resist any longer, I slide over her, prop myself on one forearm, and drive into her warm and welcoming flesh.

"Pippa." I grit my teeth, the sensation of her tight passage clenching around me undoing me. She grips my arms with her hands as if needing to ground herself. I watch her the entire time; I don't think I'll ever tire of watching her. I want to know everything she likes, everything that brings her pleasure, and give that to her.

She throws her head back as I ease in and out of her. Breathing in harshly through my nose, I grasp at my self-control. She comes undone before me, and I want to imprint the sight on my retinas.

Balancing myself on one forearm over her, I level my lips to her breasts, taking one nipple into my mouth and flicking the other one with my fingers. Pippa's hips buck off the bed, writhing underneath me.

Abruptly, I pull out, grabbing her ankles and placing them on my shoulders. I lift her ass, shoving a pillow under it. Then I enter her to the hilt until my balls slap against her ass.

"Oh, God," she cries out. "This… Too much."

"You like it, deep like this?" I ask through gritted teeth.

"I do. I can't…."

Her words fade into moans as I push my hips into

a maddening rhythm. I drag my thumb across her lips, then slide it inside her mouth. She bites it gently, and energy strums through me. Every muscle in my body contorts with effort. When she gasps my name, fisting the sheet, my control snaps. I slam harder into her than before. Her breasts bounce with my thrusts. Christ, what a sight that is. She rocks against me with equal desperation. Slipping a hand between us, I stroke her clit. Pippa rewards me by digging her nails in to the bed and crying out my name. She's sexy and wanton, and I fucking love it. A red hue spreads on her soft skin, flushing her gorgeous curves as her sex twinges around me. Her puckered nipples beckon to me and, on a groan, I lean forward and twist one between my fingers. I increase my rhythm like a man possessed until Pippa cries out loud, riding her orgasm while I come harder than I ever have.

After discarding the condom, I lie next to her. It takes a few minutes before my breath regains a somewhat normal rhythm. Pippa lies with her eyes closed and a smile playing on her lips. That's how I like to see my woman, thoroughly satisfied. The smell and feel of her damp skin are beckoning me. She shifts on one side, and when I take her in my arms, she wiggles her sexy ass against my crotch.

"Bonus points for spooning," she whispers, almost asleep. "Are you staying the night?"

"I'm not going anywhere, Pippa. My place is right here, next to you."

For now. I watch her fall asleep, unable to do the same. *How will I let this woman go?*

Chapter Thirteen

Pippa

"Rise and shine, sleepyhead." Eric's voice resounds throughout the room as if he's using a goddamn megaphone.

"No," I protest, covering my face with a pillow. I blink my eyes open and then narrow them. Sheets of light flood my bedroom, thanks to the large windows. Once my eyes grow accustomed to the light, I gradually open them wider. "It's Saturday. I want to sleep in."

"It's not Saturday," he says. "It's Wednesday, and it's ten o'clock."

I bolt upright in the bed, suddenly panicked. "Oh, my God. I made plans with my siblings to watch Dad in shifts. I was supposed to be at the hospital two hours ago and—"

Eric holds up a hand, interrupting me. "I spoke to Alice this morning. Blake and Sebastian are at the hospital, so you can relax for a little longer."

I push my hair out of my face, feeling bone-tired. Eric stands at the side of the bed, sizing me up with worry.

"Did she tell you how Dad's doing?"

"He's out of ICU and doing okay."

I breathe with relief. "Why aren't you at work?"

"I wanted to stay with you and make sure you're okay. You went through a lot yesterday."

His words reach somewhere deep inside me, in a place I've never wanted to let anyone go before. My heart thuds in my chest, and I channel the wave of emotions into a smile. "Thank you. I'm —" I almost say *all right*, but the truth is different. "I'm happy you're here with me."

Sitting at the edge of the bed, I enjoy the feel of polished wood beneath my bare feet. I decorated my bedroom in a rather minimalistic fashion, with a large bed with nightstands and a dresser made of cherry wood.

"Great. You're about to get a lot happier."

"Why?" I ask suspiciously, hoping to get another round of mind-blowing sex.

"I bought breakfast." He announces this proudly, as if he deserves a medal for it.

"Oh, okay." I try to infuse my voice with enthusiasm, but breakfast is a poor offer when I was looking for an orgasm.

"You were thinking about sex, weren't you?" He sits on the bed, eying me closely.

"Maybe."

In a fraction of a second, Eric flattens me on the bed, climbing over me. He pins my hands above my head and positions his knees at my sides, effectively trapping me under him. I'm stark naked while he's fully clothed.

"Tell the truth," he bellows, though he smiles.

I lift my head a few inches until it's dangerously close to his lips. Looking him straight in the eyes, I say, "I'm taking that secret to the grave."

"That's your final stance?"

Challenging him is such a sweet temptation. What will he do? Wrestle me into agreement? Kiss me into oblivion? Make love to me until I spill my deepest secrets? I look forward to every option. Better still, I hope he'll resort to all three of these techniques.

"Yes, it is." There's no hint of hesitation in my voice, but as his smile morphs into a devilish grin, I wonder if I didn't make a mistake.

"You asked for it," he announces.

Eric tightens the grip on my wrists with one of his hands, bringing the other to my breasts. Then no kissing or wrestling or lovemaking follows.

He tickles me. The bastard actually tickles me. I erupt in laughter as he tortures my armpits and the sides of my boobs. *Damn it. To hell with all of it. Who is ticklish on their boobs?*

"Stop," I shriek between bursts of laughter. Far from obliging me, Eric continues to tickle me.

"Have you changed your mind?"

I barely hear him over my own laughter. I'll be damned if I don't hold my ground, even though I might faint from laughter. Is death by laughter even possible?

"No," I say eventually.

"Then I won't stop." His damn fingers continue

to torment my armpits, driving me bananas.

My hips buck off the bed and collide with his.

"Fine, fine," I confess. "I *was* thinking about sex."

Instantly, he lets go of my hands, falling beside me on the bed, laughing alongside me.

"You play dirty," I accuse after regaining my breath.

"If it means I get my way," he replies. Turning on one side, he props his head on his elbow. "Coercing you into confessing wasn't the only reason for the tickling session."

"You had an ulterior motive in that evil mastermind of yours?"

"I like your laugh, so I made you laugh," he says, dragging the back of his hand up and down my cheek.

His words warm my insides. "That wasn't laughing. That was shrieking."

"True," he admits. "With a few pig-like snorts in between."

"I do not snort."

He lifts an eyebrow, and I sigh.

"Okay, I do, but a gentleman wouldn't bring that up."

Cupping my jaw, he pulls me close to him until our lips almost touch. "I'm no gentleman." He touches the hinge of my jaw and then my lower lip with the pad of his thumb.

"So, you woke up with sex on your mind."

"You know, words spoken under duress shouldn't count," I say.

He tugs at my lower lip with his teeth for a brief second, setting all the nerve endings on fire. "So, say you beg me to kiss you the next time I make love to you. Should I discard those words too?"

I blush. "That's something else."

"Double standards. I see." Shifting back, he drags his tongue over the skin between my breasts, then nuzzles one of my nipples. He swirls his tongue exquisitely slow, as if he wants to savor every lick of my skin. I want to do the same to him. I push my hips up, colliding with his hard upper body. He slides a finger inside me, his thumb pressing on my bundle of nerves.

"That feels so good," I whisper, grinding my hips against him. Eric smiles devilishly at me. Then kissing, wrestling, and lovemaking follow. In that particular order.

Afterward, we shower together and head to the living room. There is coffee, croissants, cookies, and waffles on the table.

"Not that I'm complaining, but why did you only buy sweet stuff?" I inquire while wolfing down a waffle.

"It's comfort food."

"I know, but how do *you* know that?"

"Julie," he answers simply. "Wait, why are you laughing?"

I bite my lip, evidently unable to hold back my smile.

"Do your workers have any idea the shark is a softie with his daughter?"

"If you ever repeat that in front of my employees…," he says in a faux menacing tone.

"You'll do what?" I challenge, holding my chin high.

He doesn't hesitate. "Tickle you."

Damn.

We finish breakfast in companionable silence, sitting across from each other. Our feet touch the entire time, and our hands occasionally too, across the table. He can't stop touching me, and the feeling is mutual.

Midway through breakfast, his phone vibrates. Eric glances at the screen, groaning.

"What's wrong?" I ask.

"Problems in Boston. I'll have to have a conference call with the office there when I get to work."

My throat clogs at the mention of Boston, which is silly. I know the deal.

"How do you like the work you do here?"

Eric sips from his coffee, furrowing his brow. "I like it more than I thought I would. Things in Boston run like a well-oiled machine. There are occasional hiccups, but nothing major."

"You don't feel challenged enough."

"Exactly. Setting things up here is different, more dynamic. I like it."

I fidget with my fingers in my lap, a question burning on my lips. "Why don't you move here?"

Eric doesn't answer, and my heart shrinks to the size of a pebble.

"Forget I asked," I murmur.

He leans his arm across the table, opening up his palm and gesturing me to place my hand there. I do that, startling when my skin touches his because it feels like I'm placing a piece of my heart in his palm.

"If it were just me, I'd consider it," he says in a soft voice. "But Julie's whole life is there. She's changed four schools in the last five years because she had trouble adjusting. Kids bullied her because of her leg and the inhaler, and things only settled down at her last school. I can't make her start fresh again."

"I didn't know that," I whisper. "Who would bully her? She's such a great girl."

"Yeah, but kids can be downright mean. Also, my mother is there. We're not very close to her, but Julie needs more family than me. I can't uproot her."

Retracting my hand, I lower my gaze to my plate. "Of course. I understand. Family is important."

He nudges my feet under the table. "Hey. Let's not think about Boston, okay?"

Nodding, I force myself to smile.

"That's not a real smile. I have to change that." Rounding the table, Eric takes my hand, bringing me to my feet. He pulls me in to a quick kiss, and then his fingers caress the side of my boob over my robe.

"Is this also an attempt to make me laugh?" I inquire, now smiling for real.

"Nah, this is me being a pervert, looking for every excuse to feel you up."

"Mmm… Someone's naughty," I murmur.

"Hey, we both still have a lot of sexual tension

bottled up inside. It's for everyone's benefit if we work it out before we go out into the world again."

He twirls a strand of my hair around his fingers, his lips brushing my cheek seductively.

"So, this is for the good of everyone else?"

"Exactly," he answers.

"Liar," I whisper. "This is very irresponsible of us, you know. You have to be at work, and I have to be at the hospital."

"Pippa." His tone changes from playful to serious in a split second, startling me. Licking his lips, Eric cups my face between his hands, watching me straight in the eyes. "You make me want things I shouldn't want. Things I haven't allowed myself to want."

"Like what?" I whisper.

"Like wanting to be irresponsible. If I could, I'd lock myself up with you inside this apartment for days."

"I'm that irresistible, huh?" I joke.

"You are. You're warm and funny, and I can't get enough of you."

"Let's be irresponsible for one more hour," I say, giving in to his kiss. His lips are everywhere: on my mouth, my neck, descending further down.

As sensations overcome me, drowning all reason, one thought stands out. This man is worming his way into my heart, one kiss, one touch, and one tickling session at a time.

Chapter Fourteen

Pippa

I was expecting to find Sebastian and Blake sitting in silence outside my dad's room at the hospital, allowing him to rest. Instead, the entire family is camping inside the room, talking loudly. Christopher is here as well. Right, so much for spending time with him in shifts.

Dad is sitting on his bed with Mom at his side. He looks pale, tired, and very grumpy. Almost everything in the room is white, but the color doesn't seem as austere as it did yesterday, though the smell still bothers me.

"I won't stay here for an entire week, no matter what that snotty know-it-all in the white coat says."

My dad has had a deep distrust of doctors for as long as I can remember. It's anyone's guess why, but I have a hunch it's because he doesn't like to take orders, and a doctor's word is law.

"That know-it-all happens to be the best surgeon on this coast," Sebastian deadpans. "You're staying whatever time he's saying plus one day, to be on the safe side."

"You won't—" Dad begins, but stops as Sebastian holds his hand up.

"With all due respect, Dad, you scared us, and this is not up for discussion. You'll stay here for as long as the doctors want you to."

"I'm strong as a bull," Dad says.

"And as stubborn," I say under my breath, then raise my voice so it's audible above all the chatter. "Hey, why don't you all go back to your business and leave me with Dad? It's my shift now."

Alice gives me a particularly smug look as she ushers everyone out.

"How did your morning shift go?" she whispers knowingly.

"I'll spill all the details later. Take Mom home. Knowing her, she hasn't slept a wink the entire time, and she'll want to stay. It's my watch for now."

"Yes, boss," Alice says, leaving the room. After pushing the door shut, I walk over to the bed, rearranging the pillows so he can sit or sleep comfortably.

"You don't need to baby me, Pippa," Dad says in a gentle tone. "I'm all right. I'm—"

"Dad," I say in a low voice—almost a whisper—while keeping my eyes on the pillow. "I know you're strong, but you scared all of us last night." Also, right now, with the gray hospital gown covering his pale, sweaty skin, he looks anything but strong. He looks weak and fragile, two words I have never associated with my father before. But I don't tell him that. Instead, I decide he needs some tough love to realize how serious this is. When I speak next, my voice is strong and severe.

"Mom was in shock. You have any idea what it was like to see her in that state while you were having surgery?"

Dad jerks his head back, his lower lip trembling slightly. "No."

"It was horrible and scary. I don't think she'd ever recover if she lost you. Follow the doctor's instructions. Please, Daddy."

I keep my fingers crossed behind my back because Dad is not one to listen. However, he nods at me.

"All right, I will."

Feeling bold, I decide to try my luck. "Also, I don't want you to go back to the ranch to oversee the reparations."

"Pippa—"

"No, Daddy, it has to be that way. You'll put yourself in danger again, and I... What?"

"You haven't called me Daddy since you were nine years old." His eyes are wide and glassy, as if he's holding back tears.

"I... Why did I stop?"

He smiles at me. "I believe your words were, 'It's not cool.'"

"Well, I was an idiot. Promise me you'll stay put."

"I promise you, sweetheart," Dad says, and pulls me in for a hug that makes me feel nine years old all over again. Every muscle in my body relaxes as I wrap my arms tightly around him.

"Great, now you're in for a few hours of babying,

whether you want it or not."

***
Eric

I'm in and out of meetings the entire day, skipping lunch and only taking a break around four o'clock when I receive a call from my mother.

"Hello, Mother," I say into the phone as I shut the door to my office. "Happy birthday."

"Thank you for the gift and the flowers, Eric."

"It's not every year you turn seventy."

"Shh, don't say that out loud," she admonishes me, and I can't help smiling. My mother stopped owning up to her age about twenty years ago. She's tried to pass off as being in her late fifties for the better part of the last decade. To her credit, she does look incredible for her age.

"So, how old are you unofficially? Is it still fifty-nine?" I notice a burger on my desk and immediately attack it. I make a mental note to thank my assistant—it's part of my plan to be nicer to people. In my experience, being strict always works, but maybe Pippa's on to something.

"At my age, numbers are a taboo subject. If anyone in my bridge club brings it up, I stop inviting them to come over."

"Sounds *very* reasonable," I tease her.

"The bracelet you sent me is absolutely beautiful," she continues.

Ever year on her birthday, I send her roses and jewelry. This year, I sent her one of Pippa's creations. Unable to sit anymore, I grab the burger in my free hand and pace around my office, stretching my legs.

"I'll let the designer know." After a brief moment of hesitation, I add, "I'm dating her."

"I've been waiting to hear you say that for years. I'm glad you're finally giving yourself a chance."

"What do you mean?" I stop in front of the window, frowning.

"Since Sarah died, you've closed yourself off. You—"

"Mom, I've been busy. Raising a daughter and running a business isn't easy." Why did I ever think sharing this piece of information was going to be a good idea? Now I'll never hear the end of it. Fact is, though, Mom genuinely worries for me. She tried more times than I can count to set me up with some bimbos—daughters of members of her bridge club.

Between Mother's matchmaking attempts and those of the Bennett clan, I'll take the Bennetts every day.

"That's not an excuse," she continues. "You make time for the people you want in your life, like me and Julie. If you'd wanted to make time for a woman, you would have."

My mother rarely confronts me about my personal life—usually preferring to set me up behind my back—but when she does, she's spot-on.

"Moving on is not a bad thing," she continues. "Like I did with Gerald."

"Mom, let's not talk about this again."

Three years after my father's death, Mom announced she had a *boyfriend*. At first, I thought it would never last because Gerald is the opposite of Mom in every way. Where Mother is concerned with appearances and following rules to a T, Gerald is a laid-back guy. He's a buffoon of sorts, but he makes her happy, so I've come to like him, even though his sense of humor completely escapes me. My mother had her fair share of pain, and she deserves to be happy. She handled pain much better than I did; she didn't fall into a black hole. I always thought it was because she had time to say her good-byes to Dad. He died after a two-year battle with leukemia, whereas I lost Sarah to a car accident.

"How are Julie's etiquette classes going?" Mom's voice snaps me out of my thoughts.

"Fantastic." The lie rolls off my tongue without effort. Mom insisted that twelve was the 'proper age' to start taking official etiquette classes. She's been teaching Julie on her own for years and feels it's time for formal lessons. Having been through that crap myself when I was a kid, there's no chance I'll put my daughter through it. It was so boring and over-the-top I wanted to poke my own eyes out. But Mom doesn't have to know that. What she doesn't know won't hurt her, which calls for a change of topic.

"When are you leaving to go to the Hamptons?"

Mom's best friend lives there, and they've been visiting each other regularly for as long as I can remember.

"Oh, I won't be going anymore. Bette is coming to Boston this year. I signed us both up for Krav Maga. It'll shake things up."

"Krav Maga?" I ask, suddenly on alert. "Isn't that a self-defense technique? Did you check with your doctor about this first?"

"You don't have to baby me. I can take care of myself, thank you very much."

Yeah, I bet Pippa's dad said the exact same thing right before he landed himself in the hospital.

"Well. I'll leave you to your own business," she says quickly, in an obvious attempt to get me off her back. "But consider this. If your seventy-year-old mother deserved a second chance at love, so do you," she continues.

A second chance… The words feel like a knife to my ribs. I hadn't thought about it like that. I've been so focused on making sure I'm not asking Pippa for something she's not ready for that I haven't stopped to think about anything else. She and I are kindred spirits, and yes, *maybe* on the lookout for a second chance. Caring is dangerous, though. The more you care, the more debilitating the loss. I learned that years ago. But Pippa makes it impossible not to care for her. After last night, I want more than ever to be part of her life.

The woman is irresistible, and I can't get enough of her—talking to her, kissing her, making love to her. Every time I make her laugh feels like a small victory. Pippa Bennett will be one spoiled woman for as long as I'm here.

Chapter Fifteen

Pippa

After my shift is over, I hurry home and dress to impress, even though I'd much rather stay at home, order some food, and curl up on my couch with a steamy romance book. I'm putting on the finishing touches when my phone rings. I beam when I see Eric's name on the screen.

"Hello, handsome," I say.

"Hi back. How are you feeling? How's your dad?"

"Dad is okay, I think. And I'm tired, but I still have to go to a charity event for a few hours," I say as I apply my signature red lipstick for such events.

"You can't get out of it? Your dad is in the hospital. I'm sure they would understand."

"They would, yeah, but I don't want to disappoint them. I'm the guest of honor, and it would be bad form not to show up. It's for a good cause."

"You're an amazing woman," he says softly, causing me to blush. "I was hoping to see you tonight."

"Me too," I admit. "Do you want to join me?" I bite the inside of my cheek, wondering if I'm pushing my luck. I have no idea if he wants to be seen at a relatively public event with me. We haven't yet defined the boundaries of our… relationship.

"Sure. I'll pick you up from home. I planned to spend the evening with you. I told Julie you need me more than she does right now, and she understands. Ms. Blackwell is with her."

"Thank you. I—" My voice catches, so I clear my throat before continuing. "Can you be here in half an hour?"

"Sure."

I'm grinning like an enamored teenager when I disconnect the call. He arrives twenty minutes later, and my grin stretches even wider when I see him in the doorway.

"I love your lipstick," he says. Tilting his head to one side, he adds, "Take it off."

"Why?"

"Because I want to thoroughly kiss you, and it's in the way."

I hurry to the bathroom without complaint and wipe my lips clean. When I return, Eric pins me against the wall, savoring me as if I'm a fine dessert. I sigh against his mouth, my entire body melting against him. Having Eric by my side tonight is such a treat.

Part of the charity gala was supposed to take place outside, but as we arrive at the location and I climb out of the car, I instantly know the weather will not be on our side tonight. It was cloudy the entire day, but now the sky is a violent swirl of purple, blue, and gray. The wind is stronger than it was when we left my apartment, and the sound of creaking leaves gives me chills.

The head organizer, Felicia, goes through the schedule with me. I inform her that I won't stay long, then climb up the stage in the center of the place, delivering the opening speech about the importance of the cause—education for underprivileged children. It's a cause that is dear to my heart. Growing up, I looked at higher education as something that was out of my family's reach. Our luck changed, and now it's the least I can do to make sure others get a chance too.

During the speech, my eyes sweep the room and settle on Eric, who is watching me with a serious expression. I wonder what's on his mind.

Felicia takes over the microphone after I'm done, and I scurry off the stage.

"You were wonderful," Eric whispers in my ear as I take my place at the table next to him. I take deep breaths, suddenly feeling faint. I haven't eaten much today, but for some reason the appetizers on the table don't look too appealing.

"I need to go to the bathroom," I whisper back. At his inquisitive expression, I merely shake my head. I try to be as inconspicuous as possible as I walk through the tables. Everyone is focused on Felicia's speech anyway. Once I reach the bathroom, I splash some cold water on my face and grip the sink with both hands, breathing in deeply.

Not ready to return to my table yet, I decide to go

outside for a few breaths of fresh air. When I step in the dimly lit corridor outside the bathroom, I instantly sense something's not right.

"Pippa," a familiar and unpleasant voice greets me. I stiffen, sweat breaking out on my forehead.

"Terence," I say in a clipped tone. "What are you doing here? You hated these events."

"I do, but I knew you'd be here. Your name was on all the publicity materials. The golden girl representing the illustrious Bennett family." He wobbles on his feet, clearly drunk—which is odd. He's never been much of a drinker. I brace myself for what's to come. Our last public encounters have been bad, but this has disaster written all over it. I don't want him to cause a scene. At least the corridor is sheltered from the main room.

I decide to take the bull by the horns. "You won't get one cent from me. Whatever you have to say to me, do it through your lawyer."

He snorts, spitting on himself in the process, but he's so drunk he doesn't even notice. He looks worse for the wear—much worse. His suit is old and worn. The Terence I knew never stepped out of the house looking anything other than immaculate.

After we broke up, he kept what he bought during our marriage—a small yacht, a sports car, and a collection of expensive watches. If he'd been smart and sold those, he would have had enough money that he didn't have to work for years. Of course, Terence has never been smart. That's why he's contesting the court decision. He's desperate.

"My lawyer is excellent."

"He's a sleaze," I say calmly. "Otherwise, he wouldn't have taken you on as a client."

"Damn it, Pippa. I deserve something in return for spending so many years with you. I listened to your ramblings, tolerated your family. I touched you, slept with you, fucked you. It was worse than a fucking job."

I blink back tears. "You should have gotten a job, and then you wouldn't have had to live off my money."

He stomps forward and knocks into me. I stumble backward until I hit the wall, with Terence half collapsing on me. He grips my shoulder for support and straightens up, and I freeze. He's never been violent, but the aggressive look in his eyes tonight chills me to the bone. "I will receive my share."

"If you hurt her, I'll kill you," Eric's says, right before pushing Terence off me. I hadn't seen him coming, but I've never been happier to see him.

"Who the fuck are you?" Terence spats at him.

"That's right. I forgot to introduce myself. I'm Eric Callahan." Then he raises his fist and hits Terence straight in the center of the face. I shriek, covering my mouth as Terence stumbles back. His nose is a bloody mess, which he realizes when he covers his face with his palms. He steps back quickly, as if determined to put as much distance as possible between himself and Eric.

Eric steps forward, his intent clear. He's not done with Terence. Before I can open my mouth to beg him to stop, two heavily built men step in—security, judging by their outfits and the microphones in their ears.

"We've been alerted there's been an incident here," one of the men says.

"He assaulted me." Terence points at his nose and then at Eric.

"He was defending me," I say in a strong voice. "That man is my ex-husband, and he attacked me. Eric was merely defending me."

Eric puts his arm around my waist, kissing my forehead. "Are you okay?" he murmurs in my ear.

I nod, leaning in to him, soaking in his warmth.

"We are sorry for this, Ms. Bennett," one of the guards tells me. "We will escort him off the premises right now. Do you want us to call the police and press charges?"

I shake my head.

"Pippa—" Eric begins, but I cut him off.

"No," I tell him in a strong voice. "I need to go home." Turning to the guards, I say, "Please inform Felicia of the incident, and that I'm leaving." I can't step in the spotlight again tonight.

"Of course," the man says. "Please accept our apology."

Eric and I walk to the car, neither of us speaking. Eric is still too mad, and I am still too shaken.

"How's your hand?" I ask once the car is in motion.

"Fine," he says through gritted teeth. "How are you? Did he hurt you?"

"No, he... It was weird. He stumbled and grabbed me for support. I don't think he meant to—"

"Don't fucking defend him."

"I'm not defending him," I say, starting to feel mad too. "But Terence is not a violent man. He was drunk tonight."

"Why didn't you want to press charges?"

I sink lower in my seat, resting my hands on the silk top of my dress. Looking out the window, I say, "I just didn't."

"Do you want to call Alice?"

I snap my head in his direction. "No. I'd appreciate it if you wouldn't tell Max or anyone else either."

Eric's jaw ticks, his knuckles turning white as he grips the steering wheel tighter. "If I wasn't there, you wouldn't have told me either?"

I hesitate for a beat. "I might have told you. Now, I don't want to talk about this anymore. I'm hungry. Damn, something with sugar or caffeine would be great now."

"Huh? You want—"

"No, no. I won't be able to sleep if I drink coffee now. But can we buy some Chinese food and dessert?"

Eric nods and squeezes my hand lightly.

***

We walk inside my apartment a while later, and I sashay to the kitchen to unwrap the food. "I've been dreaming about a cozy night in with a book and take out the entire day. Almost forgot about the charity event."

Eric wraps one arm around my waist from behind while I busy myself at the counter. Swiping my hair to one side, he bares my neck and kisses it gently.

"I want you to relax. I'll do everything."

"You don't have to," I tell him. He turns me around, caressing my cheek.

"Right, but you had a tough day, and I don't want you to do anything else right now. Okay?"

Sighing, I lean in to his caress, a little overwhelmed by so much attention and care. "Thank you for coming with me tonight. At the charity and now back here. You don't have to spoil me."

"Oh, but I do." He kisses my forehead and adds, "You deserve to be spoiled. And I want to be the man to do it."

"Okay," I say, almost breathless, stepping aside. "How was your day? I'm warning you, I don't want to talk about what happened tonight, so you'd better talk. I want to hear something nice."

"My mother sends you her compliments," Eric says as we sit at the small table in the living room, eating. "I sent her one of your bracelets as a birthday present."

"When was her birthday?"

"Yesterday."

"You should fly over and celebrate with her."

He shakes his head. "I'll take her and Julie to dinner when I return to Boston. That's our tradition."

"She doesn't like parties?"

He smirks, almost looking amused. "Her idea of a party is a high-brow bridge game with her friends. Julie and I try to get out of them as often as possible."

"I see. Well, Ava's birthday is coming up. You'll see how my family celebrates birthdays. Come to think of it, I'm not sure if the party is still on. It was supposed to take place at my parents' house…."

"How is your dad feeling?"

"Okay. Trying to blackmail the doctor into releasing him sooner."

Eric chuckles. "But your family is there almost round the clock. It's as if he is home."

"I think he feels powerless there. I think that's been his problem lately. He wants to prove that he can still do things on his own."

"Ha! He sounds like my mother."

A few minutes of silence follows before he says, "Pippa, I don't want to be pushy, but I think we should talk about tonight. That douche bag—"

"He was not himself," I murmur.

"Don't make excuses for him." His tone is so cutting that I flinch. "I heard what he told you. He made you feel like you were not important, like you were dirt. He deserved getting punched for that alone."

"I really wasn't important to him," I clarify. "Can we change the subject now?"

I rise from my chair, taking our plates and

bringing them to the kitchen. Eric follows me.

"It would be good for you to talk about this," he says, hugging me from behind while I pretend to scrub off the plate on the counter.

"I already talked to you about Terence."

"There's more. Why are you afraid to open up to me?"

Slowly, I turn around, fixing my gaze on the top button of his shirt. "Because you're leaving."

Eric tilts my head up until I have no choice but to look him in the eyes. "That doesn't mean what we have isn't real," he says.

"I know."

He cups my cheeks between his hands and leans his forehead against mine. "Let me make you happy while I'm here."

"You are making me happy," I whisper.

"Then trust me. Talk to me." His voice is as calm as it is controlled, and I know on the spot that he's the kind of man who never yells. Good, because I've had enough fights that involved yelling with Terence to last me a lifetime. "Don't close yourself off to me."

"Can I ask you something first?"

"Sure."

"What happened to your wife?"

He stills. "Car accident. She was speeding. I'd returned a day earlier from a business trip, and she was eager to meet me at home. Julie was in the car too."

"I'm sorry," I murmur.

"It was a long time ago."

"That doesn't mean anything."

Eric sizes me up and down, his expression unreadable. "I keep thinking I should have been able to protect them—save them, somehow."

"Eric, it was an accident."

He shakes his head. "I know. I... My biggest fear is that something bad will happen to Julie." Silence stretches for a few seconds, and then he smiles again. "Your turn."

"Talking about my ex puts me in a bad mood. I'd rather show you my good sides," I say on a playful note, but Eric's gaze is unwavering.

"First of all, there are no bad sides to you, but you've been through good times, bad ones, and ugly ones. All that made you who you are today. I want to know *you*. I want to know the good, the bad, and the ugly, Pippa."

I sigh. "You're so good with words, Eric. Why do you have to be so good with words? It makes fighting you hard."

"Oh, you want to fight me?" He's smiling at me now.

I shake my head, leaning with my lower back against the counter. "No. I don't like fighting. I'm not good at it, if I'm honest. We always talked out our problems in my family. I guess we had to. With so many people, keeping things from each other and bottling tension would have escalated quickly."

To my astonishment, Eric's eyes are doubtful. "I have one question. Were you a talker or a listener?"

"Listener and advice-giver."

"Thought so."

"You're good at reading people. Even better than I am."

"I have my talents," he answers, a determined look on his face. "But I'm all in. Don't push me out. I won't let you."

"Okay." Taking a deep breath, I start explaining everything. "A while ago, my lawyer informed me that Terence is appealing the court decision in our divorce. He's trying to get some money."

"And?"

"And my lawyer's handling it."

"Have you told your family?"

"Yes, I have, and I asked them to stay out of it, which to my surprise they accepted. I am going to ask you the same thing."

"Okay, but can I give you some advice at least?" Eric asks.

"Sure."

"You are too gentle. You treat everybody with kindness and respect. Some people don't deserve that. Sometimes you have to stoop to their level to beat them."

Crossing my arms over my chest, I consider the merit of his words. Maybe I have been too gentle with that moron.

"There's something more bothering you," Eric continues.

"I'm trying to figure out if I had a greater share of blame than I like to admit," I confess.

"What do you mean?"

"He married me for money. But he spent years with me, and I couldn't make him fall in love with me. What does that say about me?"

"That you were with the wrong man. Don't for one second think you're unworthy of love."

Which is exactly how I feel, of course. It's scary how easily he can read me, but reassuring at the same time.

"Well, my family loves me," I say with a smile, "so I know I'm not entirely unlovable."

Without any warning, Eric swipes me off my feet, lifting me in his strong arms, and walks toward the couch as if I weigh nothing. We walk too close to my shelves of books, though, and when my foot collides with a book that's sitting too far out, a bunch of books fall to the floor. Belatedly, I realize it's my stash of romance novels. Eric puts me down and makes a grab for the books.

"What are these?" he asks playfully.

"Books," I say quickly. Tiptoeing around him, I brainstorm for the best way to distract him, but by the look of intense concentration—and almost insulting incredulity—on his face, I know it won't be easy.

He scans the covers. "Bare chest, abs, couples kissing... I'm sensing a theme here." His eyebrows, which were already arched, now threaten to get lost in his hair. "More abs, and is that a—?"

"Give them here." I snatch the books from him and put them back on the shelf. My entire face feels hot and flushed, and Eric chuckling behind me doesn't help the situation.

I swirl around on my heels, facing him. "Do not mock my romance books, or you will not get laid tonight."

"Are you threatening me?"

"*Warning* you."

"Must you be reminded who's in charge here?" Eric's gaze is so intense it makes all my lady parts tingle. He oozes too much masculinity.

"You're presumptuous," I say, but lick my lips nervously when the intensity in Eric's gaze doesn't lessen. "Don't mock the books."

"I'm not mocking," he says, with an amused expression. "Just wondering what I'm up against."

"Ah, don't worry. You more than measure up to all the hotties on those covers."

"I see." His lip curls into a smirk. "So, when you say you're spending a cozy night in, this is what you do?"

"A girl's got to indulge," I say with a shrug.

Eric takes a step in my direction, towering over me as he slides his thumb under my chin and lifts my head. "Indulge in me."

"Sounds like something I can do."

He nods, picking me up in his arms again. "Let's resume our previous conversation. You, Pippa Bennett, are the easiest person to love, and any man who doesn't see that is an idiot."

"Ah, I have a feeling I'm about to be showered with compliments."

"Anything against it?"

"Not at all. Please work in many 'beautifuls' and 'funnys' with it too," I instruct.

"I was going to start with that." He laughs and lowers me on the couch. I immediately move over to one side, making space for him. Lying next to me, he says, "Then I would've added that you're smart and the warmest person I've ever met."

"Are your complimenting services available for hire?"

"They're free for you."

I poke his chest, smirking. "Nothing is free."

"You can pay me with sex." A devilish smile inches its way across his face.

I offer him a peek of my boob. "Is this payment enough?"

He purses his lips, as if seriously considering his words. "I might need to see the other one to make up my mind. And possibly that sweet ass of yours too."

"Did you just compliment my ass? You're cheeky."

"Hey, I call it like I see it. And you have a perfect ass."

"I do?" I ask coyly, suddenly ridiculously pleased with myself. God, this man knows how to make me smile. "Is that why you're staring at it every chance you get?"

"I do," he admits, and we both burst out laughing.

"I should buy clothes that put it more on display to see if it has the same effect on everyone else."

He pulls me in to a hug and climbs over me. "You will do no such thing."

"Can we negotiate?" I tease.

He traces my jaw with his fingers, spreading my legs with his knees. "You are mine, Pippa. There's nothing negotiable about it."

He kisses me deeply, cupping my face with one hand. I revel in the warmth of his body and the power of his lips, all the while trying to forget there is an expiration date to this.

Chapter Sixteen

Eric

"Dad," Julie says on Saturday morning, "we need to talk about something important."

I blink, placing my cup of coffee back on the table. The scrambled egg I ate for breakfast feels like a stone in my stomach. Nothing good ever comes from the words 'we need to talk.'

"I'm listening," I say.

Julie places her elbows on the table, frowning at me. Her own plate of scrambled eggs is still half-full, and she's seemed lost in thought all morning.

"Do you think I will ever have a brother or sister?"

I jerk my head back. "What?"

My daughter sighs, placing her head in her hands, looking troubled. "I always wanted a sister. Or a brother. I have two girls in my design class who are sisters, and they do everything together. I mean, I know I couldn't do everything with a sister, if I had one right now, because she'd be tiny, but I could do things *for* her. Like buy her clothes and read her stories. Then when she grows up, I can look out for her. She probably wouldn't want me to hang out with her, because when she'll be twelve like I am now, I'll be twenty-four, which is *ancient*."

Julie is now talking to herself more than to me, which is just as good, because I am utterly speechless. My gut clenches. She would have had at least one sibling if it weren't for the accident.

"So, what do you think? Any chances of me having a sister or brother?" she presses.

"I didn't know you wanted one until two minutes ago."

Julie crosses her arms over her chest. "Do *you* want more kids?"

"Yeah," I find myself saying, and I realize I didn't know I wanted that until I said it out loud. To my astonishment, this seems answer enough for Julie because her frown morphs into a smile. She leaps off her chair, rounds the table, and hugs me. I wrap my arms tightly around her.

"You should finish your breakfast," I tell her after she pulls away.

"I'm not hungry anymore. Can I go to my room and finish the homework for my design class until Pippa arrives?"

"Of course, but only after we clean the table."

She doesn't object; instead, she dutifully brings her plate to the kitchen. Ms. Blackwell is free today, so it's the two of us until Pippa arrives. She's been over at our place a couple of times lately, and I like having her here.

***

Pippa arrives around lunchtime, holding a box of sweets in her hands. This woman's smile is contagious. I can laugh just seeing her laugh, and that is perfectly fine by me.

"Hello, stranger," she says. "Long time no see."

"C'mere." I pull her inside the house, closing the door, and give her a smooch.

"Eric, won't Julie see us?"

"She's working on something on her computer. The house could collapse and she wouldn't notice."

I press her against the door, planning to kiss her thoroughly.

"Watch it." She holds the box above her head with so much care you'd think she had diamonds inside. "You'll ruin the cupcakes."

I take the box out of her hands, placing it on the nearby table, then resume pinning her against the door. This time, I grab her wrists with my hand and hold them above her head.

I drag the knuckles of my free hand down her cheeks, cupping her jaw. "*Cupcakes.* Somehow, I feel like I'm not a priority for you."

"That is absolutely not true. You have a tiny, dirty secret that'll always make you a priority."

"And that is?"

She pushes her knee gently between my legs, smiling coyly.

"I can't believe you called my dick tiny. He's offended."

"I can't believe you talked about your penis in the

third person."

"He deserves an apology and some love," I continue.

Pippa grins, grinding her hips against me, the little vixen. "Fine, I'll do that later. I'll whisper my apology to him."

"Why whisper?"

"Because it's between him and me. You're not allowed in on our secret conversation."

I eye her for a brief second, then kiss her hard. She gives in to my kiss, sighing in my mouth. She tastes like sugar, and I smile as I realize she probably ate one of the cupcakes on the way. She's fucking adorable.

After we pull apart, I kiss her cheek and the tip of her nose. That's when I notice the vulnerable look in her eyes.

"What's wrong?" I ask.

"Nothing. I love spending time with you. You make me feel like a pampered princess, even when you're not trying."

I take advantage of this brief moment of vulnerability, caressing the side of her neck. "That's the way it should be, Pippa. You deserve nothing less."

"Dad," Julie's voice resounds from the bedroom. "Is that Pippa? I heard the door."

I smile. "She just arrived."

With that, both Pippa and I head into the living room. Julie walks in with a huge orange plastic box in her hands.

"What's that?" I ask. I'm one hundred percent sure I've never seen that box before.

"Supplies," Julie replies simply. "Pippa, are you ready?"

Pippa nods. She and my daughter sit on the living floor, opening the orange box and rummaging through it.

"I'll be in the study for about three hours," I tell them. "I have a conference call with Boston."

Neither Pippa nor Julie looks my way, so it's safe to say neither will miss me.

I return to the living room two hours later, looking forward to sprawling on the couch for the remainder of the day. I want to enjoy a few hours with my girls, maybe watch a movie. When I open the door to the living room, I do a double take.

There's glitter everywhere, and I mean *everywhere*. Pippa and Julie stop midchat, greeting me with startled expressions.

"Dad, we thought you wouldn't be back for another hour," Julie says, in a tone that sounds an awful lot like an accusation.

"I know this looks like glitterland right now, but I promise you we'll clean up," Pippa says, almost breathless.

Glitterland? More like glitterhell, but I bite back the remark and say, "Looks like the two of you are having fun."

At this, both Pippa and Julie smile. "We are," Pippa says.

"Yeah. We're making mock-ups for my design

class," Julie explains.

I have no idea why that requires turning my living room into a pool of glitter; however, if it makes both of them so happy, then I'll drown in glitter if I have to. I make my way to the couch, but even that is full of tiny, sparkling bits.

"Aren't you a little too old for glitter, Julie?" I ask.

My daughter gasps, as if I've spat an offense of the highest order.

Pippa crosses her arms over her chest. "You can never be too old for glitter. I love it."

"Of course you do," I reply. She and Julie exchange glances then both grin, which can only mean one thing: they're planning a move against me. I eye the two of them, trying to figure out what it'll be. *Come on, Callahan. You're a damn CEO. Think fast. What are they planning?* My mind comes up with nothing. It seems I'm no match for these two masterminds.

"Your dad deserves a lesson," Pippa says.

"I agree," Julie answers.

The two of them dig their hands in the box, and before I realize what's going on, they attack me. I tumble back on the floor and they fall over me, shrieking with laughter as they fill my pockets with glitter, dripping it everywhere on my clothes. I burst out laughing as well, and soon the muscles in my stomach begin to hurt.

"There, now you're one of us," Julie says after she calms down. "Glitter fan."

"Mission accomplished," Pippa adds. The three of

us are sprawled on the floor, Pippa to my right, her head on my shoulder, and Julie on my left, cocooned against me.

As we all regain our breath, a recognition hits me hard. This is right, the three of us together, almost like a family. Pippa looks up at me, and I know she feels it too.

"Hey," she says softly. "I mentioned it before, but I didn't officially invite you. We're celebrating Ava's birthday at my parents' house next Saturday. Would the two of you like to come? It'll be a lot of fun."

"Yes," Julie answers before I even open my mouth. "Dad, can we go?"

"Sure." For the first time in a long time, I feel whole.

Chapter Seventeen

Pippa

My opportunity to spoil Eric arises two days later. I've meant to do something nice for him ever since he went to the charity gala with me, but I haven't had time. Now that my dad is back home—on the mend, but more grumpy than ever—my routine is somewhat back to normal. After work, I shop for groceries and head home. I enter my apartment at six thirty, which is perfect. It gives me enough time to cook until Eric arrives. He said he'd stop by at seven thirty. Apparently, Julie's design class has a movie night at the school, so we can have a few hours for ourselves.

Julie told me Eric's favorite dish is risotto, and that's what I'm preparing. I turn on the music loudly and begin to cook. God, I missed this. I forgot how much I love cooking. It's almost like a meditation for me. The mix of aromas, the combination of herbs. I can't believe I stopped doing it after the divorce. I resolve not to do that again.

One hour later, everything's done. Now the only missing piece is Eric himself. Except the minutes tick by, and Eric doesn't come. Eventually, I call him.

"Hey there," I greet him.

"Shit. I was supposed to be at your place by now. Sorry I forgot to call, but I can't make it. Something came up at the last minute, and I called an urgent meeting with my team."

Eyeing the risotto, I eat a spoonful. It's delicious. Then I pout, brainstorming how to lure him out of his office.

"Are you pouting?" he asks.

I startle. "How do you know?"

"Just a hunch. Will you still be pouting if I buy you your favorite chocolate cake and stop by later?"

I laugh. "Are you bribing me?"

"Unapologetically."

"I'll consider changing my expression to a mini-pout."

"Good girl."

I put the spoon down and decide that desperate times call for desperate measures.

"I'm naked in the kitchen," I murmur, hoping he can't tell I'm lying through my teeth. "With a bottle of wine, and touching myself—"

"Hold on," he interrupts.

"*Hold on*?" I bellow, but I get no answer. I hear Eric talk to someone else in the background.

"Right, I'm back."

"Eric Callahan, you do not tell me to hold on when I'm about to have phone sex with you."

"I will if I have an important thing to do."

"Like what?" I bite the inside of my cheek,

brainstorming for some credible threats.

"Like postponing the meeting to come home and have actual sex with you."

I straighten up. "You did that?"

"You thought I'd stay at the office knowing you're touching yourself?"

"Well, you're the shark after all," I say reasonably.

"I'm also a man."

"You're weak for flesh, Eric." My grin is so wide now that my face muscles almost hurt.

"Nah. Only for you."

And just like that, I melt.

"Hurry," I tell him.

***

Exactly fifteen minutes later, my doorbell rings. I've changed into a red silk and organza kimono and am wearing black lace lingerie underneath it. Drawing in a deep breath, I open the door. The second Eric lays eyes on me, his gaze darkens, desire glinting in it. Feeling naughty, I undo the cord of my kimono, opening it so he can get a glimpse of my panties and bra. I'm rewarded with a deep groan.

"If I knew you were wearing this, I'd have come home in ten minutes," he says.

"I take it you like what you see."

"I do." He steps into the apartment and closes the door. "Can't wait to rip them off."

I rake him in as well, my senses beguiled by every single aspect of him. There is something very masculine about a man in a suit, and Eric wears it well. Everything about him screams power, determination—and mind-blowing sex.

He hooks an arm around my waist, pushing me against the wall. Swiping his tongue over my lips, he slips it in my mouth. Eric kisses me like a man possessed, and I love every wild second of it. He's delicious.

"How can I need you so much?" he asks after we pull apart. His breath is ragged. "You're all I could think about when I was at the office."

My breath becomes increasingly shallow as desire ravages my body, driving me to roll my hips against him. Eric lets out a groan from deep in his throat, one of his hands finding its way in to my hair, gripping the back of my head for a brief second before releasing me and descending to cup my cheek. Unexpectedly, he presses my legs apart with his knee, his fingers push aside the fabric of my thong, and he dips his thumb into my slit. My knees instantly weaken as a quiver runs through me. This man knows how to drive a woman crazy.

"Let's go in the bedroom right now, or I swear I'll take you here against this wall."

"Then do it," I challenge.

Something snaps inside him—I think it might be his control. He kisses me hot and hard again. I ache for him *everywhere*. My hands fumble with the buttons of his shirt, undoing them one by one, barely resisting the urge to rip them off. I run my hands over his muscle-laced arms as I push the shirt off him. Taking a step back, I greedily watch his ripped chest and abdomen. My clit begs for his attention, and my puckered nipples press against the fabric of the bra.

"You're sexy," he says with a groan, his eyes on my bra. I swell with pride. I spent a good amount of time at Nadine's shop picking out racy lingerie with Alice nagging that I'm wasting my time, that men never care much about the lingerie, only what's beneath it. Well, Eric is appreciatively growling at my bra. For all of five seconds, before he unclasps it and my breasts pop free. He kneads them in his hands, focusing on my almost painful nipples. "I'm going to make you feel so good, Pippa."

"Stop stalling, start proving." I ache for him to be inside me *right now.*

"You're an impatient little thing."

He doesn't spare my panties one glance before removing them. Okay, so Alice had a point.

I undo the fly of his pants, pushing them and his boxers past his ass. This man has a gorgeous ass. I dig my nails in to it briefly to show my appreciation. Eric chuckles, cupping my face. I turn my attention to his erection next, stroking him. I sink down the wall to my knees and take him in my mouth while continuing to move my hand up and down, applying pressure. He swallows hard, his Adam's apple dipping, while his hand moves to grip my hair. With satisfaction, I observe his control ebbing with every stroke of my hand. When I swipe my tongue over his tip, he mouths my name on a groan, shuddering. Eric pulls back, kicking his pants and boxers away, but not before whisking out a condom from his pocket. He pulls the condom over his erection, then pulls me to my feet.

"Spread your legs," he commands. I swallow hard before doing as he instructs. Dipping a finger inside me, he kisses me roughly, and I love the taste of him—all man. Grazing my earlobe with his teeth, he whispers, "I love feeling you so wet for me. And I'm going to reward you for that."

He adds a second finger, stretching me, teasing me before pressing his palm over my clit and moving his hand in rhythmic beats. I clench with need around his fingers, greedy for more. He lowers himself until his lips are level with my waist and traces a fine line with his tongue from my navel to my clit. I pinch my eyes shut, losing myself in the sensation.

When he rims the sensitive flesh of my core with his thumb and then with a lash of his tongue, my knees buckle dangerously.

"You're the one who challenged me to make love to you here," he teases.

"I—yeah," I mutter, and lick my lips. "Not my best idea. I'll fall."

"No, you won't." Gripping my ass with both hands, he adds, "I've got you, baby."

As his mouth works magic on me, I run my fingers through his hair, pulling him even closer.

"I need you inside me now," I beg. Eric obliges me almost instantly, rising to his feet and hoisting me against the wall. Almost without thinking, I hitch my legs around his waist, opening myself wider to him. He captures my mouth with his, driving inside me at the same time. He doesn't move for a few moments, just holds me. I lace my fingers together at the back of his neck, enjoying the nearness, the skin-on-skin contact. His heartbeat is almost as frantic as mine.

"Being inside you feels so good, Pippa." He gives me a chaste little kiss on my cheek. "Like home."

His words touch me in a way he can't possibly know. I rock my body in to him, seeking warmth and passion. Keeping his eyes on mine, he slides in and out of me, the angle of his hips perfect, touching me on the inside in places no one did, luring moan after moan out of me. My heartbeat quickens as something powerful stirs in my center. Tightening my legs around him, I dig my heels in his ass cheeks, needing to be even closer to him. I press my hips flush against his, seeking his mouth as I pulsate around him, desire coursing through me. I graze my fingernails over the expanse of his chest and shoulders as pleasure sears me. A thin sheet of sweat dots his upper lip, and I lean forward and kiss him. He tastes a little like salt, a lot like a man. I explode in a million pieces of pleasure when he widens inside me, clinging to him for dear life as I cry out my release. He does the same then leans his forehead against mine, his breath shallow.

"I missed you." He whispers the words, smiling against my lips.

"I missed you too," I confess.

We remain entwined like this for a while before he

puts me down.

"Do I smell risotto?" he asks, sniffing the air.

"Yep. I asked Julie what your favorite food is," I say proudly. "You didn't bring any chocolate cake, like you said you would."

"I brought myself." Eric shoots me a conceited look. "Not enough?"

"I'm still deciding. Let's eat."

When he lets go of me, my skin feels cold in the places he touched me before. I can't bear thinking how I will feel when he lets go of me for good.

Chapter Eighteen

Eric

The Bennett house has three levels and a bright red roof on top. The garden is full when we arrive. There must be at least fifty people here, and I spot at least six kids, some of Julie's age. Most of them stand at the edge of a makeshift soccer field, yelling and cheering for those playing. I recognize Alice, Summer, Sebastian, and Logan on the field. Another group is gathered around what I assume is the grill, judging by the smoke coming out.

Mr. Bennett is sitting under the shadow of an oak tree further away from the field, watching the game. I can't make out if he's happy or grumpy, but at least he's healthy.

"Are all these people your family?" Julie asks Pippa, looking around as though she can't believe her eyes as we near the soccer field.

"Sort of. Many are cousins, but some are friends—adopted Bennetts."

"What's that?" Julie asks, suddenly curious.

"Friends who are very close to us."

"Can Dad and I become adopted Bennetts?" Julie

asks hopefully. "Your family is awesome. Look, Dad, they're cheering."

Pippa raises her eyebrows at me, but I know exactly what Julie means.

"Family gatherings in the Callahan family are a different beast," I inform Pippa. "Mom's idea of an afternoon in the family resembles a high-class ball where everyone dresses elegantly, and catering of the most expensive kind is consumed while playing cards. It's highly boring for both Julie and me, and we try to skip those events as often as we can."

"Doesn't that upset your Mom?" Pippa inquires.

"No, I'm subtle when I serve her an excuse."

Pippa chuckles. "I bet she's pretending. Moms pick up on these kind of things, and subtlety is *not* your strong suit."

"That's not true." I rub my stomach while watching the smoke rising from the grill. "I'm starving."

"Hey, Pippa," a red-faced Summer calls, leaving the field. "Do you want to replace me? I'm so done."

Pippa doesn't hesitate. "Sure."

"I'm on Logan's team," Summer says. "Alice and Sebastian are kicking our ass. Here, take my sneakers." Sitting on the grass, she takes off her shoes and hands them to Pippa, who immediately puts them on.

"See you in a bit." Pippa winks at Julie and me before hopping onto the field. Summer lies sprawling on her back, barefoot.

"I can't even feel my legs," she tells Julie, as Mrs.

Bennett arrives with plates filled to the brim with meat and bread. At the sight, Summer pushes herself in a sitting position. She grabs one of the plates without any words and digs in. I can tell what Julie is thinking. At Casa Callahan, lying barefoot on the grass is akin to a deadly sin. It would earn her a scolding, not a plate of food. The chaos here is unbelievable, but I have to admit I love it. It has a *family* feel to it.

"Eric, Julie, I'm so glad you could make it," Mrs. Bennett greets, holding out the other plate she was carrying. "Here, I hope you're hungry."

"We are," I answer. Taking the plate, I immediately start gulping down food, and Julie follows my lead.

"Julie," Mrs. Bennett says, "I can introduce you to some of my nieces and nephews. I think you'd love them."

Julie nods enthusiastically, peering at me. "Can I go, Dad?"

"Sure," I reply. "But don't you want to eat some more before?"

"I'll eat later." She's positively glowing.

"Off you go."

She and Mrs. Bennett leave, joining the kids' group. I turn my attention to the soccer field next. Pippa is in her element among her family, though right now she's frowning in concentration. I'd like to say she kicks ass, but her team is losing. She wasn't kidding; Alice is a pro.

"Logan's going to be grumpy again if he loses,"

Mrs. Bennett comments. I hadn't noticed she joined me again. "You have a great daughter, Eric. Pippa told me a lot about her. You did a fine job raising this girl on your own."

"Thank you, ma'am," I say. Most of the time, I think I'm doing a decent job raising her, but hearing this from a woman who raised nine kids somehow legitimizes my efforts.

We fall into silence for a few minutes, but I can sense I'm about to get a variation of 'the talk' from her.

Sure enough, she eventually says, "You have a great influence on my daughter. She's the Pippa I remember again."

"What do you mean?"

Mrs. Bennett tightens her lips. "It takes little to make my daughter happy, and a lot to make her miserable. She was unhappy in her marriage. She didn't say anything for a long time, but I could tell. Now, she glows again. It has something to do with you."

"Ma'am, the world is a better place when Pippa smiles. If I'm contributing to that, I'm proud."

To my astonishment, Mrs. Bennett seems on the verge of laughter. "Pippa is right. You *are* a charmer."

"I do my best," I reply with a straight face.

The crowd around us erupts in cheers, signaling the end of the game. Pippa walks straight in to my arms.

"That was fun," she announces.

"You do know you lost, right?" I ask as I wrap my

arms around her waist and pull her to me.

She shrugs, pushing strands of her hair away from the damp skin on her face. "No one cares—besides Logan and Alice. I like playing. So… I saw you and Mom talking."

"That's right."

"How did it go?"

"She didn't scare me off, if that's what you're afraid of."

"Of course she didn't. That's my brothers' job. But don't worry. I'm here to protect you."

"You are?" I ask, tightening my arms around her.

"Yep. I am Pippa the Protector and Keeper of Secrets." She announces this with a completely straight face, and I want to kiss this woman senseless.

"You know, monikers aren't very valuable if you appoint them yourself."

"What would you call me?" she asks coyly.

"Hmm, let's see. Pippa the Cupcake Attacker."

"Shut up."

"No, wait, I have a better one. Pippa the Cookie Devourer."

"Hey," Blake calls from behind me. "Stop being so cute. You're surrounded by single people. Have some respect."

"Go find a girl, Blake," Pippa calls to him. "Or I'll put you next on the matchmaking list."

***

Pippa

The day goes by in a haze. We celebrate Ava's birthday with an immense cake and by showering her with gifts, and I divide my time between hovering around Dad and making sure Eric and Julie have a good time. Julie is in heaven. She hits it off right away with my cousins' daughters, and she doesn't pay Eric or me any attention. We spend most of the time outside, even though the weather isn't as warm as we hoped. Then again, San Francisco is never as warm as I wish, not even in mid-July.

When my siblings—except Christopher and Max, who aren't here yet— set out for another soccer game, it's clear Eric wants to join. I watch the game with Julie by my side, cheering, insulting Logan for playing dirty, and whistling. During the second part of the game, I realize Julie's disappeared. I look over at the kids' group, but she's not with them. My heart leaps in my throat. I ask my nieces about it, and they shrug, saying she went inside the house a while ago. Fear stabs at me as I enter the house. Where's my girl? Does she have her inhaler with her?

"Julie," I start calling. "Where are you?"

"In the kitchen," a muffled voice sounds, and my heart regains its normal rhythm. I hurry to the kitchen and find Julie looking out the window to the backyard with wide, fearful eyes.

"What's going on?" I ask her.

"I don't understand," Julie murmurs. "How can

Max be in two places at once?"

"Two p—? Oh, no," I groan, realizing what this is about. Opening the door to the backyard, I yell at no one in particular, "Christopher, Max, show your faces. Both of you." My prankster brothers. They said they'd join us later because they had some business downtown, but I didn't see them arrive. Within seconds, both of them walk to us, and I can't help grinning. They are both wearing dark burgundy polo shirts and jeans. The jeans aren't identical and neither are their haircuts, but for someone who doesn't know them, I can see how this can be confusing—and scary. Christopher also looks much more tired than Max. He has dark circles under his eyes, and it's not surprising; he's been traveling back and forth from Hong Kong lately.

"Julie, my brothers are—"

"Identical twins," Julie exclaims. "Max, you never told me you have an identical twin. That must be *so* cool. I can't believe I didn't realize it at the wedding."

"What were you thinking?" I admonish them.

"When you told us she was coming, we realized she's the only person here who doesn't know we're twins. We couldn't pass up the opportunity," Christopher says. Or it might be Max. Goddammit, I can't believe I have trouble telling them apart even now. I concentrate on their haircuts, trying to remember who had the longer hair. It was Max, okay. So my first instinct was right. He's the one talking. "For old time's sake, you know."

"You scared the living daylights out of her." I

work as much severity in my tone as I can. But one look at Julie reveals that all traces of fear are gone from her expression. She's giggling.

"You're adults," I tell my brothers.

"A fact we like to forget whenever we have a chance," Christopher says seriously. "Most of the time, we aim to achieve that as soon as we're out of the office."

"And especially when we're in the company of a fellow like-minded young lady," Max adds. Julie's expression lightens up at being dubbed 'young lady.' Typical of my brothers to charm everyone into forgiving them.

"Pity we don't have any nephews yet," Christopher says. "So many new possibilities for pranks."

Max opens his mouth, then closes it again as the sound of loud cheers reaches us from the front of the house.

"Looks like the game's over. Let's see who won," he says.

The four of us walk outside, and I turn to Julie, informing her, "Julie, I need to teach you basic survival skills in the Bennett family."

"Sounds exciting," she says.

"Whenever someone pranks you, you have to make them pay." I give my brothers the stink eye.

Julie frowns. "How?"

"You have the right to ask them to bring you whatever you want."

"Nah, don't teach her that," Max complains in a

low voice.

"You mean like ice cream and stuff?" Julie asks.

"Exactly. The key is to make sure whatever you want isn't easy to get. Make them jump through hoops, and be obnoxious," I elaborate.

Julie turns to the twins. "I can't decide yet. I'm thinking either cheesecake or ice cream from my favorite *gelateria* downtown."

"You're a pro at this," I say appreciatively.

Christopher sighs, telling Max, "Man, I just met her and I'm whipped already."

That's when I notice Eric watching us from afar. He stands at the far end of the makeshift soccer field, away from everyone else. I leave Julie with my cousins' girls again and then jog to my man, who's a little sweaty from the game and a lot sexy.

"Great game, Callahan. Word on the street has it your team won."

"We did." He pulls me in to a quick kiss and then goes inside the house. Mom has a number of T-shirts ready for people to change into after a game.

I wonder why my brothers haven't ambushed Eric or flexed some of those alpha muscles they're so proud of. They are being remarkably civil, and whenever they talk to Eric, they stick to business topics. By late afternoon, most of the guests are gone, except for the kids, who will stay here overnight. My mom has grown attached to the little ones. They belong to some cousins from my dad's side, who moved to San Francisco about four months ago. Mom has been inviting their children for sleepovers almost every weekend during school days, and now that they're on vacation, they're here during the week too.

"Mom is in dire need of grandchildren," Alice remarks. Right now, Eric and I sit outside at the table with her, Sebastian, Ava, Logan, and Nadine. "She keeps organizing sleepovers for all her nephews."

"Don't look at us," Nadine says at once, then points at Sebastian and Ava. "They're married already. They should have kids."

Sebastian gives Logan an uncharacteristically smug smile.

"Now, now," Logan says, patting Nadine's arm. "If we could set our wedding date—"

"Oh, my God," I blurt, realizing what Sebastian's smug smile was about. Looking from him to Logan, I ask, "You two are still trying to win that bet, aren't you?"

"Pippa," Logan and Sebastian warn me in unison, but it's too late. Nadine and Ava are already glancing at me curiously.

"What bet?" Nadine asks.

"Nothing," I say quickly.

"Pippa Bennett," Ava admonishes, "spill it."

My brothers are shooting daggers with their eyes at me.

"Well," I say, "they made a bet about ten years ago about which one of them will have the firstborn in our family."

Nadine elbows Logan. "So that's why you're in such a hurry to have the wedding?"

"We're going to be the first ones anyway," Sebastian says.

"We'll see about that," Logan counters. There's so much testosterone at the table it's nearly suffocating. Nadine and Ava look at their men, both incredulous *and* proud.

"There goes your Keeper of Secrets title," Eric whispers to me.

"There's something else I wanted to talk to you about," Sebastian says, his tone serious again. "The ranch renovations are going well, but Dad wants to keep a closer eye on the team. Thankfully, he understands he can't do it himself. It's a miracle that he's on board with it."

I smile to myself, certain that my little tough love speech at the hospital is the reason for that, but seeing how I just outed my brothers' bet with my big mouth, I'll keep the bragging to a minimum.

"We could oversee the construction project by rotation," Max suggests.

"Yeah," Christopher agrees. "I'll be flying back to Hong Kong in two weeks, but I can help until then."

"I was going to suggest we do it by rotation too," Logan says. "Sebastian and I worked out a schedule."

Logan takes out a folded paper from his pocket, which I suspect is the schedule. Blake, who is inspecting the paper from behind Logan's shoulder, whisks it from his hands, staring at it incredulously.

"Logan, if you spend so much time at the ranch, your fiancée might decide to dump your ass," Blake says, and adds with a wink to Nadine, "In case she does, there are plenty single Bennetts waiting to take your place."

Nadine immediately protests, and Logan is red in the face. It's almost hilarious watching how quickly Blake can rile up Logan. Sebastian, who has his arm around Ava's waist, merely cocks an eyebrow.

Daniel and Blake exchange glances, and the former steps up. "Yeah, you two have pretty women waiting for you back home. Why don't you leave the shifts to the single men in the family?"

"That's a great idea," Max jumps in, then turns to Sebastian and Logan. "Besides, you two shouldered a lot of the work at the ranch when we were kids. Time for us younger ones to pick up the slack."

No one speaks for a few seconds, and the air is thick with emotion.

"Thanks," Sebastian says eventually. "Logan and I will stop by on weekends anyway."

"Your family is interesting," Eric says as we leave the group a while later, walking toward the house to find Julie and leave.

"What do you mean?"

"I don't know. The way you go from annoying each other to working together like a team."

"Never a dull moment with the Bennetts. I couldn't imagine what being a single kid is like."

"Much duller." Eric's eyes cloud for some reason, and he shakes his head as if to clear his mind. "What were Max and Christopher doing with Julie earlier?"

"Initiating her in the arts of being a Bennett," I explain.

"She looked very happy."

"Yeah, I think they want to teach her some of their mischief skills. You might have a lot on your hands afterward," I warn him.

Eric flicks his hand. "I can handle mischief."

"Like you handled the glitter episode?" I ask as we step inside the house. I love my parents' home. It's warm and cozy, perpetually smelling of something delicious. Right now, I detect cinnamon and vanilla in the air.

"That was an ambush. Big difference." He hooks an arm around my waist, pulling my body against his. We're alone in the hallway, but with so many people on the property, it's very likely we'll be interrupted soon. Still, feeling the hammering of his heart against his chest makes all my girl parts tingle and yearn for him.

"You look happy too," I murmur.

"I am. I would've loved this as a kid. Family gatherings were always formal. I had to dress up like I was going to the opera every time."

I raise an eyebrow. "Did you wear a bow tie?"

"Of course. It was obligatory. Cufflinks too."

"Oh, my God, you must have been so cute. I mean, you're cute now too."

"I refuse to be described as cute." Eric steps back, folding his arms over his chest as if he's serious.

"Why?" I ask, baffled.

"It's not manly at all."

"How about if I add shark to it? Cute shark."

"How about Master of Pleasure? I can also work

with Master of Orgasms." The fact that he says this with a straight face makes me laugh.

"You're singing your own praises," I tease.

"Are you saying I don't deserve those names?"

"Mmm," I say coyly, shrugging.

"I'm warning you, that is a dare. I will make you regret teasing me." Eric accompanies his warning with a heated gaze, and even though my entire body flames up under his intense scrutiny, I hold my own, not breaking eye contact. Within seconds, the sexual tension between us is so thick you couldn't even cut it with a knife. You'd need a machete.

Or my mother.

She clears her throat loudly, and I snap my head in the direction of the sound. She and Julie are walking toward us like two women on a mission.

"Eric," Mom says, "would you let Julie spend the night here with the other girls?"

His expression grows tense within seconds. "She has—"

"Please, please, please, Dad," Julie says. "All the other girls are staying overnight, and they are awesome."

Her eyes are wide and pleading. Ah, she's bringing out the big guns.

"She'll be safe," I murmur to Eric.

"Whose side are you on?" he asks me. I wink at Julie, and Eric shakes his head. "Fine."

Julie smiles brightly, and Eric all but melts looking at her. "You are the best dad in the entire world."

"Mrs. Bennett, when should I pick Julie up

tomorrow?"

Mom waves her hand. "Give me a call in the afternoon. You and Pippa enjoy the time together."

I blush furiously as Eric bids her good-bye and takes Julie to one side, presumably to give her instructions to be on her best behavior. As if it's necessary. This girl is precious.

"Pippa, can I give you a piece of advice?" Mom asks me.

Uh-oh.

A truth that should be universally acknowledged is mothers are always right—whether they give you advice or a warning. It took me a while to accept this truth. I've never been rebellious, though I did have a wild streak here and there toward the end of high school. My rebellions were more of the 'Of course I'm going to wear this mini skirt, even if it's below zero outside' type, despite my mother's advice. I'd remember that when I got sick. In my mid-twenties, I progressively realized all of my mother's warnings turned into reality. At thirty, I'm almost afraid her words have prophetic qualities.

"Sure." I eye my surroundings, wondering if I can find an excuse to make a quick escape. Not likely. She cornered me in the hallway.

"If you find a good thing, don't let it go."

My heart squeezes, and I blink rapidly. "Mom—"

"I want you to be happy again." She pulls me in to a hug I return.

"I am happy," I whisper in her hair. "I have all of you."

"There are several kinds of happiness, Pippa."

I pull away from her as Julie and Eric approach us. He attempts to hug Julie good-bye, but she pushes him off, mumbling, "Dad, I'm too old for hugs in public."

"You're never too old for hugs," I tell her, but she shakes her head. Eric looks taken aback by her declaration, and I feel for him, so I squeeze his hand lightly. After *verbal* good-byes to Julie, he and I walk to the car together.

Once inside, he says, "We are about to have some alone time."

I sink lower in the seat, blushing. "Yeah. The evening got much more interesting."

"Let's not forget the night too," Eric says in a husky, delicious tone, which sends a jolt right through my center.

"What about the night?" I tease.

"So many possibilities," he whispers. "All of them involve you staying up and screaming my name."

"Eric." The word leaves my mouth almost on a moan.

"Stop saying my name like that, or I'll pull over somewhere dark and make love to you right here in this car."

"Then drive faster, Callahan," I challenge. "Can you do that for me?" The skin on my entire body tingles. I can't believe all it takes for me to ache for him is some sexy banter.

***

I will never know how we made it inside my apartment.

"Your couch is about to see some very X-rated action," Eric says, lowering me on it.

"I think it can take it," I assure him. "It's a naughty couch, like its owner."

"Oh, you're not just naughty." He brushes his thumb against my temple, kissing the tip of my nose. "You're feisty and sexy."

"Admit it," I say. "I'm perfect."

He pauses a beat before answering in a serious tone, "You are."

Levering himself over me, Eric brushes his mouth against mine, then gently nips with his teeth at my lower lip. His eyes sparkle with desire, and something deeper.

"I love having you in my arms, Pippa. You belong here."

I quiver under him with unspoken emotions. I needed so much to hear that. Eric's grip on my waist tightens, and he sighs against my neck. The muscles on his arms tense under my touch.

"What's wrong?"

"You make me want to give you more."

"More what?" I ask, confused.

"More of me. The trouble is, I loved and lost, and I don't know what's left of me."

This moment is so real and raw that it almost frightens me. As does the realization that he has my heart, I have his, and neither of us knows what to do about it. I take his hand, turning it palm up and planting a kiss in the center, watching him all the while.

"We'll find out together," I whisper. "You have so much to offer, Eric, and you have given me so much already."

There's uncertainty in his eyes, and I know that words alone won't change that. I resolve to show him, in every way I can. He smiles and nods, but his vulnerability is almost palpable, and all my instincts want to put him at ease. That's why I kiss the corner of his lips, adding, "I like what I'm seeing so far."

"You do, huh?"

"Yeah. A man who is loving and caring." I kiss down his chin, his faint stubble grazing my lips. "It doesn't hurt that you have a hot body too," I add as an afterthought, and his face instantly lights up with the Cheshire Cat grin I love so much.

"If I didn't know better, I'd say you're sweet talking me so you can use my body. You're taking advantage of me."

"Who knows," I tease. "Maybe I am. But I do really like you, though."

"I suppose that makes it all right." Eric laces his fingers with mine, pushing my arms against the couch. The corded muscles of his thighs press my legs together. He's trapping me beneath him, and he leans in to a deep kiss, his tongue exploring my mouth tenderly for long minutes, until I whimper with need and desire. He moves down my neck, nipping and biting me gently. I roll my hips in to him, beyond aroused, but Eric merely shakes his head, a smile playing on his lips.

Staring me straight in the eyes, he presses the head of his erection against my thigh. I fight to keep my composure, but my shallow breath gives me away. When he rubs himself slowly—oh, so slowly—against me, I nearly lose it.

"Oh, God." I lick my lips, writhing under him, the feel of his hot length against my skin almost too much. "I need you."

Eric takes off my shirt and jeans, nudging my knees open with his, and then he slides back, kissing my neck before descending to my breasts. My nipples pucker, begging for his attention, but he ignores them, sliding further down. The bastard. He stops at my navel, swiping his tongue over it. The gesture sends deliciously hot and cold shivers all over my skin. He moves to my thighs, completely ignoring my throbbing center.

"What are you doing?" I ask him.

"Discovering your sweet spots," he answers without hesitation.

"You missed the most important one," I joke, pointing to my clit.

"I'll take care of it later," he rasps, while planting his lips on my inner thigh. He nuzzles my skin with his mouth, tracing a line until he reaches the side of my knee. Raising my bent leg, he swipes his tongue over the sensitive skin at the back of it. Bliss and torment course through me at the same time. I'm going to break out of my skin if he doesn't take me soon.

"See?" he asks, satisfied. "Sweet spot."

"I'm so aroused that every inch of skin is a sweet spot," I murmur. "You'd better hurry up, mister, or I'll make love to your face or fingers. I don't mind either."

"You threatin' me?" he asks.

"Obviously."

"I guess I have to tease you some more." His scorching-hot mouth continues back up my thighs, resting above my folds.

"You'll pay for it. You'll—"

Pushing my panties to one side, he sucks my clit gently into his mouth, and I forget my words, enjoying every second of the sweet torture. Desperate for more, I shove my hand in his hair, tugging at it all the way to the roots. Unexpectedly, he pushes himself up on his elbows, taking my hand.

"What are you doing?" I ask. The look in his eyes is raw and primal, oozing masculinity in a way that turns my knees to mush. He pushes down my panties and does away with my bra. Next, he discards his own clothing and leads us to the side of the couch.

When we're in front of the armrest, he says, "Turn around."

"You're bossy," I challenge.

"That's right. Turn around. I want you from behind. I want to feel your sweet ass against me when I'm buried inside you."

Oh, God. My insides clench almost painfully, heat

pooling low in my body. I do as he says. When my back is to him, he nudges my thighs open with his knee, spreading me for him, and says, "Lean forward and don't look back."

Licking my lips, I obey, resting my hands on the arm of the couch. My ass is almost pressing against his crotch. He grips my ass cheeks with his hands, parting them slightly. The anticipation is nearly undoing me. When I feel him dip his tongue once between my cheeks, a jolt of heat sears me from my center all the way to my toes. My knees buckle violently, almost giving way.

"Eric," I hiss through gritted teeth, my breath coming out in heavy pants. He feathers his mouth over my spine, starting at the base and then tracing all the way to the back of my neck. He's only a breath away from me, teasing me.

"You're so sexy, Pippa," he says with a groan. "I like seeing you all flushed and ready for me."

He drags his tip up and down the seam of my sex, slapping my clit. Shards of need pierce me with every gentle slap. He'll be the death of me….

"We don't need a condom," I whisper. "I started taking birth control pills ten days ago."

Eric kisses the side of my neck, and every fiber of my body screams for him.

"Are you sure?" he asks.

"Yes. Unless you don't want to… I'm clean. I got tested a while ago," I say quickly.

"Of course I want to. I'm clean too, but this is a big step. I want you to be sure about it."

I melt, remembering this man didn't bring a condom on the boat because he didn't want to rush things.

"I am," I say. "Completely sure."

"You drive me crazy, Pippa." His words come out more like a groan.

My center pulses with anticipation when Eric takes my hips in a possessive grip, slamming into me. The sensation of him stretching me, filling me more with each stroke, causes pleasure to radiate through my very bones. The sound of his hips slapping against my ass is as much a turn-on as hearing him call my name in the throes of passion. His voice, hoarse and masculine, spurs something deep inside me.

Kissing my neck, he brings one hand to my clit, pressing his fingers against it.

"Right there. That's so good." I rasp the words, fervently looking for more. The pulse of my orgasm forms inside me already. Panting, I give in to the sensations he awakens inside me, until my inner muscles close in around him, and I cry out. Eric finds his release while I'm still quivering in his arms.

"You okay?" he asks.

"Mmm, better than okay." I push away a strand of hair that sticks to my sweaty forehead. "I'm trying to decide which name fits you better, Master of Pleasure or Master of Orgasms."

He kisses my earlobe, then grazes it between his teeth. "You know what I need to hear."

"Let's shower."

***

After the shower, we return to the living room and snuggle on the couch. I lean in to his touch like a kitten looking to be spoiled, then relax completely… until my phone beeps with an incoming e-mail from my lawyer.

"Sorry," I murmur to Eric. "I have to read this."

I toss my phone away after reading it. "Can't postpone this much longer. I'll have to face Terence in a mediation meeting."

Eric takes my hand, squeezing it gently. "You know my opinion about this. Don't run away. Fight him with his own weapons."

"Sounds more tempting with every passing day," I admit.

"If you need me, I'm here. I'll do whatever you need me to do, such as punching him again." The nonchalance in his tone makes me chuckle.

"Why would I need that?"

"It would make you feel better." Eric kisses my temple, pulling me in his arms again.

"I'll handle this," I assure him. "Let's forget about it."

"Okay, but if you need help or to talk about it, I'm here. I want you to know that."

"I appreciate it."

"I love your hair," he says, twirling a lock of blonde mane between his fingers. "Especially after you wash it."

I eye him suspiciously. "I didn't put any hair product in. It looks wild."

He shrugs. "It has its own personality, like you." Eric leans over me, dragging the back of his fingers down my cheeks. *Uh-oh.* I know that look in his eyes—desire. Normally, I'd jump at the opportunity to snatch some more sexy time with my man. But right now, I have a very important appointment... with my TV, which is why I insisted we come to the living room instead of the bedroom after our shower.

"What's wrong?" He pulls back, watching me with concern.

"My show is starting in three minutes," I say quietly.

"Your... Huh?"

"TV show." I wiggle out from under a stunned Eric, grabbing the remote and starting the TV. "It's on every Saturday." The intro music is already on.

Eric sits up, grumbling. "A crime show?"

"Yep," I reply proudly, as the main detective appears. He's a hottie.

"You read romance novels but watch crime shows?" Eric asks, mystified, as if the two things are mutually exclusive.

"Yep. I have multiple personalities. They all drool at the sight of him," I explain seriously, pointing at the hottie on the screen.

"Can't you record it?"

"No can do. The Internet will be full of spoilers if I wait."

"But if you record it, you can skip all the

commercial breaks," he insists.

"I love the commercial breaks. I get to fret and wonder what will happen next. Watching it live is part of the experience. It's like a soccer game. Much better live, right?"

He nods at this, and I congratulate myself on drawing this comparison.

"I can't believe I'm being cockblocked by a show." He smirks, and I almost expect him to whip out his phone or find some other way to work, but instead he grabs my feet, pulling them in his lap. His eyes are fixed on the TV.

"What are you doing?" I inquire.

"Watching with you. There's already been a crime in the first minute. Sounds like my kind of show."

"Do you want this to be our show?" I ask. My stomach somersaults, and I'm aware my excitement level is a tad ridiculous, but I can't help it.

"Okay," he answers. "Does this mean I get to spend time with you every Saturday night?"

Oh. I hadn't even thought about that. "Do you want to? I mean, you don't have to—"

Without warning, he pulls me toward him until my ass is almost in his lap, and he silences me, putting his forefinger to my lips. "I'd love to. I'd spend every night with you if I could."

Until I leave.

The unspoken words hang between us, but as much as they make my heart clench, I don't want them to shadow this moment. It's too precious.

So I nod. "It's a date." Then I realize he might

prefer to do something else Saturday nights, or at least today since Julie is with Mom. "If you want, we can go out afterward."

"I don't care what we do as long as I'm with you, Pippa. And I like staying in."

"Me too. I'm a homey kind of person," I confess.

"I've gathered that. Also, staying in will be much more fun. "

"In what way?"

"Plenty of ways. I'll show you." His voice becomes throatier with each word. "I promise they will all make you ache."

"I can't wait," I say, suddenly breathing hard.

Chapter Nineteen

Pippa

The next two weeks are something out of a dream. The only downside is that both Eric and I are working crazy hours, so we try to sneak in as many lunch dates and dinners as possible. We mostly live for the weekend, though, especially since Mom insists on Julie sleeping over at their house.

I arrive late and flustered in Sebastian's office on a Monday morning, smothering my hair and skirt and hoping I don't look like someone who's just had mind-blowing sex. When I step inside the office, I find Max there as well.

"'Lo, sis," Max greets me.

"Hi." I slump in the chair next to him, drawing my breath from so much running. Sebastian eyes me seriously. "How come Logan's not here?"

"He and Blake are at the bank," he says.

I perk up at this. "Those two are clicking, aren't they?"

Sebastian shrugs. "I'll have a talk with Blake soon. He does his job all right, but I can tell that something's bothering him."

"So, what's this about?" I ask.

"Christopher told us he's looking to replace himself in Hong Kong," Max says.

My heart does a somersault. I'm so giddy I could jump from my seat and hug my brother, but I try my best to be professional and asks, "Why?"

Max shrugs, rising from his chair, and starts pacing the office. "I think he wants to be back home."

"He'll return here as Chief Operations Officer," Sebastian says, which I expected because that was his old job. Max took the job of International Development after his return from London.

"This is great. So, when will he be back?" I ask.

"It'll take a while to find the right person to take over there," Max remarks. "Took me long enough to find a replacement for myself in London."

"At least we have you back." I grin.

"Don't set your matchmaking eyes on me, Pippa," Max says.

"I'm not," I lie. But it's just half a lie. I was thinking about how great it'd be to finally have everyone home again. Matchmaking him *might* have crossed my mind.

"Yes, you were," he says with an annoying certainty as he drops in the seat next to me again. "I can practically see the wheels turning in your head."

I pout, leaning back in my chair.

"You've been gone for too long, brother," Sebastian says. "If you want to lead a peaceful life, you can't win against Pippa."

"What he just said," I say with a nod.

"You don't get to make any plans for me, sister. Are we clear?" Max asks.

"I can neither confirm nor deny that," I say seriously.

Max gawks at me. "Who are you, the CIA? Speaking of, what's up with you and Callahan?"

"We're dating," I mumble, wondering where this is coming from. I'm used to Logan and Sebastian meddling in my affairs, not Max. "We like spending time with each other."

"You seemed... serious when you guys were at Mom and Dad's," Sebastian says.

"We are."

"But he'll go back to Boston at the end of summer."

I can hear the unspoken continuation. *Last time we talked, we all thought it was a good way for you to have fun.*

"Way to be tactless." Max shakes his head at Sebastian.

"I don't want you to get hurt again," my older brother says.

"I won't. Don't worry. I've got my big girl panties on," I reply with a heavy heart.

Sebastian eyes me in silence for a few seconds, then casually asks Max, "What's the valuation of his company? Can we buy him?"

I drag my hands across my face, shaking my head. "Sebastian, stop."

Neither of my brothers pays me any attention. Typical.

"Logan and I ran the numbers. His company is worth almost as much as Bennett Enterprises. There's no way," Max says.

For a few minutes, I'm too stunned to speak. I don't know what surprises me more. That they are talking so casually about buying an entire company to keep Eric here, or that Max is involved in this. It shouldn't surprise me, though. After all, Sebastian and Logan set up a company for Terence back in the day, so the asshole could name himself CEO even though he didn't have the brains or willpower to work to deserve that title. At the time, I thought his growing resentment for me was because I was earning more than he was, and he was feeling inferior in front of our friends. No, turns out he was an ass.

"Sebastian, Max," I say, in a voice as calm as I can muster, "I appreciate your concern for me, but I don't want you trying to solve my problems. Last time you did, it didn't go over so well. It's time I handled my own issues."

"We don't want you to get hurt again," Sebastian answers in a concerned voice.

I sigh. "Neither do I, brother. Neither do I."

Chapter Twenty

Pippa

I spend the rest of the week working late every night, whether I stay at the office or take work home with me. Today, I've decided to leave the office early and work from home.

It's six o'clock when my doorbell rings, startling me. I wonder who it is. I haven't ordered food.

When I open the door, my face instantly cracks into a smile. Eric. At the sight of him, my heart somersaults, filling me with energy. I've been running on caffeine and sugar for the past few hours, and they had started losing their effectiveness, but seeing him fills me with a jolt akin to having a caffeine pill.

I take his hand, pulling him inside and closing the door.

"What are you doing here so early?" I ask him.

By way of answering, he pulls me in to a kiss, plastering me against the wall and pressing his body against mine.

"I wanted to surprise you," he says after we pull apart. Eric walks straight to the couch and I climb in his lap, lacing my fingers at the back of his neck.

"Julie might like your mom more than she likes me. She's now sleeping there twice a week, in addition to the weekend."

"Mom loves Julie, and I believe she's trying to give us some couple time."

"Ah, makes sense."

"Anyway, since Julie is sleeping at my mom's house today, I thought you'd stay up late at the office."

"Well, I was in a meeting and thought, 'Do I really want to spend the entire evening talking to the insufferable dickheads in my office, or with my woman?' You won."

I pinch his abs, which is no small feat considering how ripped he is.

"Glad I rank above insufferable dickheads. I rank you above vegetables and flat shoes too."

Eric frowns. "That's a random combination of objects."

"No," I insist. "It makes perfect sense. I don't like to eat vegetables or wear flat shoes."

"Your mind will forever be a mystery to me." He cups my jaw, pulling me into a smooch. Afterward, he adds, "I'd hope to rank above cupcakes, at least."

"Only if you rank me above risotto." In a small voice, I add, "You wormed your way into my heart, Eric."

His smile falters as his eyes become more serious. "Back at you," he says, and the words fill me with warmth and joy.

"So now I have a hole inside that's mine?" I ask.

He smiles my favorite smile, his arms encircling my middle. "Yeah, you do."

"A big one or a small one?"

He drags his thumbs over my lips, and I bite it slightly. He groans as he says, "You're very focused on size, you know that?"

"Of course," I reply seriously. "Size does matter. Anything else is a myth. So... how big is that hole?"

"Come here." He cages me between his arms, leaning his forehead on mine. "You're becoming so important to me it scares me, Pippa."

"Let's be scared together," I whisper, shuddering with emotion. As I pull back a notch, the skin on my arms has turned to goose bumps. Eric must notice this because he smooths his hands up and down them.

"It's been a long time since I felt this way," he continues. One of his hands finds its way to my hair, fisting it and pulling me to him. "I don't know what to do about it. But I know you're mine."

"Yours," I whisper in agreement. Our lips meet halfway, as our hands roam hungrily over one another. I want more of him, right away. I flatten myself against him, seeking his warmth, and he wraps me in his arms tightly.

After we pull apart, we remain silent for a few minutes, listening to each other's breaths. I sit up, squirming in his lap.

"You had to do that, didn't you?" he asks, a smile playing on his lips.

I shrug, as if it's purely coincidental. "It's the most

comfortable spot. And someone's happy I'm here," I add, feeling his erection.

"Always." With a swing of his arms, he pushes me sideways, laying me on my back and climbing over me. "I had a crazy thought today."

"Tell me," I beckon.

Eric's eyes turn serious as he twirls a strand of my hair between his fingers. "Would you move to Boston with me?"

Wham. The impact of his words knocks the wind out of my lungs for a few seconds. I remain speechless, simply because I can't wrap my mind around the idea. I try to visualize how my life there could be. With some adjustments, I could continue working for Bennett Enterprises, and I would be with him and Julie, but I break a sweat at the thought of not having my family around me.

"I could never live so far away from my family," I answer honestly. Uttering every word feels like I'm stabbing him and myself at the same time, but it's the truth, and he deserves it.

He gives me a sad smile, looking away. "I feared you might say that. I wanted to ask anyway. Hearing you confirm that hurts more than I thought it would."

"Eric...," I whisper.

"I don't want to let go," he says. "I won't know how to do it."

I run my hand at the side of his face, and he leans in to my caress with a vulnerability that completely disarms me and beckons me to peel back my own layers.

"I don't know how either."

"Let's not think about it anymore then, and just enjoy each other," Eric whispers, nuzzling my neck with his lips.

"Okay."

***

When I wake up the next morning, I find Eric at the foot of the bed, with an amused expression. I love having him sleep over.

"Hey, stranger," I greet him, rubbing my eyes. "How long have you been standing there?"

"A while," he informs me, a smile playing on his lips. "I like watching you sleep."

"Why?"

"Because you're peaceful, and sweet, and *very* kissable."

I huddle my blanket to my chest, feeling oddly displaced. My flirting talents don't spring to life before I've had my first coffee, so I just smile.

Oblivious to my predicament, Eric continues, "Also, you have a lovely snore."

This instantly jolts me out of my morning haze. "I definitely don't snore," I reply indignantly.

"Thought you'd say that." With a smirk, he pulls his phone out of his pocket. "But I have proof."

He presses a few buttons on his phone, and a weird wheezing sound comes from it. Then it hits me.

"That's me? You recorded me sleeping?"

"Yep, couldn't resist it."

I cross my arms over my chest. "That's not snoring, it's purring."

"Aha," Eric says, furrowing his brow in mock concentration as he listens to the recording again. "Loud purring."

"Turn that off."

He does as I say, remarking, "You're grumpy today."

"Weird mood this morning," I inform him, yawning.

"Also, it's six thirty."

I nearly choke in shock. "Why would you wake me up so early?"

"So I could spend a few minutes with you before I have to leave. Be right back." He rises from the bed, heading out of the bedroom, and returns a few minutes later holding a plate and a cup.

"Coffee and cookies," I exclaim.

"Yep, freshly bought for you. Feeding your sugar and caffeine addiction."

"Very smart of you. I'm no fun to be around if I haven't had either of them for the day."

"You don't say." He shoves the plate in my lap, placing the cup on the bedside table. Immediately, I dig in to the cookies.

"Oh, my God, you're the perfect man." I close my eyes, savoring the sweet flavor. Pushing myself straight up in the bed, I grab the coffee cup from the bedside table and sip. "Wait, is there a reason you bought this?"

"Are you implying I need a reason to spoil you?" he asks. I shrug, and he continues, "Okay, full disclosure. I do have an agenda that involves making you less grumpy. I figured you might wake up a little... off."

Yeah, from our conversation last night.

The fact that he had the foresight to do this warms my heart. I resolve to find a way to pay him back.

"You're a smart man." Munching on another cookie, I add, "I love that you know what will make me less grumpy."

"What else do you love?" He cocks his brows suggestively.

"That you make love to me against the wall."

Eric leans forward a tad, tugging at his lower lip with his teeth. "We're surrounded by walls."

"Are you talking dirty to me?"

"Yes, and I'm not even trying to be smooth about it."

A tingling sensation of arousal singes my body. "Go on, I like it."

"Pick a wall," he says in a low, rumbling voice.

My cheeks heat, and as I squirm in the bed, my body responds to him even before my mind is awake. The realization is downright scary.

Peering around the room, I point to the one facing the south.

"That one looks sexy enough," I suggest.

Eric rises from the bed, offering me his hand. I

take it without hesitation and jump out of bed, following him.

Pressing me against the wall, he drags his knuckles down the side of my cheek, finally cupping my jaw. I instinctively arch against him.

"You're so responsive to my touch," he says. "I was thinking of all the things I want to do to you while watching you sleep."

He pins me against the wall, kissing me thoroughly. His tongue does delicious things to my mouth, while his hands find their way under my baby doll nightgown, traveling up, grasping my breasts underneath the fabric.

"I changed my mind," I tell him. "Let's go to the kitchen."

"Huh?"

"That's a room we haven't made love in already," I say out loud. What I don't say is that I want to feel his presence everywhere long after he's gone. Also, I have some cream in the fridge, and I thought of a brilliant use for it.

I shimmy to the kitchen with Eric on my heels. Once inside, I take out the can of whipped cream, presenting it to him as if it's a prized possession.

"You woke up naughty today."

Licking my lips, I nod. "Blame it on the cookies. They had extra chocolate."

Hooking an arm around my waist, he pulls me close to him. "How about attributing it to my charms?"

"You're so full of yourself," I tease.

"And you can't wait to be full of me," he whispers in my ear. I blush violently at his wicked words, which is exactly what he intended, of course. Eric hoists me up on the table in the center of the kitchen, taking off my nightie and pushing me on my back. Need surges through me as he puts whipped cream in one thin line from my navel up to my chest. Then he smears it with his finger in circles around one nipple. He does so with an exquisite slowness that drives me crazy. Watching it unravel before my eyes turns me on to no end. By the time he proceeds to the other nipple, I'm so turned on I feel I'll break out of my skin. I need him *now*, but I know he's not done teasing me. I should have known this would come back to bite me in the ass. Pulling back a notch, Eric smiles at me, giving my clit a gentle smack. I shudder, gasping. Then he places his mouth on the same place and nips at my tender spot.

"No more whipped cream?" I ask.

"Not here. I want to taste *you*."

He slides his tongue inside me, mimicking the act of making love, and I nearly come undone. Suddenly, I become desperate for skin-on-skin contact. I pull myself back, pleased when Eric takes my cue, straightening up and unbuttoning his shirt. I unzip his jeans and pull them down together with his boxers. He cups my ass in his hands, pulling me close to him while I lean back, propping myself on my elbows. My breath catches when he enters me, slow and deep.

"You're a wonderful woman, Pippa Bennett," he

says, right before making passionate love to me.

Chapter Twenty-One

Pippa

I'm the first to arrive in my office. Despite Eric's lovemaking and the coffee he brought me, I'm bone tired. Waking up before 8 a.m. tends to do that to me. Opening my computer, I intend to dive in working through my e-mails, but end up researching Boston.

Eric's question plays in my mind repeatedly. Could I give this a shot? Boston is beautiful, of course. The truth is, even if the city were hideous, it wouldn't matter; I'd love it simply because Eric and Julie would be there. The problem is that it's a six-hour flight away from my family. I love being able to talk to my brothers at any time of the day, or drop in on one of my sisters whenever they need me. I can't lose that. The one time I lived a few hours away from my family was during college, and I was miserable. I can't do it again. With a heavy heart, I close all websites I had open about Boston. I have my answer, it seems. I can't even consider moving away without almost having a panic attack.

On the strength of that decision, I send another e-mail—this time to my lawyer, explaining to him what our next steps should be. It's high time I took Eric's advice. Terence won't know what hit him.

As I lean back in my chair, feeling proud of myself, my phone beeps with an incoming message from Blake.

Blake: Did you have breakfast?

Pippa: Yes, but I won't say no to some goodies. I'm in my office. You want to stop by?

Blake: Sure. I'll buy breakfast for me. Two muffins for you?

I smile as I type back.

Pippa: You know me well, brother.

Blake arrives twenty minutes later, looking as if he hasn't slept all night.

"Have you been partying all weekend?" I inquire as he places the muffins in front of me and drops in the chair on the other side of my desk. "You look dreadful."

"Good morning to you too, sister," he answers. "If you keep throwing around insults, I'll keep your muffins for myself."

I shrug, but immediately pull the muffins closer to me and out of his reach. "I'm just saying. The post-party look isn't the best office look to build credibility."

"Who says I was partying?" Blake shakes his head and then takes a bite from the sandwich he brought for himself. "How come when Logan rides my ass, I want to punch him, yet when you do it, I think you're adorable?"

I smile coyly. "Because I'm all-around adorable."

He sighs. "I have no balls whatsoever when I'm around my sisters."

"Right, I don't ever want to hear you talk about your balls in my presence." We fall into a companionable silence as we eat, and I use the time to inspect my brother. He has dark circles under his eyes and is pale, but this is not his usual after-party look, which makes me think he might indeed not have been partying. Maybe he simply has a lot on his mind, and he couldn't sleep.

"What's wrong?" I ask.

"Me being at Bennett Enterprises... It's not working out."

"Oh." I can't help but feel a tad disappointed, but I don't want to let him see that. Instead, I want to make him see that it is working out, or at least get to the bottom of why he thinks it's not. "But Sebastian says you've been doing great. Logan too. I was afraid you'd be butting heads more often, but you make a good team."

Blake runs a hand through his hair, looking frustrated, and it worries me. I've never seen him so unsettled.

"We do. The problem is that, around here, I'll always be the younger, player brother. Or at least for a long time. I mean, it's my fault. I expected I could waltz in and start with a clean slate, and everyone would treat me the way they treat Sebastian or Logan."

"I know it's a cliché, but Rome wasn't built in a

day, brother. Neither are reputations. It'll take time to—"

"Yeah, yeah. But I'm already tired of defending myself all the time. Every time I meet a new partner or whoever, they start with a joke about me. When I was with Logan at the bank, we wasted the first hour talking about a party I was at a *year* ago."

"So, what's the plan?"

"I want to start my own business," he announces.

"Wow. I'm impressed."

"I helped a few friends set up bars across the country."

"Yeah."

This was a running joke in our family, that he 'consulted' them because he had a lot of experience partying, but my brother's smart.

"I want to open my own bar, and who knows. If it does well, maybe more of them."

I lean back in my chair, nodding at him. "Sounds exciting. Do you need any money?"

"No, I've saved a good chunk from the shares revenue I received over the years."

"Now I'm *very* impressed. I thought you blew through all of it."

"Your confidence in me is astounding," Blake says, but he's grinning, and I'm relieved to see my brother morphing back to his usual self.

"Have you told Sebastian and Logan?" I ask.

"No, I wanted to tell you first."

"Why?"

"Because I wanted your opinion. Sebastian always

has his poker face on, and I can't tell what he's thinking. Logan will be disappointed, but he usually is where I'm concerned. The point is, I don't want any of you to feel I don't appreciate everything you've done for our family, because I am. I truly am. But I want to branch out on my own, prove myself."

"Logan and Sebastian won't be disappointed. They'll be proud. I am proud."

In the vision Sebastian initially had when he founded the company, he'd hoped all of us would find their place in it. When Alice announced she wanted to open a restaurant and Summer became a professional painter, Sebastian, Logan, and I were proud of them, even if it was bittersweet. This will be exciting, just like it is every time a Bennett sibling starts a new venture. It's an opportunity for all of us to rally together, offering our help. Assisting Blake in setting this up will be fun.

"Okay," he says, "I'll talk to them later today." Rising from his chair, my brother rounds the corner of my desk and bends down to kiss my cheek. "I don't know what I'd do without you."

"Now, go break your news to our brothers."

"I will. Can't believe I'll finally have a job where my CPO title will be official."

"What's CPO?"

Blake wiggles his eyebrows. "Chief Party Officer."

Chapter Twenty-Two

Eric

"What do you mean you want to stay there for an entire week?" I ask, looking at my daughter in disbelief. It's eight o'clock in the morning, and Julie blindsided me with her request.

"Well, the girls' parents are going on a vacation, so the girls are staying with Mrs. Bennett. They invited me to stay with them. It'll be like going to camp. And summer school ended, so I'll be bored anyway."

"You've never wanted to go to camp," I say.

"But I want to stay with Mrs. Bennett and the girls," Julie pleads.

"Why do you like sleeping there so much?"

Julie shrugs. "Mrs. Bennett is cool. She makes us Pop-Tarts and even plays Twister with us."

"But isn't she *old* by your standards?"

"Dad, there are cool old people and uncool ones," Julie says in her 'You know nothing, Dad' tone. "You're going to be an uncool old person."

I nearly choke on my coffee. "What? Why would you say that?"

"Because I've spied on you sometimes when you

speak on the phone with people at your office, and you're grumpy all the time. You only smile when you're with me or Pippa."

Wow, kids certainly don't hold back punches. Scratching my jaw, I try to find the best words to tell her that she shouldn't get used to Mrs. Bennett and the squad. After all, we'll be leaving here in two weeks. But as Julie watches me with wide, pleading eyes, I can't bring myself to break her heart, so I say, "Okay, you can go."

Just thinking about her being gone for a week makes me sick. I have to get used to this. As she grows up, she'll prefer to spend more time with her friends rather than with me. Still, a difficult pill to swallow.

"Yay! I have to be at Mrs. Bennett's on Saturday. So I can call my friends and tell them we'll be staying together?"

"Yeah. You do that," I say.

Julie practically jumps up and down as she darts to her room, pressing the phone to her ear. She's growing up way too soon.

***

Pippa

On Friday night, I'm at Eric's place. Alice should arrive in about an hour, so we can start the girls' night out we planned. Ava, Nadine, my sisters, and I collectively decided we need to let off some steam tonight. It's been months since we've done it. Julie is leaving for my mothers' tomorrow for a week, and Eric insisted I sleep here for the entire period, starting with tonight. He also insisted that I should bring enough clothes, so now his bedroom is full with dresses, shoes, and makeup items.

Preparing for the night can wait, though. Eric can't. Julie's out with Ms. Blackwell, so it's the two of us alone for a little while. I'd better take advantage of it. I find him in the living room, barking orders on the phone while typing on his laptop. He and Julie will have the evening to themselves, and they'll spend it watching movies. He's having the blues because she's leaving tomorrow, and he couldn't be more adorable. Well, he's adorable to me. I'm sure the person on the receiving end of his orders would disagree.

"Stop looking for excuses and start finding solutions," Eric bellows into the phone.

Right, time for an intervention. I wait until he finishes the conversation then ambush him.

"You said you're being nicer to your team."

"I am until they screw up."

"You work too much." I push his laptop away, climbing in his lap. I undo the belt of my kimono, giving him a view of my naked skin, hoping that'll take his mind off whatever troubles he's having. Judging by his sharp intake of air, I succeed. He pushes the fabric off to the sides, completely baring my breasts. He looks at them with a delicious hunger, riling me up to no end.

Instead of touching me, though, he drops his

hands to his sides. All right, two can play at this teasing game.

"You carry a sketch pad in your bag," Eric remarks.

I shrug. "You never know when inspiration strikes. Let's make a deal for this week. If one of us thinks the other is overworking to death, we step in. You scratch my back, and I scratch yours. What do you say?"

"Deal." He pushes my kimono off my shoulders and drums his finger on the bare skin below my neck. His brow is furrowed as if he's considering something.

"What?" I squirm in his lap, trying to get a feel for the situation. Oh, yeah, there's definitely a *hard situation*. This man's libido is working in overdrive, and I love it.

"So, do we have to scratch the back, or can it be something else?" He kisses my jaw, then my neck and descends the valley of my breasts. I lean back, giving him better access.

"'Cause I have a much better suggestion." He whispers the words seductively against my skin while he feathers his fingers over my nipples, turning them to hard nubs.

"Like what?" I meant to say the word as seductively as he did, but my voice is an uneven mess.

"This." His thumb circles my sweet spot, applying pressure to it.

My hips instantly buck up as I cry out. "I… *Ah.*

This is…."

"You can't form full sentences, Ms. Bennett. Now, why would that be?"

His thumb continues to torture my bundle of nerves, and despite wanting to give this bastard a snappy reply, the only word making it past my lips is "Fuck."

"Orgasms relieve stress, you know." Eric's eyes are hooded with desire, and I shudder when he pulls me to him, fisting my hair.

"Prove it," I whisper. And he does.

***

"Thank God, it's Friday," I exclaim an hour later, dropping on Eric's bed while munching on a slice of pizza.

"You should eat healthier," Alice reprimands.

"Oh, stop being such a buzzkill. I intend to keep my unhealthy habits for as long as I can get away with it."

"At least you're showing up at the gym regularly," Alice says appreciatively.

"Pick your shoes, so we can start our girls' night," I instruct. I've already decided on a dark blue sequin dress and white pumps. My sister is currently trying to decide whether she should go with black or golden strap sandals. Since the short dress she's going to wear is also black, I'm in favor of the gold ones.

Eric enters the room, staring at the multiple pairs of shoes lined up in disbelief.

"What's with the shoe parade?" he asks, and Alice shoots daggers at him with her eyes.

"Eric," I warn. "If you know what's good for you, you won't say anything else."

"Yeah," Alice adds. "Don't get between a woman and her shoes."

Eric holds up his hands in defense, saying, "I'm open to learning. I won't comment anymore."

Alice whips her head in his direction, saying, "You're a keeper."

"Right," Eric says. "I'll leave you two to change."

An hour later, Alice and I are ready, and we look sexy as hell, if I may say so.

"We're ready," I call out to let Eric know he can come into the bedroom if he needs to. Predictably, he steps in not two seconds later.

His eyes rake over my body, resting on my curves much longer than polite since we're not alone, and for some reason, he sets his jaw. All right, I was expecting a compliment. I cock an eyebrow at him.

Alice catches the wordless exchange and eerily says, "I'll wait for you in the living room."

"What's wrong?" I ask.

"Let me get this straight. Is a 'girls' night out' code for picking up guys?"

I chuckle. So that's what this is about. "No."

"You shouldn't look this irresistible unless you go out with me."

"You think I'm irresistible?" I bat my eyelashes at him, pushing my left hip out as if I'm posing for a photo.

In a fraction of a second, Eric closes the distance

to me, hooking an arm around my waist from behind.

"You look gorgeous, Pippa." He trails his finger over my bare shoulder, drawing the movement out with exquisite slowness. "Beautiful." He stops touching, and instead kisses me there. I'm on fire instantly. "But these shoes... They shouldn't be allowed out in public."

"Where should they be allowed?" I ask in a breathy voice.

Swiping my hair to one side, he kisses my neck and whispers, "In bed with me." His tone is low and suggestive, sending shivers down my back.

Eric turns me around, pins me against the door, and kisses me passionately. The last coherent thought before I'm ravaged by sensations is *Good thing I'm not wearing any lipstick*. He is not holding back. His mouth is hot and hard on mine, exploring me like a man possessed. His lips are rough, demanding, and I love it. With one hand, he pins my wrists above my head, gripping my waist tightly with the other.

"Fuck," he says on a groan. "I want you."

"Back at you," I whisper, savoring his taste on my lips. "But I have to go."

Eric lets go of me, stepping back and glancing at me up and down, then says, "I'll drive the two of you to the bar."

"Okay," I reply, surprised by the sudden offer. "Julie—"

"Ms. Blackwell will stay with her until I return."

"Right. Let's go." Now I'm not just surprised, but

downright suspicious.

"Well, that's very gentlemanly of you," Alice remarks when I inform her Eric will drive us. "Thank you."

I have a suspicion his offer to drive us has nothing to do with being a gentleman. He shrugs, pointing at the door, as if saying, 'After you.' Alice and I say good-bye to Julie, who looks at us longingly, as if jealous that she can't join us.

"Have fun with Ms. Blackwell until your dad returns," I tell her.

"I miss Ms. Smith. Ms. Blackwell is no fun," Julie says with a dramatic sigh. I remember Eric telling me Ms. Smith is her other nanny in Boston. Next to me, Eric chuckles, but his smile fades when Julie says, "I can't wait to stay with your mom, Pippa."

Ah, if Eric feels blue because she wants to spend a week at my mom's, he'll be depressed when she's a teenager. Now I'm depressed because I won't be around them to experience it. Way to start my night out.

The bar is located in a posh area downtown. Predictably, the traffic is a buzzkill. Eric throws me hot looks every few minutes, and I do a poor job of ignoring him. Every time I feel his eyes on me, my skin heats up. If we continue like this, I won't even get out of the car. After a million minutes, we arrive in front of the bar. Ah, a night infused with estrogen and girl talk. This is exactly what I need. The evening air has a pleasant smell—a mix of jasmine and cherry.

Eric rounds the corner of the car, and when he's

right in front of me, he surprises me by hooking an arm around my waist and pulling me in to a kiss. He swipes his tongue over mine first, then slides it in my mouth, kissing me ferociously. I respond in kind.

"What was that about?" I ask after we pull apart.

"Now every guy in this bar knows not to try anything because you're mine." He says this with a smug smile, as if it's the most foolproof plan in the world. This has too much potential for fun for me not to poke holes in it.

"You think every man inside was watching us?" I ask.

"Trust me, they'll know."

"What if we change bars? We might barhop tonight. Tequila here, cocktails across the road."

His arm tightens around me possessively. "Are you serious?"

"If I say yes, will you take me in every bar and kiss me like that again? 'Cause then it's yes all the way."

"Don't tempt me." He strikes his thumb over my lower lip, his eyes zeroing in on my mouth.

"Okay," I whisper.

"Have fun with the girls."

"I will," I promise. I step on the sidewalk, waving to him as he leaves. I turn to Alice, who waits for me by the entrance, whistling loudly.

"That was one hell of a kiss. I could sense the alpha vibes all the way over here," she comments.

"Yep. My knees are still feeling the effects of so much testosterone. That was *hot*."

"No disagreement here. Let's go inside. The girls

are already here."

The bar is buzzing with voices—laughter, giggles, arguments, everything. The lights are dim, bathing the entire room in an intimate atmosphere. Intimate and edgy, as if sinful things are about to happen here. Well, not for me; I'm here to have fun with my girls. But once I return to Eric's house, we'll get sinful all the way. With his kiss still lingering on my lips, I stalk toward the girls, energy strumming through my body. Ava, Nadine, Summer, and Caroline, who is a good friend of mine, are sitting at a round table, looking like they're up to no good. The second Alice and I join them the atmosphere becomes downright infectious.

"Okay," Caroline says, "I say we order a round of tequila, and then each of us starts sharing her news."

"I won't drink tonight," Ava says sheepishly.

"Why ever the hell not?" I ask.

Blushing, she glances quickly at Nadine before saying, "I think I'm pregnant."

The rest of us simultaneously erupt in a parade of "congrats" and "greats," and we take turns hugging her.

"Don't say anything to Sebastian, though," Ava says after everyone's quieted down. "I want to wait until I can be sure."

"Wow," Alice remarks, "so Logan lost his bet."

"He'll live," Nadine says.

"You warmed up to Seamus, in case it's a boy?" I ask, rubbing my palms excitedly.

"Over my dead body," Ava says.

"Aww, come on. It's cute," I reply, which doesn't earn me any points with Ava. The name seemed ridiculous when Sebastian first came up with it, but now I'm kind of fond of it.

To make up to my sister-in-law, I offer, "I am going to be your wingwoman tonight, and I won't drink any alcohol either."

Nadine purses her lips. "Now you're making me feel guilty for not offering first."

"How about we're all alcohol-free?" Alice suggests, and we all nod in agreement.

Once we're armed with an assortment of mocktails and teas, we clink glasses, and Caroline asks, "So, what will it take to get the three of you to dance on the bar tonight?"

Alice, Summer, and I groan in unison.

"I know we put on quite a show at the bachelorette party, but I'm not up to a repeat of the experience," I announce.

"Besides, we don't have the balls to do it without any alcohol," Alice says.

"I do," Summer counters unexpectedly. "But not if I'm the only one."

Alice and I stare at her.

"Who are you, and what have you done with our sister?" I ask.

Summer merely shrugs, glancing from her mocktail with an innocent look.

"You girls were epic," Ava says.

"I still watch the video from time to time," Nadine admits.

258

"I can't believe you filmed it," Alice states.

"Are you kidding me? That night went down in history as TNTBGWW."

"What?" my sisters and I ask in unison.

"The Night the Bennett Girls Went Wild," Nadine says, clearly on the verge of bursting into laughter.

So yeah, my sisters and I might have gotten a *bit* carried away at Ava's bachelorette party, and we somehow ended up dancing on the bar. And Nadine filmed us. We did a dubious impression of the French cancan. We made total asses of ourselves, but it was fun.

"What do you think the guys did at the bachelor party?" I ask, genuinely curious. "I tried to get it out of Blake, but the bastard won't say anything."

"They went to Vegas," Ava says. "I'm not sure we want to know."

"Oh, I already know," Summer says. "But I'm not saying anything."

We all turn to her.

"Why do you always keep the boys' secrets?" I inquire.

"Cause otherwise they won't tell me all of them," Summer replies smugly, shooting me a significant look. Okay, so yeah, my Keeper of Secrets title isn't exactly warranted. I'm much better at spilling secrets. But Summer, my baby sister, has all the boys wrapped around her little finger. Once upon a time, Alice was the boys' girl. She was a tomboy through and through, especially in her teenage years. I suspect this also has to do with the fact she was crushing on Sebastian's friend and was using her tomboy status to hang out with them. "My lips are sealed."

"Fine," Alice says with a faux I-give-up air. If there's one thing Alice doesn't do, it's giving up. She will wriggle the details out of Summer eventually, one way or the other.

"Can I bribe you with a dress, Summer? Custom-made for you?" Nadine asks, batting her eyelashes at my sister. Summer has a weakness for beautiful dresses, and Nadine's designs are nothing short of superb.

For a split second, Summer hesitates, but then she firmly shakes her head. "Nope. Besides, you have enough work as it is."

"That's true," Nadine replies, massaging her neck. "Logan and I will go on a vacation next month. Can't wait. An entire week of nothing but good food and excellent sex."

I hold up my hand, shaking my head. "Stop. I don't want to hear about my brother's skills in bed. I will never be able to unhear that kind of conversation."

"I think you've been around Julie too much," Nadine says. "You're used to censored talk. You need some more dirty talk."

"Yeah," Ava agrees. "Come over to the dark side."

Alice is the only one who doesn't join the conversation. At first, I think it's because she's on my side, but then I see her smile.

"Oh, Pippa's been getting plenty of dirty action," Alice says. "Why don't you share some dirty details, big sister?"

"Wonderful idea," Nadine adds.

Oh, no. There's no way I can get out of this.

"What do you want to know?" I ask.

"Everything," Ava says, at the same time Alice asks, "Do you love him?"

Ava elbows Alice while Nadine drums her fingers on the table, slicing a threatening glance at my sister.

"You had to jump right to that, didn't you?" Nadine asks. "That wasn't the plan."

A knot forms in my throat. "You had a plan?"

"Well," Alice begins. "We were supposed to first make you tell us what you like in bed, then in general about him. The last step was to make you admit that you love him."

I decide to put the girls out of their misery. "I do love him, but that doesn't change things. He has his life in Boston, and I respect that."

"So, you're giving up?" Alice says.

"No, Alice. I'm doing what I can so I won't be too heartbroken in a few weeks."

"Are you okay?" Summer asks. For a split second, I toy with the idea of brushing her worry off as I did with my brothers, and say I have my big girl panties on. But truthfully, I'm not okay. And maybe it's time I took Eric's advice and stop with the bravado around my family.

"I'm not," I answer. "He's sweet and attentive, and I love every second I'm spending with him and his daughter. And I'm terrified that they'll be going back to Boston." Voicing this out loud has the unexpected effect of making the knot in my throat feel less tight.

The girls are silent for a few seconds, and then Summer says, "Don't worry. We'll take care of you."

"Yeah," Alice says. "We have your back, sis."

Caroline claps her hands and, in a stroke of genius, says, "Time for a subject change."

"Hear, hear," I agree. "Shoes?"

"Oooh, yes," Alice says. "I bought the best pair the other day."

We spend the rest of the night talking about everything under the sun, and I manage to relax. Come September, I will be heartbroken. I know that. But knowing I can rely on my friends and family makes this slightly easier. Just slightly.

Chapter Twenty-Three

Pippa

The next morning, mayhem reigns in the Callahan household. Julie wakes up late and goes into a frenzy as she starts packing. Eric is in a frenzy too, panicking more about Julie's departure with every passing second. He's adorable.

I spend some time talking to Ava on the phone, consoling her after she texts me with the sad news that it was a false alarm, and there will be no baby Seamus after all.

When it becomes clear that Julie and Eric are driving themselves crazy trying to pack, I put my foot down, instructing Eric to go in the living room and relax, and I help Julie.

"I don't think you've forgotten anything," I tell Julie a few hours later. We're in her room, inspecting her full bags one last time.

"I'm so excited to go." She almost squeaks out the words.

"I can see that."

She's been talking my ear off the entire afternoon about all the things she and the girls are planning to do. I've tried to sneak in as much advice as I could during our conversation, but I'm not sure she listened to any of it. She's riding high on enthusiasm right now. A loud honk resounds from outside the house, putting an end to our inspection. We ticked off everything that was on the to-pack list twice already, anyway. She's good to go.

"They're here." Julie claps her hands. My cousin Jamie is picking her up. He's driving her and his three daughters to my mom's. Two of the girls are Julie's age, and the oldest one is sixteen. Predictably, she doesn't appear to be looking forward to spending an entire week with twelve-year-olds.

I pick up Julie's wheeled suitcase. She slings her backpack on her shoulders, and then we head out of her room.

Eric is outside the house, chatting with Jamie. The younger girls sit on the hood of the car, eating ice cream and talking loudly. They slide off the car when they see Julie, and she runs to greet them.

"Ready, girls?" Jamie asks.

They all answer with overenthusiastic nods and cries of yes.

"Let's get going," my cousin says.

The moment the car is out of sight, we walk back inside the house.

"So," I tell Eric coyly. "I'm going to change."

"Why?" he asks, perplexed.

"To prepare for our date, of course." We deemed today to be date night ever since Julie told him she wants to go to my mom's.

"You look great. Though I like you naked best."

I suck in a breath, pressing my palm against his chest and pushing him slightly away. Having him so close makes it hard for me to think straight.

"You're cheeky," I murmur. "But I still have to go and change. I'm not even wearing a proper dress." Since it's warm outside, I put on a sundress this morning, which, while cute, is not appropriate for date night.

"No idea what your definition of proper is, but I love this one. All I have to do to get you naked is pull on this string."

"Your mind is in the gutter all of the time. Luckily, mine is not."

"Then I'm not doing my job right." With a wicked smile, he drags his thumb over my lips once, eyeing my mouth as if he's about to do dangerous things to it. "Time for you to be thoroughly kissed. We're not going anywhere, anyway."

"We're not?"

"Nope." He cups my cheek, his hand sliding down my neck and settling on my chest. "I'm cooking you dinner, so we can start our date right away. I bought all the necessary ingredients for starters and the main course yesterday."

"What about dessert?" I ask in a panic. "That's the most important part."

"You'll be my dessert." He gives me a heated look. "I'll be yours." Noticing my facial expression, he continues, "You don't seem impressed by it."

I chew on the inside of my cheek, wondering if

there's a nice way to let him down. I don't think there is. "It's just that dessert is the best part."

"You prefer dessert to sex with me?"

"I did not say that."

"You did not *not* say it, though," he insists. He gives me a quick kiss on my forehead before adding, "I'll order chocolate cake but, just so you know, my ego is very hurt."

"Aww." I pinch his shoulder playfully. "I'll scream extra loud during sex to make up for it?"

Eric's gaze darkens instantly. Hooking an arm around my waist, he pulls me to him. "I'll *make* you scream extra loud."

"Okay," I say, almost out of breath.

Seemingly satisfied by my answer, he interlaces his fingers with mine and leads me into the house.

"This is date night," I insist. "Are you sure you want to do this?"

"What's wrong with me cooking dinner for you?"

It's homey and sweet, and if I see you cooking, in addition to having seen you with your daughter, my ovaries might explode is what I want to say. But I don't want to sound like a hormonal wacko, so I say, "Absolutely nothing."

Once in the kitchen, I watch him pull out all the ingredients from the fridge and lay them out on the counter. He starts chopping vegetables right away.

"What should I do?" I ask, hovering around him.

"Entertain me."

"And what else?" I insist.

"Nothing."

"Eric, I can't do *nothing*. I'm a doer. I need tasks."

He puts down his knife, pinning me with his gaze. "Here are your tasks. One: Relax. Two: Smile. Three: Think about all the things I'm gonna do to you after we eat."

He says this in a serious, commanding tone, which sends a delicious shiver through me.

"Very precise instructions," I murmur, leaning against the table.

"And I shall be strict in making sure you follow them."

I perk up at this. "How will you punish me if I don't?"

"No orgasm for you tonight."

"The joke's on you, buddy. I'm perfectly capable of giving one to myself."

I meant this as a joke, but the air between us changes in an instant. When he speaks next, his voice is low and husky. "I need you to stop any dirty words coming from that pretty mouth of yours, or we won't have dinner at all."

I debate pushing him over the edge for a split second, but my rumbling stomach wins. Still, I can turn this cooking session into PG-rated territory in lots of ways. I brainstorm a few options as Eric brings a bottle of red wine and pours me one glass.

"Fine, under one condition."

"We're bargaining now?" he asks, disbelief coloring his voice.

"Yes, we are, and we established I have the upper hand." I cock an eyebrow, swiping my tongue over my lower lip, and Eric's eyes darken with lust. I don't know what's gotten in to me, but I feel greedy and feisty, and I want all of him right now.

"Pun intended?" he asks, and I take immense pleasure in the way his voice wavers.

"All the way."

"Fine. What is your condition?"

"Lose the pants," I instruct.

"You want me to cook naked?" he asks.

"Nah, you can keep the shirt." I grin devilishly. "I'm interested in your booty."

"My torso feels discriminated against right now," he says, feigning offense.

"It'll get over it. Now, strip."

"Only if you do," he replies.

"No can do. If I'm naked, we'll end up starving."

"You have little faith in me, Pippa Bennett."

"You have proven to have a weakness for flesh." My pulse leaps as I wait for his response.

"Only because you're so fucking irresistible."

My breath catches as he advances toward me and places his hands on either side of me, trapping me between him and the wall, kissing me feverishly, turning me into a heavy-breathing mess when he lets go of me. "You're not getting a peekaboo at my ass. I'll save that for the bedroom." Seeing me pout, he adds, "You know, I'm becoming suspicious that you're only using me for my body."

"You're so full of yourself. Unbelievable."

"You mean I shouldn't pride myself on rock-hard abs, an ass you can't take your eyes off even when

I'm dressed, and a big cock?"

I form an O with my mouth. "You're shameless." Dropping my voice to a whisper, I add, "But I can't contradict you."

He goes back to chopping ingredients, and watching him is like foreplay.

"You're cooking Italian food," I exclaim.

"Yeah. Bruschetta for starters, then spaghetti arrabiata for the main course."

Right. Hearing him talk about food is a freaking turn-on. I hop on the counter, observing him. Once everything's cooking, I decide it's confession time.

"I had my lawyer set up a meeting with Terence next week," I say. "On Tuesday."

Eric looks up with a frown from the pan where the arrabiata is cooking. "Why?"

"He thinks it's to discuss a settlement, but I have a plan." With a wink, I add, "I'm going to channel my inner shark. I wanted you to know."

"Thank you for trusting me." He plants a quick kiss on my forehead. I grip the hem of his shirt with my fingers, unwilling to let him step back.

"Thank you for making me hope again," I whisper. "For making me fear less."

Eric stills. "Pippa, are you saying good-bye to me?" His voice is low and uneven.

My heart clenches as I watch his tormented expression. "No, absolutely not. I won't say good-bye until you board that plane."

"Good." He lets out a heavy breath. "Good."

Eric steps between my thighs. His mouth feels

soft on mine as he kisses me tenderly at first, then more intensely until I moan in his arms. His hand moves up my thigh, higher and higher—

The unmistakable sound of sauce overflowing on the stove forces us apart.

"Don't burn the food, Callahan," I tease, wanting to lighten the mood as he's trying to save our dinner. "It'd be bad form to let me starve."

"It's bad form to tempt me the way you do," he volleys back.

"Oh, you want me to stop doing it?" I pretend I want to jump off the counter, but Eric stops me, placing a firm hand on my thigh.

"Don't move." His eyes have a dangerous glint to them. "Tempt away, Bennett."

***

I keep my promise to Eric and tempt him constantly for the next few days, which results in little sleep for both of us. Tuesday arrives after a night of tossing and turning in bed. I wake up covered in a cold sweat. Eric isn't next to me, but I expected that since he always wakes up before me. I go through the motions of showering and dressing in a somewhat robotic mood, trying to imagine how my meeting with Terence will go.

When I step into the living room, a mix of aromas I love greets me—coffee and muffins.

"Very thoughtful," I say to Eric, who is sitting at the table with a Cheshire Cat grin.

"I was told it brings luck to start the day by eating your favorite breakfast."

"Who told you that?"

"My mother."

"I like her already." I sit across from him and dig in to my breakfast. My palms become sweatier as the minutes pass by, a fact I try to keep from Eric.

"You don't have to drive me there." I grip my coffee cup with both hands, gulping down the last drops of liquid.

"Not negotiable." Eric's voice is soft and firm at the same time. I have no idea how he's doing that. "I'll wait for you outside the office. I'll be there in case you need me to cheer you up or punch someone."

"There will be no punching," I say in a warning tone.

"Only if needed. I solemnly promise."

I'm remarkably calm when I enter my lawyer's office half an hour later. He tells me Terence is already in the meeting room—alone, as I requested. Terence's lawyer is sitting in the waiting area, eyeing me with curiosity. He's donned an expensive suit, a watch, and a self-assured smirk to match.

His smirk becomes more pronounced by the second, sickening me. Unwilling to spend more time than necessary here, I walk straight into the meeting room.

Terence is sprawled lazily on one of the chairs, and I sit opposite him. He sports the same self-assured facial expression his lawyer does—clearly assuming I'm going to offer him money for disappearing from my life. Before the divorce was final, I was mostly silent during mediations, letting my lawyer do all the talk, and doing my best not to provoke Terence. I'm no longer that same woman, though. He's in for a rude awakening.

"Let's get this over with," I say by way of greeting. I prop my elbows on the wooden desk, leaning slightly forward. "You're not getting one cent."

That wipes the smirk off his face right away. Good.

"Are you joking? Did you call me here for more of the same? My lawyer—"

"Wears a more expensive suit and watch than you do right now. His retainer alone is more than a year's worth of rent for that crap-hole you live in."

This gets his attention. He sits up straighter, flaring his nostrils. "Have you had someone look in to my things?"

"Yes." Logan knows some skilled investigators, and he put me in contact with them. "They found extremely interesting information. You sold the yacht, the car, and your collection of watches so you can pay your lawyer. By my calculations, you can afford to pay him for another five months."

I can practically see the color draining from his face, and I'm far from done.

"I can afford legal fees for years and years to come," I say coolly. "Can you?"

"Once I win, I can pay," he says through gritted teeth. I think he meant that to sound menacing, but it came out desperate.

"You wouldn't win. That's a fact. You have no case. What you and your lawyer are aiming for is for me to cave and pay you off so I don't have to deal with you."

"You're bluffing," Terence replies, a vein pulsing in his temple.

"I looked in to your lawyer too. This is his strategy. Harassing the other party until they give in. Most of them give in quickly. But here's the hitch." I cross my fingers over the table, smiling sweetly at him. "Processes can last years. I can *make* this one last years, and I will if you force my hand. Oliver and I think we can prolong this for at least five years. Expensive suit out there will want his retainer during that time, and you have nothing else to sell."

"I can find money."

"Maybe you can, but judging by the look of you, you're clearly not faring well." The muscles in my arms quiver and sweat breaks out at the back of my neck as I continue. "You're betting that I'm willing to do anything so you disappear from my life. I'm here to tell you otherwise. I will drag you through courtrooms until you are broke. I'm not afraid anymore, because you mean nothing to me. I will protect my family's legacy at whatever cost."

"You bitch. You fool everyone with your nice-girl act, and—"

"Let's get one thing straight," I say loudly. "I can play dirty. I choose not to. Most of the time. I treated you fairly until now, but you don't deserve it. You have one week to drop this entire act, or I'm going after you until you are literally buried in legal fees."

Terence doesn't reply for long minutes, then says viciously, "You think he loves you, don't you?"

"This is none of your business."

"You really do believe it. God, you've always been an idiot. That's why you'll end up alone. That's what you deserve."

Bile rises up my throat, but I force myself to remain calm. Standing up, I say, "You have one week to drop this. Then I'm going after you."

I walk out of the room, nodding at Oliver, who gives me a thumbs-up. Expensive suit looks pale, all traces of self-confidence gone. I guess our less-than-friendly exchanges were loud enough for him to hear. Good.

"Let me know how this pans out," I tell Oliver.

I almost jog to the park across the office, in need of fresh air. Sweat dots my upper lip as I sit on a bench, close my eyes, and take in deep breaths to calm myself. *His words can only hurt me if I allow them to, and I choose not to.* I repeat this mantra a few times, already feeling much calmer.

"How did it go?"

I startle in my seat, my eyes flying open. "Eric. I forgot you were here."

He sits next to me, taking both my hands in his. "You okay?"

"My inner shark kicked ass."

As if on cue, my phone chimes with a message from Oliver. *Terence dropped the lawsuit. He won't bother you anymore.*

Smiling, I show the message to Eric.

"Wow, you must've been scary, Ms. Shark," he remarks. "This demands a celebration. How about we both take the day off?"

A warm, fuzzy feeling takes hold of my chest because I know how much work he has to do before returning to Boston.

"Are you sure?" I ask.

"Positive. What do you want to do?"

I stretch out lazily on the bench, contemplating whether I can tempt Eric with a movie, or some other cozy activity. Without warning, he pulls my feet in his lap.

"Let's go training," he suggests.

"I was making a mental list of all the things we could do today. Training wasn't even on the list."

By the mischievous smile stretching on his beautiful face, I know he won't give up easily.

"Working out is good for you. It makes your heart beat faster, and—"

"So do you," I interrupt before he can enumerate all the benefits. Alice already recited them to me more times than I care to remember. Struck by a genius idea, I crawl closer to him, until I almost sit in his lap. Channeling my inner seductress, I say in a low, inviting voice, "And you do it very well."

Eric cocks an eyebrow. "You think seducing me will work?"

My shoulders slump. Apparently, my inner seductress sucks. "Yeah," I admit, and Eric chuckles.

"We had fun last time we were at the gym together." He wiggles his eyebrows suggestively.

"Are you bribing me with sexy times so you can get my sorry ass to the gym?"

"Of course I am. And don't insult your ass. It's my special delight in the mornings."

"What are you talking about?" I ask, genuinely confused.

Eric trails his fingers up and down my arm, raising goose bumps on my skin.

"I wake up about an hour before you do, take my laptop, and sit on the armchair. Your favorite sleeping position is on one side with your pillow between your thighs. Your night gown usually bunches around your waist, so your ass is bare. I have memorized every inch of it."

"You watch me when I sleep?" Something about his admission touches me deeply, though I can't quite explain why.

"Yeah," he says softly. "You're sweet and peaceful. I could watch you for hours." His eyes bore into mine with an intensity that smolders. "So, one hot kiss, and we train for forty-five minutes, two kisses—an hour?"

"Three kisses buy you forty minutes," I announce. "And then I want us to go restaurant hopping."

Eric immediately bursts out laughing. "You are a terrible negotiator."

"I know, but you just admitted I can ask you for favors, or there will be no more early-morning peeking at my butt."

"Pushing your luck here, but okay. I like this, taking time for us."

I sigh, remembering there will only be an 'us' for another two weeks.

Chapter Twenty-Four

Pippa

My mood grows grimmer over the next few days. I try to enjoy every minute I spend with Eric, but the knowledge that this will all be over soon overshadows my happiness. On top of that, I seem to tear up about random things at work, and I'm exhausted no matter how much I sleep, which is why I've decided to spend the rest of the week working from Eric's house. Either I'm coming down with some terrible flu, or I have the worst case of PMS, or I'm losing it.

On Thursday, I go in for my annual checkup, and since I am feeling lousy, they take some blood. Then I have to deal with the lightheadedness caused by the blood loss on top of my weird state. When Eric comes home later that night, I try to shove his imminent departure to the back of my mind and enjoy our time as much as possible.

"How was your day?" he asks me, coming over to me and kissing my forehead. I'm sitting cross-legged on his couch with sketches spread around.

Pouting, I point to the bruise on my arm. "I had a

blood test today. The nurse couldn't find my vein at first, so she stuck me a few times."

"You're afraid of needles?"

"Yeah."

"I love how I learn something new about you every day." He caresses my cheek with the back of his hand, and I lean in like a kitten who can't get enough of her master's touch. "I'll bring you a top with long sleeves so you don't see it."

"Great idea," I say, touched. I'm wearing a silk, sleeveless sundress.

Eric returns a few minutes later, handing me a long-sleeved summer sweater. After I put it on, I notice he's holding the shirt he gave me months ago in his other hand.

"You're a little thief," he informs me, sitting next to me and pulling me in his lap. "I forgot about this. Were you ever going to return it?"

"Well, you did find it in my suitcase."

"So, you're a reformed thief?"

Licking my lips, I say, "I slept in it a few times at home." Heat creeps up my face, and I'm sure the redness in my cheeks is visible.

Eric is silent for a few beats, before saying, "C'mere." He opens his arms, beckoning me to lean in to his hug. I stay put, not meeting his gaze for some reason. I play with the sleeve of the shirt, keeping my eyes fixed on the button.

"Pippa, is everything okay? You've gone quiet."

"Everything's fine."

"Do you want to keep this?" His voice has an

edge to it that threatens to undo me. Am I imagining it, or is there pain in it?

"I'd love to, but I was wondering. Can I swap this shirt with the one you wore today?"

"Why?"

"Because this one doesn't smell like you."

"You want to sleep in my smelly shirt?"

I keep twisting the sleeve in my fingers as I say, "I want to have something that smells like you, so I can remember you."

"Pippa, look at me," he says gently.

"I love you," I whisper. In the stunned silence that follows, my heart shrinks to the size of a pea. "I'm sorry. I know we—"

"Shhh," Eric interrupts me. He puts his thumb under my chin, lifting it and looking at me. His eyes are full of warmth and tenderness. "Never apologize to me. Least of all because you love me." He pulls me closer to him, and this time, I lean in to his touch all the way. "I can't say it. I could never get on that plane if I did."

I nod, smiling against his lips. "I think it's best if you don't. Otherwise, I'll start crying."

He leans his forehead against mine, and we both draw in deep breaths.

Eric pushes my hair to one side, then nuzzles the exposed part of my neck.

"I want you," he whispers. His hot breath on my wet skin prompts goose bumps to form on my arms.

"Yes." We desire each other with an intensity that scares me. I grip the hem of his shirt with both hands, pulling him to me, needing to feel even closer to him, but nothing feels close enough. A familiar sexual stirring springs to life inside me. His hands travel from my shoulders to my waist, and he cups one of my breasts over the fabric of the sweater.

He groans against my lips. "You're not wearing a bra."

"You complainin'?"

"No. I thought about you all day, wanting to make love to you."

"There's nothing restricting you now," I tease.

Eric slides my dress up to my waist and strokes his finger over my thong. I shudder. With this one single touch, he sets every nerve ending in my body on fire. My nipples throb, rubbing against the dress with every small move I make. They are so sensitive that even the sheer silk is too rough for them. Yet somehow, I think Eric's tongue—or even his teeth— would not feel rough at all. He pushes his hips against me, letting me know he's hard and ready for me.

I undo the buttons of his shirt, taking it off him, then proceed to rid him of his pants and boxers, freeing his glorious erection. I swipe my tongue over the tip exactly once before pulling away.

Eric sucks in a sharp breath. "You're a bad girl."

"Very bad," I agree with him. He removes my sweater in one swift move, then hooks his thumbs in the top of my dress, pulling it down. The dress gathers at my waist, leaving my breasts exposed. Eric glances down at them, rubbing one nipple between his fingers, while slicking the fingers of his other hand over my sex. A bolt of heat sears through me.

"I don't want to let you go, Pippa. For once, I wish I could be selfish and choose my own happiness. I would choose to stay here with you."

I swallow a sob, fighting the sudden burning sensation behind my eyelids. How can a few words cause me so much happiness and ache at the same time? *I will not cry. I will not cry.* Watching the pain in his eyes, I realize I have to be strong for both of us right now.

"Let's not think about that." I kiss the corner of his lips. Unable to help myself, I add, "You're the most selfless person I know, and I love you for it."

Without a word, Eric hoists me in his arms, and I wrap my legs around him. He takes us to the bedroom, where it's pitch dark, but I don't worry. I'd let this man take me blindly anywhere; that's how much I trust him. And I never thought I'd trust a man again.

He lays me on the bed, climbing on top of me. "I love you so much it fucking hurts," he whispers in the darkness. His words accelerate my heartbeat and stop my breath.

"That makes two of us," I whisper back. Next, his mouth is on mine, and we say no more. Instead, we pour all of our unspoken words into kisses and caresses. Gentle at first, then passionate.

Eric enters me in one swift move, and he stills inside me.

"Oh, fuck. This feels too good." He all but grunts

out the words. Interlacing his fingers with mine, he rests his head in the crook of my neck. For long moments, we stay like that, listening to each other's breaths, feeling the other's heartbeat, connecting on a level I never thought possible. When he finally starts moving, he does so with long, deep thrusts, his mouth on mine the entire time. He murmurs my name between kisses, caressing my face, my neck. I run my fingers on the expanse of his back, wanting to remember every inch of his skin, and the way his muscles tense when he makes love to me.

Pushing him gently away from me, I bring my hands to his chest, continuing my journey of memorizing his body.

His precise, devastating thrusts spur a hunger deep inside me, which spreads all the way to my fingertips, until it becomes all-consuming. My hips buck off the bed, desperate for more. Eric intensifies the rhythm, his thrusts growing ferocious as he exhales fiery breaths.

My pulse ratchets up as a small quiver builds in my center, then spreads through my entire body. Abandoning all pretense of gentleness, Eric grabs my ass with his hands, digging his nails into my skin. I revel in the pleasure the pinching sensation brings. He buries his face in my neck, his chest pressing against my breasts as he drives inside me like a man possessed. I push my hips, joining him in his rhythm, needing my climax, yet at the same time not wanting this to end. Desperation shadows our desire, but we quench it with kisses, groans, and a frantic search for our release. Eric widens inside me and groans out my name at the same time my orgasm ripples through me, and it's bittersweet.

Taking deep, ragged breaths, we lie tangled in each other's arms for a long time, neither of us wanting to let go.

Chapter Twenty-Five

Eric

My last week in San Francisco starts with a boom. I have a meeting with my team first thing in the morning, going through the agenda for the week. Marcus, one of the initial employees, will be the head of the team after I leave. I will be monitoring the growth here from Boston, but I will be less involved. I'll miss this. It was a tough two and a half months, but I enjoyed it more than I thought I would. There is something to be said about growing a company yourself over inheriting a fully formed organization. When my father stepped back from his job as CEO and I took over, Callahan's Finest was already working like a well-oiled machine. Here I had to roll up my sleeves and do the dirty work myself. I loved every minute of it. Marcus still has a lot of work ahead of him, and I envy the bastard.

"Great job, everyone," I say as the meeting ends.

"We'll miss you, boss," my secretary says. I raise an eyebrow, preparing a sardonic remark, but then I realize she means it. Okay, so Pippa's advice to stop being an ass had more merit than I anticipated. I'm barely back in my office when my phone starts ringing. Looking down at the phone, I see it's Mom.

"Hi, Mom."

"How are you, Eric?"

"Busy. Trying to wrap everything up."

"So, your return to Boston is going according to schedule?"

"Yes." I flip through a report on my desk, making mental notes of everything I have to do the moment I finish talking to Mom.

"I raised you better than this."

"What?"

"I do speak to my granddaughter, you know. She tells me what's going on in her life. Your life."

"I see."

"Do you? Because right now, I'm thinking my son is blind."

"Mom, if there is something you want to tell me, cut to the chase." I push the report away, ready for her attack.

"You're in love with Pippa Bennett."

I don't hesitate. "Yes."

"And you're still not going to do everything you can to stay in San Francisco?"

"It's not that simple." I huff out a breath, drumming my fingers on my desk.

"Why not? What's keeping you in Boston?"

"It's a long list."

"Humor me."

"Julie's school—you know how much she struggled fitting in. You. The company."

"That was an exceptionally short list. Let's go over that line by line, shall we? First, the company. Can you say with absolute certainty that the company would be worse off if you hired a CEO in Boston and you moved to San Francisco, developing the business there?"

Though Mother isn't an official board member, she's up to date with the state of things in the company, always has been.

"No," I admit. "If anything, it would strengthen the company's overall position. I'd be more aggressive with our growth than Marcus or anyone else here. And I'm bored in Boston."

"Yes, that was apparent from the moment you announced you wanted to go to San Francisco yourself. So we ticked that off. Now, let's take me."

It doesn't escape me that she hasn't touched the subject of Julie yet, who was the first on the list.

"We talk on the phone and have monthly dinners. I also throw bridge parties, from which you and Julie bail every time."

Oh, hell. Pippa was right. Mom *was* pretending to buy our excuses.

"Can we agree that we can talk over the phone even if you're away, and we can meet for monthly dinners?" Mom presses. "I can fly to San Francisco, or you can fly here."

"Mom. You're seve—" I stop before I spell out the word. Bringing up Mom's age won't be doing me any favors, but a woman her age shouldn't travel back and forth so often.

LAYLA HAGEN

"Glad you stopped. Now, let's get to Julie. Have you actually talked to your daughter about moving to San Francisco?"

"I don't want her to feel like she comes in second. Ever," I say firmly.

"That's not what I asked."

"No, I haven't talked to her."

Silence hangs in the air for a few seconds, and I imagine this is how prisoners sentenced to death by guillotine felt in the seconds before the blade fell. Mom's next words slice through me.

"It is as I thought. You're using all these arguments as excuses."

"Mother...."

"Do you love Pippa? Do you see yourself spending your life with her?"

"Yes."

"Then stop looking for excuses and start finding solutions."

I smile, despite everything. This is my punchline whenever I feel someone's slacking, which Mother knows well. Also, she might be on to something. It's not something I want to admit, but maybe I *was* looking for excuses.

"Thank you, Mother. I—" The phone starts vibrating, alerting me that there's another incoming call: Julie. "Julie's calling me. I'll catch up with you later."

I switch off this call, taking Julie's.

"Hi, pumpkin," I greet her.

"Hi, Eric," Mrs. Bennett says.

My insides clench instinctively. "Did something happen to Julie?"

"She cut her arm the other day," Mrs. Bennett says quickly.

"Is she all right?"

"She didn't tell me about it, so it got infected. I found out today, and I'm about to take her to the hospital. I—"

"I'll come to your house and get her," I say, barely keeping my voice even. "I want to speak to my daughter."

"Hi, Dad," Julie says. "It hurts."

"You'll be okay, sweetheart." My gut clenches, and I hurt for her. "Do you want me to stay on the phone with you until I arrive?"

"Yes, Dad."

I spend the next twenty minutes with her on the phone, soothing her, trying to take her mind off the pain while speeding through the city.

Mrs. Bennett waits with my daughter and her suitcase in front of her house. I pull over and hurry to them, my eyes on Julie's arm. Fuck! It's red and swollen, far too swollen for a simple infection. Julie sobs and wraps her healthy arm around my neck as I hug her.

"You will be all right," Mrs. Bennett says, patting her head. To me, she says, "These things happen to kids all the time, Eric."

"Yeah," I say through gritted teeth, lifting Julie in my arms. My anger is directed more at myself at this point, but I don't want to discuss this with her or I might end up being disrespectful. "We're going now."

Mrs. Bennett pats my shoulder but doesn't reply. I secure my daughter in the car, then climb in the driver's seat and gun the engine. All the way to the hospital, I speak about everything under the sun, trying to distract Julie. If I'm honest, I'm trying to distract myself too. Her arm doesn't look good at all.

At the hospital, it takes forever until a doctor finally sees her. I'm pacing in the corridor for fifteen agonizing minutes until the doctor comes out.

"Your daughter needs surgery," he informs me.

"What?"

"We need to open up the area to clean it, and also to determine what kind of bacteria caused the infection so we can treat it. She'll need to stay here a few days. Don't worry. It's not serious, and she'll be fine, but we need to keep her under observation and change her bandages once a day."

I clench my fists at my sides. "Of course."

"We'll take her to the fifth floor for the surgery. It will be short, fifteen minutes tops." He gives me some more details, and then the waiting begins.

I go up to the fifth floor and pace up and down the corridor, unable to stay put. This is my worst nightmare come true. Damn it, I shouldn't have let her stay with Mrs. Bennett. I've let my desire to have more alone time with Pippa get in the way, and that's unforgivable.

Being in the hospital brings back my worst memories of another wait, many years ago. I tell myself the two things are completely unrelated, but I can't shake the memory. It strangles me. The smell of medicine and disinfectants only serves to intensify the memory, as does the austere white paint. I swear, hospitals look the same everywhere.

I remember being in a waiting room not unlike this one in Boston, waiting for the doctors to inform me about the fate of the two people I loved dearest. When one of the doctors finally came out, he told me that Julie would make it. Sarah would not. She was pronounced dead almost as soon as they brought her in. Just like that, my world turned upside down.

This is different. This is very different.

I'm lost in my spiral of negativity when my phone rings, Pippa's name appearing on the screen.

"Mom told me everything. I'm in the hospital. Which floor are you on?" she asks.

"Fifth."

Clicking off, I pace around the waiting room when a nurse walks up to me. "Your daughter is now in a room. You can see her."

As the nurse leads me out the corridor, I see Pippa jogging to us. She takes my hand when she reaches us, squeezing it lightly.

"How is Julie?" she asks.

"We're going to see her now."

The nurse comes to a stop in front of an open door, motioning us to enter the room. There are two beds, and my daughter is in the one nearest to the door.

"Dad, Pippa. I'm so sorry," she murmurs the

second she sees us. The doctor is at the side of her bed, standing stiffly, his arms crossed.

"You have nothing to be sorry about, love," I tell her. Pippa sits at the edge of the bed, hugging my daughter.

"It still hurts," Julie whispers to her.

I turn to the doctor. "Why is she hurting?"

"She's been in a surgery with a local anesthetic, which is starting to wear off. She'll be fine."

"Give her something for the pain."

"Painkillers are not candy," he says in a deadpan voice. "She will receive them at certain intervals."

"I will not have my daughter be in pain—"

"Then I suggest you look after her more closely, so incidents like this don't happen. Now, I suggest you step out of the room until you calm yourself down."

Who the fuck does this moron think he is? I grind my teeth, barely restraining myself from replying.

"Eric," Pippa says softly. "Calm down. Let's go out for a little while."

Nodding, I follow her out, leaving Julie with the doctor.

"She'll be fine, Eric," Pippa says once she's in the corridor.

"Jesus, why does everyone tell me she'll be fine?" My tone is harsher than I intended, and Pippa flinches, taking a step back. "That's not the point. The point is that this could have been much worse."

"Eric—"

"I shouldn't have allowed her to go anywhere."

"You're blaming Mom?" Her voice is incredulous.

"No, I'm blaming myself. I lost focus." I avert my eyes from her. "I should have kept watching her. Instead, I was…."

"Busy with me. Are you really going down this route? She's a kid, Eric. They play. They get hurt. This could have happened even if she were with you at home."

"No, it wouldn't," I say sharply. "Let's not talk about this now. I'm not—"

"Why aren't you even looking at me?" she asks in a small voice.

At that, I drag my gaze to her, frowning. "I don't know. All I can concentrate on now is my daughter. I'm going to make some calls to inform the team I'll be working from the hospital until Julie's out."

"We can take care of her in shifts, and—"

"Maybe it's better if we don't," I find myself saying.

"What do you mean?"

Silence looms between us as I search for the best words, but one look at Pippa tells me she already knows where I'm going with this. Damn it, the last thing I want on this earth is to hurt this woman.

"Are you breaking up with me?" Her shoulders slump, and I bite the inside of my cheek, watching the woman I love shrink before my eyes.

"I'm leaving in a week anyway." My voice is even, but only barely. Something inside me breaks with every word, but what hurts most is knowing I hurt her.

"One week is not today," she whispers.

"What's the point?" I ask, and instantly know it was the wrong thing to say. Pippa's expression changes from hurt to furious. Glaring, she advances toward me, a strand of hair falling from her bun and over her forehead.

"If you don't know what the point is, then you haven't been paying attention. When my dad was in the hospital, you told me not to push you out. You said you wanted to be there for me when things are bad. Now, you're pushing me out and using Julie as an excuse. I love you, and I love Julie, and this is *not* how what we have is going to end." She presses her lips together, and her nostrils are flaring. "Don't you have anything to say?"

I'm so stunned I can't even think straight, let alone form a coherent sentence.

"I've never seen you so mad," I say eventually, still too blindsided to come up with anything smarter. Judging by the color storming her cheeks, and by the strength with which she clenches her fists, it was the wrong thing to say. Still, seeing her mad at me is much more of an improvement over seeing her hurt. Maybe if she hates me, she'll suffer less.

"I haven't even begun being mad. When you have more important things to say to me, you know where to find me. And by God, if you board that plane and leave for Boston without talking to me first, you will see me truly *mad*. Kiss Julie for me."

Then she turns around on her heels and leaves.

Damn.

Chapter Twenty-Six

Pippa

I'm still shaking when I storm inside my apartment. *Breathe in, breathe out, Pippa.* Yeah, that's not going to help me. My usual go-to comfort food is cupcakes, but strangely, the thought of them makes me nauseous. That bastard. How dare he take the coward's way out?

I pace around my living room, rubbing my palms up and down my arms, unable to stop the tears. If I can continue being mad at him, maybe I won't hurt so much. My heart begs to differ. It already hangs heavy in my chest, making it a chore to breathe.

I'm about to open my fridge and search for some comfort food when my phone rings. It's a number I don't know, but I pick up anyway.

"Hello."

"Is this Pippa Bennett?" a female voice asks. I recognize it; it belongs to my doctor.

"Yes."

"This is Dr. Edwards. I have your test results."

"Oh, great. Please tell me I don't have some life-threatening disease, because my day has taken a nosedive as it is." I slump on my couch, not even able to muster the energy to worry about whatever she's about to tell me.

"I have great news for you, Pippa. You're not sick. You're pregnant."

My mouth goes dry, and for a few seconds, I don't register her words. But when I do, I choke, unable to breathe.

"A—are you sure?" I stutter.

"Positive. Your blood tests prove it."

I clench the phone tightly in my hand, bringing my knees to my chest and resting my chin on them.

"But I was on birth control," I argue, sure there must be an understanding. "I took pills from my gynecologist, then stopped using condoms."

"Maybe you stopped using the condoms too early? You were supposed to wait ten days."

I start counting in my head, convinced I waited the right amount of time. "I think I waited nine and a half," I say, defeated.

"Pippa, are you all right?" she asks, worry lacing her voice. "You've wanted to have kids for a long time."

"Yeah." She would know all about it. Ever since I first got married, I've dreamed about the day I would be a mother. I hug my knees tightly to me, processing it. My eyes are misty. Damn it, I have to stop crying.

"I know you and Terence are divorced," she says quickly, my sobs clearly not going unnoticed. "And I'm not sure if you're in a relationship, but don't be discouraged. There is a lot of support for single mothers."

"I'm happy about the baby. These are happy tears." *But I'm also hurt and afraid.* "Can I call you back later?"

"Sure. You should make an appointment with the gynecologist as well."

"I will," I assure her, before hanging up.

I lie on the couch, hugging a pillow, curling around it. A *baby.* I break out in sobs and, too tired to fight them, I give in. I'm not even entirely sure why I'm crying. Gritting my teeth, I steel myself. I know the kind of man Eric is. He won't turn his back on me.

But what if he will? What if he thinks I'm trying to trap him? An old fear wakes inside me, and the memory of the dreadful night that marked the end of my marriage rushes back to me.

***

I'd been feeling faint and my period was late. I thought I was pregnant and was so ecstatic on the way to the pharmacy, where I bought five tests. I've always wanted a big family, like my own. Whenever I brought up the subject of kids to Terence, he put it off, saying we were still young, that we didn't have to hurry. But I did want to hurry. I wanted my little bundle of joy. Selfishly, I also hoped our unborn child would save our marriage. At the very least, I hoped it'd make the evenings Terence didn't spend at home less lonely. There was only so often I could spend my evenings with friends or family. They had lives of their own.

When I arrived home, Terence was in a rage. Then again, he was lately always in a rage. He never hit me, but our arguments were vicious. He froze when he saw the bag in my hands. The package was visible through the near-transparent plastic bag.

"What's that?"

"Pregnancy tests."

"We use protection," he said incredulously. "We always use protection."

"Yes, but nothing's 100% safe, and I've been unwell. Plus, I didn't get my period this month."

"You're not pregnant." His tone sent chills down my spine, but still I smiled, trying to ease the tension.

"We'll find out soon, right?" I held up the bag, smiling like an idiot. "I know you think we're not ready, but—"

"Are you trying to trap me? I don't want a child with you," he spat, taking a step back from me. "All I want is to do my ten years and get the hell away."

I will always remember those words, that precise moment when my world snapped. *Do my ten years.* It sounded like a prison sentence. In that moment, I realized that was exactly what our marriage was for him. I just hadn't realized all of it.

"What do you mean?" I whispered.

"After ten years, the prenup will be void."

"The money," I whispered, the pieces suddenly falling into place. "You want the money."

I had imagined many scenarios of why he resented me. The most plausible one was that he was not feeling like a man because I earned more. That's why Sebastian and Logan set up a company for him. Yet here it was, the simple truth. He'd married me for my money, and gradually he realized that ten years is a long time to spend faking love.

The pain in my chest was so strong it felt as if someone had sliced it open with a knife. I could barely breathe, or even stand, but I knew what I had to do.

"Get out of my sight. Take your things and leave," I said. "Better still, just leave. I will send your things."

"Pippa…." He advanced toward me, raising his arm as if to touch my shoulder.

"Don't you dare touch me. Leave."

"I want to know if you're pregnant first."

"I'm still divorcing you, even if I am pregnant."

"I want to know. I won't abandon a kid of mine."

Terence grew up with his dad. His mom took off early on, and he didn't even remember her. It was perhaps his one redeeming quality, not wanting to do to his child what his mother did to him, but it was too little, too late.

I went to the bathroom and did one test. It came out negative. Through sobs, I did the other ones. They all came out negative. I didn't have the energy to leave the bathroom, so I cracked the door open and said, "They're all negative. Now, leave."

"Thank fuck. And don't you think I'm walking away from this marriage with nothing. I did three years. That has to count for something."

His reply set off a wave of devastating pain. Then he left. I spent the night in the bathroom, hugging my knees to my chest, rewinding the past years in my head, analyzing everything. Retroactively, everyone's smarter; I saw signs everywhere. But at the time I met him, I didn't. He was charming and went out of his way to please me. He didn't even seem interested in my money.

When Sebastian and Logan told me they wanted Terrence to sign a prenup, I immediately agreed, because the two of them had set up Bennett Enterprises. It was their right to want to protect it. Terence kept his cool when I told him about it. I suppose he didn't realize how long ten years were.

At least it was over.

***

Lying on my back on the couch, I hug my belly, even though it's still flat. There is a small baby in here. My lips curl in a smile.

"Well, hello, little one," I whisper. "We haven't met yet officially, but I already love you very much. You'll be the first Bennett baby, and you'll have so many uncles and aunts you'll lose count of them. They will spoil you even more than I will. God, I can't believe I'm rambling already. You should get used to it. We'll have lots of talks over the next nine months. If you're a boy, your name might be Seamus."

Chapter Twenty-Seven

Eric

The room is quiet as I wait for Julie to wake up. At my demands, the doctors gave her a room of her own, so it's just the two of us here. I'm sitting on the couch that will also be my office for the three days she will be here.

They administered a pain reliever in the evening, and she slept through the night. I couldn't sleep a wink.

There is something very peaceful about watching my daughter sleep. As a matter of fact, it's the only peaceful thing right now. I keep replaying the talk with Pippa. Now, with a clear head, I can finally think straight, and I identified the problem. I don't want to go after Pippa to bid her good-bye.

I want to go after her and tell her I won't let her go. Of course, that's assuming she still wants me. My gut clenches at the idea that she might not.

Sometime between watching her walk away and jolting awake from my stupor, it's become clear that I want this woman in my life for good. I have to find a way to make it happen, and at the same time not let my kid down. As Mother said, it's time to stop looking for excuses and start finding solutions.

Moving here will not be easy on Julie. She will have to adapt to a new school and a new life. She will have to leave her friends behind, but there are strong arguments in favor of moving here.

The most important one is Pippa, obviously. She loves my daughter, and my daughter loves her back. Then there is the Bennett family, which embraced Julie like one of their own.

I drum my fingers on the armrest of the couch, waiting for Julie to wake up so I can discuss all this with my baby girl.

She stirs hours later, and the first thing she says is, "You're here."

I move from the couch to the edge of her bed, patting her cheek with the back of my hand. "Of course I'm here, sweetie. Does it hurt?"

Julie shakes her head, yawning. "I slept a lot, didn't I?"

I chuckle. "Yeah."

"You slept here too?"

"Yes."

"You're the best dad in the world." She leans her head on my arm, sighing. "Where is Pippa?"

"She... Uh...." Why didn't I anticipate that this would be one of her questions? Julie pulls away from my hug, frowning at me.

"Pippa left yesterday, and didn't come back. Is it your fault?" she asks.

"What do you mean?"

"I know Pippa. If she's not here, it means you said something to upset her."

"Why would you think that?"

"Because Sophie, the older girl at Mrs. Bennett's house, had a boyfriend, and they argued on the phone because he said *a lot* of stupid things."

I open my mouth and close it again when I realize Julie's not done.

"She said stupidity runs in the Y chromosome. I learned in biology that the X chromosome is for the females and Y for the males, s—"

"*Where* did I send you?" I ask, flabbergasted. Shaking my head, I add, "Don't you worry about anything. There is something I want to talk to you about."

At that, Julie's expression brightens, and she shifts more to one side as if to make space for me on the bed.

"How would you feel about moving here permanently? I looked up schools—"

Before I can finish my sentence, Julie pushes herself up on her knees and wraps her good arm around my neck, yelling in my ear, "I want to stay, Dad. I want to stay."

I hug her tightly, careful not to touch her injured arm, while my heart beats at a million miles an hour.

"I love it here. I like Mr. and Mrs. Bennett more than Grams, but don't tell her that." She slips out of my arms, sitting back on the bed. "And I love Pippa. She's like a mom. She'll never replace my mom, of course, but I love her. Don't you?"

"I do, pumpkin."

"Let's stay."

My beautiful baby. She will never cease to surprise me. I should have known she wouldn't even want to hear my arguments, that she'd decide with her heart. If I'm honest, I did the same. Still, as her father, it's my duty to lay out all the pros and cons, to make her aware of them so she can walk into this with her eyes open. I want her to think this through, to see all the implications.

"It won't be easy, though. I know you had a tough time acclimating to your school. But I researched some here and found some you might like. We can also try homeschooling."

"Can I go to the school where the Bennett girls go? Pleeease. I'd already have two friends that way."

"Sure, I will look in to that. You wouldn't see your friends back home often, or Ms. Smith. You said you missed her."

Julie shrugs. "Yeah, because she was more fun than Ms. Blackwell. But Ms. Smith is my nanny. Pippa would be my mom."

"It would be a big change, sweetie."

"I *know*, Dad. I'm a big girl. And in six years, I will go to college, and you will be alone. If you marry Pippa, you will never be alone again."

"Way to break my heart, kiddo."

"You know it's true."

I watch her determined look for a few seconds, and I have to give it to her. She's not a baby anymore; she is a big girl, and I have to trust that she can make a sound decision.

"Are you one hundred percent sure?" I ask one more time.

"Yes," she answers with a firm nod.

"Okay. Do you mind if I leave you here alone for a few hours?"

"No, go and find Pippa."

"Be a good girl."

Rising from the bed, I kiss the top of her head and head to the door. I'm going to get my woman.

My mind is racing with arrangements and solutions. I can stay here and grow the company, and I'll need to replace myself in Boston. None of that matters, though. All I needed was to know if my girl was on board with this. I can make everything else work. Now I have to make sure Pippa still wants me.

I'm barely out of Julie's room when I find myself flanked by Max and Blake. *This will be interesting.*

"You son of a bitch," Blake says. Ha! I glance at Max, hoping for some support, but judging by his expression, I will have no ally today. Which serves me right, I suppose.

"Look—" I begin, but Max immediately cuts me off.

"Our sister is hurt," he booms. "We demand an explanation."

"I was an idiot," I reply coolly.

Blake raises his eyebrows. "I wasn't expecting a confession so quickly." Looking at Max, he adds, "We're that intimidating."

"I don't have time for this," I inform them, starting to get annoyed. "Is Pippa at home?"

"Yeah," Max answers, and he takes a step back, his expression transforming from aggressive to curious.

"You goin' to grovel?" Blake inquires, now equally curious.

"Yeah."

"Let's hear it," Blake says.

"What?" I ask.

"We want to hear your groveling plan." I don't know what's more fascinating, that he's saying this with a straight face or that these two actually think they can question me.

"How's that your business?" I retort.

Max answers. "She's our sister, Eric. She's been hurt before by a dickhead. You seem like a decent guy, but you've hurt her too. We want to make sure it doesn't happen again. Anything less than a plan which includes you not fucking off to Boston isn't going to cut it."

I have to give it to them; the Bennetts stick together. And I have to admit, if I had a sister, I'd do the same. Hell, I'd do the same if someone went out with Julie. Come to think of it, any guy who'll go out with Julie will go through a worse interrogation than this one.

"I plan to stay here and propose to your sister. How does that cut it?"

Blake and Max look at each other, and then nod.

"Okay," Blake says, "We should give him

pointers."

I stare at them, astonished by the change in attitude, but I'm not about to complain. "What do you mean?"

"Our sisters are there," Max says. "They'll eat you alive."

"We should go with him, distract Alice and Summer," Blake tells his brother.

"I'm not going to have a committee when I talk to Pippa. I'll handle Alice and Summer," I assure them.

Blake elbows his brother. "This one's so full of himself. We have way more experience with the women in our family than you do."

"Tell Alice that you have a plan and that you're sorry," Max says.

"And say it the second you see her, or she'll cut off your balls," Blake adds seriously. "And tell Summer some romantic stuff. That'll soften her up right away."

"I can handle this," I repeat. "Have a good day."

With that, I walk past both of them and into the elevator.

Chapter Twenty-Eight

Pippa

After an entire night during which I did not sleep a wink, I decide I need my sisters, so first thing in the morning, I send them both a message.

Pippa: S.O.S. Can you both stop by for breakfast? I'm throwing a pity party, but I need some company.

They both reply *yes* within minutes. I walk like a zombie into my kitchen, inspecting my fridge. Looks like I'll have to go shopping for my girls. Alice likes bagels and Summer has cereal and yogurt for breakfast, and I have none of these things. If I'm making them come here, at the very least I can feed them their favorite breakfasts.

I risk a glance in the mirror before I leave the house and sigh. I look the way I feel: exhausted, sick, and scared. My eyes have dark circles under them, in addition to being puffy from crying. That's how I spent the first part of the night. I dedicated the second part to looking up baby clothing on the Internet while pondering how best to break the news to Eric. Sweat coats my forehead, and my throat clogs.

Logically, I know Eric is nothing like Terence, but I can't help fearing that he'll turn his back on me, thinking I'm trying to trap him. Or worse, that he'll stay with me just for the sake of the baby.

There is nothing logical about fear, and it paralyzed me the entire night. Judging by the numbing sensation in my stomach, it's about to overcome me again. *No.*

Gripping my bag tightly, I stare straight at my pale reflection in the mirror and berate myself. "You're a grown-ass woman, Pippa Bennett. You've handled worse. You can handle this."

It doesn't work, the knot in my throat is tighter than ever, but I refuse to dissolve into a puddle of fear and insecurity again, so I grit my teeth and leave the apartment.

I return fifteen minutes later, and my mood has improved somewhat. I set the table and brew fresh coffee. When the doorbell rings, I nearly trip over my own feet in my haste to open it.

"Morning," Alice says, while Summer hugs me without a word.

"Why are you hugging me?" I ask, breathing in her light jasmine perfume and hugging her back so tightly I'm surprised she can breathe.

"You look like you could use one," she mumbles, then pulls away.

Alice says, "You look bad."

I shake my head in answer, my eyes darting to the bags in her hand. "You didn't have to bring food."

Letting them in, I lead them to the living room, pointing to the dining table. "I went shopping after I texted you."

"Pippa!" Alice's sharp tone instantly sets me on alert. "You don't know how to do this pity-party stuff, do you?"

"You're not supposed to take care of us," Summer adds. "It's the other way around."

I can't help smiling. "I wasn't aware there was a way to do it."

"That's because you haven't done it before. Now you know," Alice says firmly.

My sisters eye each other, and then Summer asks in a small voice, "What happened?"

The three of us sit at the table, and in as few words as possible, I tell them what happened with Eric at the hospital.

"Well," Alice says, munching on her bagel, "proof that even the best of men aren't very smart."

Summer frowns at her. "Sometimes you're too cynical for your own good. I think he was just too worried about Julie to focus on anything else. I mean, maybe being in the hospital brought back memories from losing his wife."

I hadn't thought about that. "That's not all, though. I'm pregnant."

Alice freezes in the act of biting her bagel, and Summer leaps from her seat, hugging me for the second time today. Alice joins us in a group hug, and for a few brief moments, I lose myself in their arms, soaking in their happiness and care.

We move to the couch next, and they start questioning me about the pregnancy, and if I feel sick. Euphoria overcomes me as I give them details, until Alice asks, "Have you told Eric?"

"Not yet. I found out less than twenty-four hours ago, and I wanted to regroup. I'll speak to him soon. Right now, I need some quality time with my sisters."

"Okay," Alice says with a clap of her hands, as if preparing herself to order us around. "I say we do this Bennett-style. We have to adapt. Wine's out of the question, but I bet you have hot chocolate, and I can have obscene amounts of food delivered from the restaurant. We can also watch some romantic comedies. The best way to feel better about yourself is seeing other people screw up."

"I'm game," Summer says.

"Me too."

Bennett-style usually involves the three of us, plus Caroline, and lately Nadine and Ava getting together and gossiping over wine. Hot chocolate makes for a great substitute, though.

For the next twenty minutes, my sisters hover around me, not allowing me to do anything and taking care of everything. The food my sister ordered arrives so quickly I wonder if Alice had someone prepare it beforehand, just in case.

As they bicker over which romantic comedy to watch first, I have a vision of us being eighty, wrinkly, and having the exact same conversation. Some things will never change, and that's a good thing.

"Girls, come on. Stop bickering."

To my astonishment, they do.

"This line has never worked before," I mumble.

"Yeah, but you're pregnant now. We can't upset you," Alice says reasonably, which makes me grin. I will use every single advantage this pregnancy will bring.

I turn on the TV as the girls settle on a movie, and I almost tear up when I see what's on the screen.

"Pippa?" Summer asks tentatively. "You're... Are you crying?"

"No... I don't know." I point to the TV, as if that alone explains everything.

"This is your favorite crime show. Can't blame you, the lead detective is a hottie," Alice says. "I'm not following. What's with the tears?"

"Eric and I decided it's *our* show a while back. We didn't see it on Saturday, and I recorded it for later." A tear rolls down my cheek. "How am I supposed to watch the show without him?"

Alice and Summer simply stare at me. It's official. If out of all the things I have to worry about, a damn show takes center stage, I'm losing it. Is it too early to blame the hormones for my weird priority list?

The girls have the decency not to reply. We settle on a movie eventually, and we're halfway through it when the doorbell rings.

"I hope you didn't order more food, Alice," Summer says.

"No, but maybe they forgot to drop off something. I could swear everything was in the delivery boxes, though".

"Do you think if we ignore them they'll go away?" I groan. "I'm in a food coma already. Can't even move."

"I'll get the door," Summer announces. I let out an undefined noise, pausing the movie, as my little sister scurries out of the room.

What follows catches me completely unprepared.

"What are you doing here?" Summer asks.

"I need to talk to Pippa."

Every muscle in my body freezes. Before I can even wrap my mind around the fact that Eric's here, Alice leaps from the couch and joins Summer. I don't see what's going on in the corridor, but I can hear everything.

"You idiot," Alice says. "I thought you'd—"

"Alice," Eric booms, and the sound of his voice snaps me out of my stupor, leaving a place for panic and excitement at the same time. What if he's here to say good-bye? What if he's here *not* to say good-bye? I become aware of my pitiful state—the dark circles, the crazy hair—and groan. I'm a mess.

"I'm sure you have some more insults up your sleeves," he continues, "but I'm here to talk to Pippa, not you. For what it's worth, I know I made a mistake, and I'm here with a plan. A good plan." He lowers his voice, so I don't hear the next words, but Summer exclaims, "That's so romantic."

And just like that, he charms my sisters, which is a remarkable feat. It took my brothers years to learn how to tiptoe around them and say exactly what they

LAYLA HAGEN

want to hear. Summer and Alice poke their head in the room and adopt apologetic expressions.

"Pippa, we will have to resume our pity-party later on," Alice says.

"Yeah, we're leaving now," Summer says.

All I can do is nod, and the two of them leave.

***

Eric walks into the living room, and as I take in his appearance, my heart soars and dips at the same time. He looks pale. I wasn't the only one who couldn't sleep last night.

"I wasn't expecting you." I don't move away from the couch, feeling a chill creep in to my veins.

"I'm sorry. I shouldn't have let you leave yesterday." Sitting next to me, he reaches for my hands, but I keep them in my lap, shaking my head.

"You pushed me away."

"I know, and I'm sorry. Being in the hospital and seeing my daughter in that bed brought back ugly memories."

"Eric. Why are you here?" My throat tightens as I keep my eyes on my fingers, unable to meet his gaze.

"Not to say good-bye."

A wave of tension bleeds away from my body, like a poison being sucked out. His words are like a balm.

"I wasn't thinking straight yesterday. I kept replaying in my mind the night of Sarah and Julie's accident. Just being in that waiting room knowing my daughter was hurt felt like a nightmare. I was scared.

But that was no excuse for being an ass to you and to your mom. I snapped at her when I picked Julie up. I called her on my way here and apologized. Julie and I are here to stay, Pippa. I love you, and I don't want to be somewhere you're not."

I hug him wordlessly. He wraps his arms around my waist, keeping them there.

Pulling my head back a notch, I look up at him. "But Julie's school—"

"I talked to her, and she wants to go to the same school as your cousins' daughters." Cupping my cheek, he adds, "Let's talk about us right now."

"But your company, and—"

"Pippa, relax. I'm taking care of everything."

"And you'll be happy if you move?" I ask.

"I'll be the happiest man alive having you by my side. Back at the hospital, I chose to let fear dictate my actions. I chose fear. I won't do that again. I choose *you*."

The air between us charges with the weight of his words. He laid himself bare for me. I decide to do the same.

"I have something to tell you. It might scare you," I say, then choke up and am unable to utter any words. Unsure how to break the news to him, I take his hand and put it on my belly.

Eric's eyes slowly widen with understanding and excitement. "You're pregnant?"

I nod feverishly, and my heart seems to have grown twice in size. "Yes. I found out yesterday. My doctor called me after I left the hospital."

Without notice, Eric pulls me onto his lap, kissing me senseless. Feeling his mouth on mine is like taking a much needed breath of fresh air.

"You should've told me the second I walked in," he whispers, covering my cheek and my neck with kisses, his hand still on my belly.

"I was afraid you'd think I wanted to trap you," I say in a small voice.

"Oh, you can trap me all you want, love, especially between your thighs."

I attempt to chuckle, but it doesn't come out right.

"I'd never think that. I love you, Pippa Bennett. Whatever happens, never forget that. I know you've been hurt and disappointed before, but that's not going to happen again. Not because of me. In fact, I'm going to make sure no one else does either. Once you're my wife, I'll have an official license to make sure no one harms you again."

"Was that supposed to be a marriage proposal?" My hands tighten on his shoulders, but my heart flips in my chest.

"Shit! It didn't come out right, but yeah."

"Are you asking me to marry you just because I'm pregnant?"

"Why would you think that?"

"Maybe because you proposed ten seconds after I told you?"

"I want to marry you because I love you. I've wanted this for some time, but I didn't admit it to myself. Seeing you walk away at the hospital was a wake-up call."

"Because it scared you?"

A grin flickers on his lips. "No, because you have a sexy ass. I realized I couldn't go without it, and I had to marry you."

"Wow," I whisper, squirming in his lap for good measure. "My ass must be more impressive than I gave it credit for."

"You haven't given me an answer."

As I'm about to open my mouth, a sob forms in my throat, so I pinch my lips tightly together, shaking my head slightly.

"You won't marry me?" he asks, stricken.

"Yes," I say, after swallowing the sob.

"A shake of your head means yes? I'm learning something new about you all the time. But I'm looking forward to it."

I lace my fingers on the back of his neck, shifting even closer to him. Eric drops his hands to my hips, gripping them firmly.

"You deserve the best, and I'm going to remind you of that every day," he murmurs.

"How are you going to do that?"

"I'll surprise you with little things and big things."

"Well, whatever *things* entail, throw a foot massage and ice cream in there."

Eric lets out a low and throaty laugh. "Demanding, aren't we?"

"I'm pregnant. That's going to be synonymous with entitlement to be spoiled for the next nine months." I'm already excited about all the possibilities.

"It'll be my pleasure to spoil you, future wife. I can't wait for this little one to be out." Eric glances down at my belly longingly. "The best thing about babies? They love being hugged. I'll appreciate this more the second time around. I didn't know the cut-off age for being hugged in public is twelve."

"I love hugs," I say coyly.

"I know." He kisses the tip of my nose, then my jaw, prompting delicious shivers to run through my body. "Don't worry. You'll receive plenty too."

"Tell me more about babies," I encourage.

"They're small, pink, and smell like sugar."

"Eric Callahan, you've been holding out on me. You can't wait to be a dad again."

"Yeah. But I need to sharpen some of my skills. They probably got rusty."

"What skills?" I ask, confused.

"You know... Finding the perfect rhythm to swing my arms for the baby to fall asleep, and—"

"You are *adorable*," I exclaim, melting in his arms. "You speak so seriously about it, like it's a science."

Eric offers me a smirk. "Wait until you have a crying baby on your hands, and you'll make a science out of it too."

"Luckily, you'll be there to help."

"I will be there. Always. For everything." The playful twinkle in his eyes diminishes, seriousness replacing it, and I cocoon in his arms, feeling his heartbeat against my chest. He covers my mouth with his, while letting his hands roam freely over my body. His caresses speak of promises, his kisses taste like dreams. I believe every single word because he is this kind of man. This is why I love him.

"I can't wait for you to be Mrs. Callahan," he whispers.

"Oh, that. Umm… I don't want to change my name."

He blinks. "What?"

"I want to keep the Bennett name."

"Not happening. That would be a severe blow to my ego. How will everyone know you're my wife?"

"You're protecting your bragging rights?"

He chuckles, and the sound is music to my ears. "Can you blame me? You're smart, beautiful—"

I leap from his arms, rising to my feet and swinging my forefinger at him. "Don't think you can sweet talk me into this."

"A man can try, can't he?" Eric advances toward me with sure steps, and I feel like I'm about to be trapped. I backpedal as fast as I can, until I bump into my bookshelves. Eric places his arms at my sides. Trapped. "Besides, I'm not saying anything that isn't true. How about Pippa Bennett-Callahan?"

I pout, even though I know I'll give in. His proximity is too much for my senses, and it's hard to resist him when he pins me with his gaze like this.

"It's bad form to upset your pregnant wife-to-be."

He closes in on me. "We're not even married yet and you're trying to emotionally blackmail me."

I smile, wrapping one arm around his neck. "Not such a terrible negotiator after all, am I? Fine, let it be Pippa Bennett-Callahan."

"Our first compromise. To tell you a little secret, you'll get away with almost everything else." Eric pulls out of my hug, lowering himself until his eyes are level with my belly. "Little baby, you'd better be a boy, so you can be on my team. Otherwise, I won't stand a chance against your mother and two girls."

"We'll have so much fun, the four of us," I say.

Chapter Twenty-Nine

Pippa

"I'm fine," I repeat, though I feel anything but fine. I'm curled up in Eric's bed, afraid even to move, because it might trigger another wave of morning sickness. For the past few weeks, I've spent my mornings either in bed or with my head over the toilet. Sometimes the afternoons go the same way. I'm hoping things will get better after the first trimester.

A flustered Eric sits at the edge of the bed, looking at me as if I'm about to break, moving his thumb in small circles on the back of my hand.

"There has to be something I can do," he says. "I feel powerless."

"Join the club. It should pass soon now," I reply, smiling at him encouragingly. The door opens, and Julie peeks inside, then enters the room. She holds her open laptop in one hand, and she has our favorite online baby shop open in her browser. Ever since we broke the news to Julie, she's been almost as obsessed with searching for baby items as I've been.

Wordlessly, she climbs into the bed, next to me,

showing me her newest findings. I push myself into a sitting position, offering my opinion.

"So this is the cure to morning sickness?" Eric asks with a shake of his head. "Shopping?"

I shrug, pinching his arm. "It helps. I already feel much better."

Julie sighs, bringing up the *wish list* she made, which is segmented into *girl things* and *boy things.*

She's thorough. I love this girl to pieces. Hugging her tightly, I wink at Eric. He and I have been doing our own lists. Buying a suitable house is high on our priorities list. My apartment is too small, and the owner of this house isn't selling. Planning our wedding is also very high on our priorities list, though my family is helping with that.

"Okay," Eric announces, rising from the bed. "Time to go or we'll miss the appointment."

Julie almost leaps from the bed, but I take my sweet time. Jerky movements don't do my morning sickness any favors.

Ten minutes later, we're in the car on our way to have my first ultra-sound. Neither of us is speaking, but the excitement is palpable.

"I can't believe we still have to wait months to find out if it will be a boy or a girl," Julie exclaims. In the rearview mirror, I notice she's rubbing her palms in excitement.

"We're going to find out if everything is all right with the baby today," I explain, "and we'll hear the heart beating."

Julie beams, and Eric puts his hand over mine in

an attempt to soothe me. He can feel I'm nervous.

"Everything will be fine," he murmurs to me, squeezing my fingers lightly.

My doctor, a kind woman in her fifties, is all smiles when the three of us walk into her office. She explains the procedure and assures me that I will be completely comfortable.

Lying on that exam table, though, I'm anything but comfortable. I drum my fingers on the surface beneath me, my heart in my throat as I watch the monitor. Eric stands next to me, holding my hand, and Julie is on his other side.

Everyone is silent as the monitor comes alive, and the doctor nods.

"This is the heartbeat," she announces triumphantly. "Everything looks normal. Oh—"

Eric's hand goes rigid in mine, but he relaxes as the doctor chuckles. Pointing to the screen, she says, "Here is the second heartbeat."

Julie is the first to react. Squealing, she looks from the doctor to me and then to Eric. "Does this mean I'll have two brothers? Or two sisters?"

"Or a brother and a sister," the doctor tells her. "It's too early to say."

Julie squeals again, and this time I join her celebrations, laughing with her. A misty-eyed Eric murmurs, "I love you," only for me to hear.

"Are you sure you can't tell if they are boys or girls?" Julie asks the doctor. "Not even if you look *really* close?"

"I'm afraid not," the doctor says.

Julie gives me a hug as best as she can.

"There's a history of twins in your family, Pippa, right?" the doctor asks.

"Yes."

"So, what do you figure we'll have?" Eric asks. "Party twins? Serious twins?"

I chuckle, thinking about the two set of twins in my family. "No idea, but I know one thing: they'll be double trouble."

Epilogue

One month later
Pippa

"To the first shotgun wedding in the Bennett family," Alice exclaims. In the mirror, I see her and Summer clink glasses with champagne.

"Girls, why don't you focus on zipping up my dress now and drink later?" I plead, terrified they'll spill champagne on my dress.

"You're the boss." Alice puts the glass away immediately, and Summer follows her lead. Then they both turn their attention to my veil.

I admire my dress in the mirror, sighing happily. It's an A-line shaped ivory dress with delicate lace on the upper part and flowy organza from my waist down. Nadine designed it, and she's outdone herself. There's only a tiny baby bump in sight, but there's still time for it to grow.

The wedding is taking place at our old ranch, which looks brand new right now. Renovations were completed two weeks ago, but the B&B isn't open for business yet.

It made perfect sense to have the wedding here.

For one, it's a small wedding with only immediate family and our closest friends attending. It's simple too, with a small ceremony officiated by a close friend who is ordained. The party will be in a beautiful and elegant tent outside in the garden.

I have a connection with this place, which is hard to describe. The second I stepped inside, it felt like home, even though it looks nothing like it used to.

The room we're in right now used to be our bedroom. Alice and Summer had twin bunk beds, while I had one for myself, which garnered me progressively more jealous looks from both of them as they grew up. The walls were a light pink color with a stain next to the door that never went away. Even though it's gone, I can point out exactly where it was. The walls are a beautiful yellow now, giving the room a bright and cheerful appearance, as does the king-size bed.

"Nervous?" Summer asks, watching me in the mirror.

"No." I smile at my sister, who looks a little unconvinced. I can't explain why I'm not nervous. Last time I did this, I was a wreck the entire time during the preparations and the wedding itself. I was borderline nauseous the entire day. Now, I'm oddly at peace. I have butterflies in my stomach and a grin I can't seem to tone down, but I'm not *nervous*.

A knock at the door startles the three of us.

"Can I come in?" Mom's voice resounds from outside.

"Sure," I reply.

The door opens, and Mom steps inside with Julie at her side. Julie is lovely. She's wearing a white satin dress, looking like a princess.

"Julie, you are so pretty," I say.

"So are you," she replies.

Mom doesn't say anything, merely pulling me in to a hug. She was right, of course. There are several kinds of happiness. As I stand here, surrounded by my family with the man I love waiting on the other side of the door, I feel happier than I ever have.

"Mom, don't ruin her hair," Summer calls.

"It's okay," I assure her, and linger in my mom's arms for a while longer. My blonde hair is styled in waves with a few pins here and there, so there's not much to ruin about it.

"Oh, look, I did undo one of your pins," Mom says as I pull out of her hug. She focuses on righting my pin next, but I think it's an excuse for her to regain her composure because she's misty-eyed.

"Mom," I whisper. "I'm not nervous at all. Is that weird?" I look at her in the mirror, holding my breath.

"No, honey. It means you know deep down it's right." She offers me a warm smile and squeezes my hand. Julie is quietly looking at me, as if she wants to say something but doesn't have the courage.

"What is it, sweetie?" I ask her. She glances at my sisters and Mom, then to her feet.

"We'll go outside to see if everything is okay," Alice says, getting the drift. "But you should hurry up. It's starting in ten minutes."

The three of them leave me alone with Julie.

"Let's both sit on the bed, and you can tell me what's wrong," I say, leading us both to the bed.

"I asked Dad and he said yes, and I'm hoping you will too."

"Okay."

She licks her lips several times, wiping off some of her cherry lip gloss. "Can I call you Mom? I know I'm not going to be your baby the way they will be," she says quickly, pointing to my stomach, "but—"

I hold up my hand, stopping her. "You are my baby. Don't think for a second that I will treat any of you differently. And I'll be honored if you call me Mom." I pull her in to a hug just like my own mother did with me moments ago. Damn it, I'm way past misty-eyed. I'm downright tearful.

"Sister," Max's voice comes from the corridor. "You'd better come out soon."

"We'll be right out."

Julie opens the door for me. I walk out of the room with small steps, careful not to step on my dress. Max is at the end of the short corridor, which opens into the spacious living room. My family waits there, along with Eric.

He wears an elegant navy suit that highlights his blue eyes, and a small strand of his rebellious hair shadows his left eyebrow.

The first part of the ceremony passes by in a haze. I don't pay attention to one word being read to us, and neither does Eric. We are both too preoccupied stealing glances at each other and sharing accomplice smiles. It's only when I hear the words "You can exchange your rings now" that I seem to come back to my senses.

Julie brings us the rings on a pink, silky pillow. I take Eric's with a trembling hand. I notice there is a slight tremor in his hand too as he reaches for mine. We interlace our fingers briefly, strengthening the other. Then we put the rings on.

"And now, the vows."

Eric winks at me, his lip curling up to a smile. Writing my vows has been a true adventure, mostly because he was doing everything to find out what I was writing. I hid them well, I hope. I wanted this to be a surprise.

He takes my hands in his, clearing his throat. Waiting for him to speak sends my pulse into overdrive.

"Pippa, I promise to take care of you, love you, and respect you. I promise to anticipate your need for sugar and caffeine, and always have a quick fix at hand."

I chuckle and blink back tears of joy. Eric isn't done, though.

"I promise to be there through everything. Cheer with you on the good days, cheer you up on the bad ones. Work through everything and never give up. Love is an honor and a choice, and I will choose to love you every day."

I tear up, there's no denying it, but my voice is remarkably steady as I recite my vows. "Eric, I promise to take care of you, love you, and respect you. I vow to only find appropriate nicknames and never give you reasons or opportunities to tickle me, though I do promise to give you reasons to laugh often. I vow to fight for our happiness every day."

He cups my cheeks in his hands, pulling me in for a kiss. His lips brush mine softly, lingering there too long for the kiss to be considered chaste. My body hums at his nearness, and he drags his fingers down my neck in an almost sinful touch, which is full of promise. *Later.*

Hand in hand, Eric and I step outside the house, with the rest of the gang on our heels. We're going to take a group photo.

"Damn," Max exclaims, squinting as the sun blinds him. "Too much light outside."

I chuckle, elbowing my brother. "Too much alcohol at the bachelor party. Why did you do it the day before the wedding?"

"Hey." Blake appears at my other side. "Shotgun wedding, shotgun bachelor party. What did you girls do for your party?"

"None of us got a hangover the next day," Alice answers from behind the boys. "But I have muscle cramps."

"Yeah," Nadine chimes in. "Safe to say we can dub it The Night All Girls Went Wild."

Blake nods, impressed. "I'd call our party The Night the Party Brothers Behaved, and the Serious Brothers Went Wild."

Max scoffs. "I'm going to shortcut that to The

Night I Can't Remember."

"On my count," the photographer says, and we all turn to him, smiling. He takes a number of shots, some with the group, some with just Eric and me.

After the photo session, we all walk toward the tent, chatting happily.

"Ready for the first dance?" Eric asks, wiggling his eyebrows.

"No funny moves," I warn him, remembering our wild dance at Sebastian and Ava's wedding. We rehearsed the first dance, but who knows what ideas my man has.

As Eric walks over to the DJ, Nadine appears by my side, rubbing her palms. "So, who's next? I'm starting to like this matchmaking game."

"Logan and I made a bet," Sebastian says, appearing at my other side with Logan.

"Since when are you making bets on this?" I ask. Logan shrugs, a devilish smile on his lips. Since Alice's guy is still a world away, and Summer is too young, I will concentrate on my brothers.

Across the dance floor, the two sets of twins are engaged in a heated discussion. I wonder who's ready for the next step. The party twins, Blake and Daniel, are still a tad too young. But I'm seeing possibilities for the serious twins, Max and Christopher, especially since Max is back from London for good. Nadine follows my gaze, grinning.

"Max," we say at the same time.

THE END

Other Books by Layla Hagen
The Lost Series

***

Lost in Us: The story of James and Serena
There are three reasons tequila is my new favorite drink.
• One: my ex-boyfriend hates it.
• Two: downing a shot looks way sexier than sipping my usual Sprite.
• Three: it might give me the courage to do something my ex-boyfriend would hate even more than tequila—getting myself a rebound

The night I swap my usual Sprite with tequila, I meet James Cohen. The encounter is breathtaking. Electrifying. And best not repeated.

James is a rich entrepreneur. He likes risks and adrenaline and is used to living the high life. He's everything I'm not.

But opposites attract.
Some say opposites destroy each other.
Some say opposites are perfect for each other.
I don't know what will James and I do to each other, but I can't stay away from him. Even though I should.

AVAILABLE ON ALL RETAILERS.

***
Found in Us: The story of Jessica and Parker

Jessica Haydn wants to leave her past behind. Hurt by one too many heartbreaks, she vows not to fall in love again. Especially not with a man like Parker, whose electrifying pull and smile bruised her ego once before. But his sexy British accent makes her crave his touch, and his blue eyes strip Jessica of all her defenses.

Parker Blakesley has no place for love in his life. He learned the hard way not to trust. He built his business empire by avoiding distractions, and using sheer determination and control. But something about Jessica makes him question everything. Not only has she a body made for sin, but her laughter fills a void inside of him.

The desire igniting between them spirals into an unstoppable passion, and so much more. Soon, neither can fight their growing emotional connection. But can two scarred souls learn to trust again? And when a mistake threatens to tear them apart, will their love be strong enough?

AVAILABLE ON ALL RETAILERS.
***
Caught in Us: The story of Dani and Damon

Damon Cooper has all the markings of a bad boy:
• A tattoo
• A bike
• An attitude to go with point one and two

In the beginning I hated him, but now I'm falling in love with him. My parents forbid us to be together, but Damon's not one to obey rules. And since I met him, neither am I.

AVAILABLE ON ALL RETAILERS.
***

Standalone USA TODAY BESTSELLER
Withering Hope

Aimee's wedding is supposed to turn out perfect. Her dress, her fiancé and the location—the idyllic holiday ranch in Brazil—are perfect.

But all Aimee's plans come crashing down when the private jet that's taking her from the U.S. to the ranch—where her fiancé awaits her—defects mid-flight and the pilot is forced to perform an emergency landing in the heart of the Amazon rainforest.

With no way to reach civilization, being rescued is Aimee and Tristan's—the pilot—only hope. A slim one that slowly withers away, desperation taking its place. Because death wanders in the jungle under many forms: starvation, diseases. Beasts.

As Aimee and Tristan fight to find ways to survive, they grow closer. Together they discover that facing old, inner agonies carved by painful pasts takes just as much courage, if not even more, than facing the rainforest.

Despite her devotion to her fiancé, Aimee can't hide her feelings for Tristan—the man for whom she's slowly becoming everything. You can hide many things in the rainforest. But not lies. Or love.

Withering Hope is the story of a man who desperately needs forgiveness and the woman who brings him hope. It is a story in which hope births wings and blooms into a love that is as beautiful and intense as it is forbidden.

AVAILABLE ON ALL RETAILERS.

Cover: http://designs.romanticbookaffairs.com/

**

Acknowledgements

There are so many people who helped me fulfil the dream of publishing, that I am utterly terrified I will forget to thank someone. If I do, please forgive me. Here it goes.

First, I'd like to thank my beta readers, Jessica, Dee, Andrea, Carrie, Jill, Kolleen and Rebecca. You made this story so much better!!

I want to thank every blogger and reader who took a chance with me as a new author and helped me spread the word. You have my most heartfelt gratitude. To my street team. . .you rock !!!

Last but not least, I would like to thank my family. I would never be here if not for their love and support. Mom, you taught me that books are important, and for that I will always be grateful. Dad, thank you for always being convinced that I should reach for the stars.

To my sister, whose numerous ahem. . .legendary replies will serve as an inspiration for many books to come, I say thank you for your support and I love you, kid.

To my husband, who always, no matter what, believed in me and supported me through all this whether by happily taking on every chore I overlooked or accepting being ignored for hours at a time, and most importantly encouraged me whenever I needed it: I love you and I could not have done this without you.

YOUR FOREVER LOVE

Made in the USA
Monee, IL
30 July 2023

40124995R00198